THE HANALEI HOUSE

BOB PUGLISI

Cover design by Asya Blue

Bob Puglisi's photograph by Robert DeLaurenti

ISBN:978-0578663012

Dedicated to my dear friend Cecil "Tootsie" Schreiber. She was a mentor and supporter who helped edit my first three books. She was too ill to edit or even read Unassisted Living. I'm sure she would have enjoyed it. There's a little bit of Tootsie in Mildred Myers. I miss my friend.

Gayle,
Thanks for reading my book.

Bob Puglisi

Also by Bob Puglisi

Novels
Railway Avenue
Midnight Auto Supply
Unassisted Living

Memoir
Almost A Wiseguy

CAST OF MAIN CHARACTERS

Mildred Meyers – a seventy-one-year-old activist, resident of the Hanalei House, former resident of the Star Bright Senior Residence in Hollywood, California, and Arthur Kulak's lover.

Arthur Kulak – an eighty-year-old resident of the Hanalei House, Mildred Meyers' lover, and former resident of the Star Bright Senior Residence.

Stanley Cutler – a hippy in his early thirties, the owner of the Hanalei House, former owner of the Start Bright Senior Residence, and Karen Eichel's fiancé.

Albert Cutler – Stanley's older brother, business partner, and attorney.

Pauline Benson – in her mid-seventies, wife of Jim Benson, resident of the Hanalei House, and former resident of the Star Bright Senior Residence.

Jim Benson – in his mid-seventies, husband of Pauline Benson, resident of the Hanalei House, and former resident of the Star Bright Senior Residence.

Neil French - thirty-nine-year-old business partner of the Cutler brothers, and Annie Larson's husband.

Annie Larson - thirty-five, Neil's wife and business partner with Neil and the Cutler brothers.

Jason French – Neil's ten-year-old son.

Sue Watanabe – the cook at the Hanalei House, a woman in her early sixties, Clark Watanabe's wife, and former cook at the Star Bright Senior Residence.

Clark Watanabe – in his late sixties, a retired landscape gardener, and Sue Watanabe's husband.

Karen Eichel – Stanley's fiancée, a thirtyish professional ballet dancer.

Irene Eichel – Karen's mother, a seventyish New Yorker.

Tony Santos – a hippy twenty-year-old, decorated Vietnam veteran, and Glo Goldberg's boyfriend.

Glo Goldberg – a twenty-year-old hippy and Tony Santos' girlfriend.

Louise Hart – an eighty-year-old Hollywood actress and a previous resident of Stanley Cutler's Star Bright Senior Residence.

Harry Leonard – an eighty-year-old retired writer and friend of Louise Hart.

Jeff Kress – a Hollywood producer and former live-in boyfriend of Nancy Meyers—Mildred's deceased daughter.

Calvin Daniels – a fifty-nine-year-old business executive and condominium developer.

Joe Thomas – in his early thirties, a newspaper reporter on Kauai.

Lucy Kapana – an elderly Asian woman and longtime Hanalei resident.

Angelo Sambucci - in his mid-sixties, Mildred's friend, former boss, and husband of Helen Sambucci.

Helen Sambucci – about the same age as her husband Angelo.

CHAPTER 1
1976

Seventy-one-year-old Mildred Meyers sat on the porch of the Hanalei House drinking her morning coffee. She was a petite woman with white hair who had been on the island of Kauai a couple of months and wondered if moving there was the right choice. Mildred was a city person; she grew up and lived in Manhattan most of her life, and for a short time she lived in Los Angeles at the Star Bright Senior Residence. Now, she was in this beautiful, isolated, garden-like setting with its impressive mountains and waterfalls.

Mildred's only other trips to the islands were to Oahu, more precisely Waikiki. For her, it was New York City with the heat turned up. She loved leaving her hotel in the morning and having breakfast at McDonald's. By the time she ate an Egg McMuffin and drank her decaf coffee, stores were opening on Kalakaua Avenue, Waikiki's main drag. She loved looking for bargains that she could bring back to New York for her friends.

Mildred now lived with her fellow retirees in a big two-story white plantation-style house on a ten-acre farm in Hanalei. The house had chipped paint that needed scraping and a paint job. They planned to remodel and update their new home and to turn the old plantation cottages where workers used to live into vacation accommodations.

The house had eight bedrooms, three on the first floor and five on the second. The first floor also had a large living room, a dining room, the owner's office/bedroom, and the kitchen in the rear of the house. The back door in the kitchen led to the farm and the cottages.

Down the road from the house, there was a hippie camp. Mildred was concerned because she heard rumors about plans to raze the camp and build condominiums.

Stanley Cutler, the owner dashed out the front door and stopped when he saw Mildred. Previously, Stanley owned the Star Bright Senior Residence in Hollywood where Mildred lived until Stanley sold that. Then, Mildred, the Bensons, Mr. Kulak, Mrs. Watanabe the cook, and her husband all made the move with Stanley to this farm on Kauai.

Stanley's appearance reminded Mildred of his upcoming wedding. He was in his early thirties had long hair, thick glasses, and looked frail. He treated his elderly residents with love, care, and respect. Stanley and his fiancée planned to live in the downstairs bedroom next to Stanley's office following their wedding.

"Oh Mrs. Meyers, I didn't know where you went after breakfast."

Mildred said, "It's so nice out here. Everything is so green. I like to sit and listen to the waves in the distance, hear the birds singing, and the palms rattling. It makes me slow down. I wish I had done that years ago."

"Oh, that's good. We've all been so busy—we haven't had time to sit and talk. How are you doing?"

"I'm doing alright, I guess. Still trying to get over Nancy and adjust to all the changes. I think about her every day and pray for her every night. I still say it should have been me."

"You shouldn't say that, Mrs. Meyers. It was Nancy's time, not yours." He was sorry he said it as soon as the words came out. He thought he was being insensitive, and said, "We should be happy for her."

Mildred had lost some of her spunk since her daughter passed away. "I don't know. Us Jews—we always think negative. We have to suffer!" She laughed.

Stanley shifted awkwardly holding a bunch of keys in his hand. "You look like you're going somewhere," Mildred said.

"Oh yeah, to the airport to pick up Karen and her mother." Mildred had a blank expression on her face. "We talked about it last night at dinner."

Mildred scrunched up her face, "I guess I forgot."

"You want to come?"

"Oh, no. It's a long ride. I'm going to help Sue in the kitchen. We're gonna have a few extra mouths to feed. She sent Clark to the farmers' market. You see what he comes back with?"

Stanley laughed remembering the first time he went to the L.A. Produce Market with Mildred, before remarking, "He's as good as you at finding bargains. Where's Mr. Kulak? He dashed out right after breakfast."

"He grabbed his surfboard and paddle and said something about a lesson."

"Oh, that's right, he's taking paddleboard lessons."

"You mean surfing?"

"It's kind of like surfing but you have an oar to row with. It's great exercise. I might try it myself."

"Sounds like a lot of work to me. I hope he doesn't hurt himself."

"I don't know. He's in pretty good shape. I hope I'm in that kind of shape if I ever reach his age."

Mildred said, "You think that marijuana you smoke is good for you?"

Stanley looked a little uncomfortable. "Please, Mrs. Meyers don't mention that in front of Karen's mother."

"And what about that smelly garden in the back of the property?"

"That's Neil and Annie's deal." He looked about nervously, not knowing how to end the conversation, then finally said, "Hey, I got to go."

Mildred waved a hand and watched Stanley spring down the stairs, jump in his white van, start the engine, and leave red dust behind as he pulled down the drive. It scattered the island's wild chickens and roosters in a panic. Stanley's van turned onto the road towards the hippie camp on his way to the main road.

Mildred turned as the Bensons came out the front door. They were in their mid-seventies and retired from the real estate business in Los Angeles. For years, they ran a successful real estate office in the Midwest. They lived in Stanley's Hollywood house for two years before the move to Kauai.

Pauline Benson was a big woman with a salt-of-the-earth personality, who spoke out of the side of her mouth. Jim Benson, with a full head of white hair, was robust, a football player in high school and college, who still suffered the effects of those years.

Mrs. Benson said, "Oh, there you are Mildred. Care to join us?" The Bensons stayed in shape by walking every day. Everyone whispered that they still had an active sex life.

"Thank you. I'm just sitting here relaxing a little."

"Isn't it beautiful here?" Mrs. Benson asked.

"I was just thinking the same thing, Pauline," Mildred answered.

One of the island's wild roosters let out a loud crow. Mrs. Benson turned in the direction of the noise and said, "But these damn roosters remind me of living on the farm in Indiana as a child."

"The only roosters I ever heard were at the produce market where I worked," Mildred said.

"They start so early. It wasn't even light out this morning and they were crowing," Mrs. Benson added.

"Where's Arthur?" Mr. Benson asked.

"He's taking a… I think Stanley said, paddleboard lesson."

"Oh, yes. He told me about that. He wanted me to join him. I don't think my knees would support me."

Mrs. Benson snapped, "Never mind, you're not going out on a surfboard."

"It's paddleboarding—not surfing." Mr. Benson corrected. "I believe it was made popular by Waikiki beach boys."

"Whatever it is—you're not doing it," Mrs. Benson said. "But… I must say it's incredible the things Arthur does at his age."

Mr. Benson frowned and said, "That's because he never played football like me."

That sounded reasonable enough to Mildred.

"You sure you don't want to come for a walk?" Mr. Benson asked.

"No, not today. I'm going to help Sue in the kitchen. We'll have two more guests for dinner tonight."

The Bensons looked puzzled. "Oh my, are we having tourists already?" Mrs. Benson asked.

"Karen and her mother..." Mildred clarified. Stanley just left to pick them up. He said he mentioned it at dinner last night. I didn't remember."

"Oh my, I don't remember either." Mrs. Benson laughed. "Well, that'll be nice..." Turning to her husband, she asked, "Shall we go Jim?"

"Yes, let's. We'll see you later Mildred," Mrs. Benson said, and they walked down the steps.

Mildred watched them go down the drive towards the road. She overheard Mr. Benson when he said, "You think Arthur is in better physical shape than me?"

"Of course not. Jim, you're my hero?"

Mildred watched them stop and kiss, then continued to walk. She smiled, admiring their love for each other.

Neil French and Annie Larson came around the side of the house and stepped onto the porch. Neil French was thirty-nine, handsome, tall, his long black hair hung in a ponytail, and he dressed in tattered jeans and denim work shirts with patches of peace signs and marijuana leaves. He had worked at Los Alamos Labs in New Mexico creating top-secret weapons until his wife passed away several days after giving birth to their first and only child, Jason. It devastated Neil. It resulted in an epiphany about the work he was doing and one day he walked out of the Lab, never to return.

He took his baby boy, and moved to a commune, just outside of Taos. There he met Annie, who helped him with the child. The couple and the boy eventually left the commune for San Francisco.

Annie Larson was thirty-five, pretty with red curly hair, busty with a narrow waist, and a sexy contagious smile. She had been a proofreader at the San Francisco Chronicle. "*Aloha,* Mrs. Meyers!" Annie said.

Mildred greeted them. "Oh, good morning." She still hadn't gotten used to saying, "*Aloha.*"

"Is Stanley inside?" Annie asked.

"No. He went to Lihue to pick up Karen and her mother."

"Oh, we were going to go with him," Neil said. "We had some errands to run."

"I guess he forgot," Annie commented.

Mildred offered, "You know he's got a lot on his mind these days… With the wedding and all."

Neil and Annie smiled. Before coming to Kauai, Neil and Annie lived with Stanley and a group of artistic hippies in a warehouse commune in the Haight-Ashbury area of San Francisco for two years.

The couple opposed the Vietnam War and protested it at rallies all around the Bay Area. Many of the protests turned violent with police attacks that left protestors beaten and bloody.

One vicious attack put Neil in the hospital with serious head injuries. He eventually recuperated but the couple soured on the San Francisco scene. They followed hippie friends to Kauai with the hope of a more *ke ola maluhia* (peaceful life).

Arriving on Kauai, they worked odd jobs and lived in some holes-in-the-wall for about a year. When Annie's father passed away and left her a large sum of money, they found and bought the farm in Hanalei where they have lived and worked for three years.

Many of their friends returned to the mainland because of lack of work, and prejudice by the locals towards hippies, especially *haoles* (Caucasians). Some of their friends remained on the island and lived at the hippie camp down the road for a while. They built tree houses to live in because of *tsunamis* and flooding. The landowner was a wealthy entrepreneur and let a handful of hippies live there for several years. In a short time, the population of the camp swelled to more than a hundred.

Mildred hadn't been inside the camp but passed it many times and noticed naked and half-naked people walking around or playing volleyball. She thought, Arthur Kulak, her lover, would like that. Occasionally, some of the hippies came to the farm looking for work. They were always very polite, and according to Stanley, they were good workers. Mildred couldn't decide how she felt about these strangely dressed and undressed young people, sometimes smelly, and reeking of marijuana. Their unkempt appearance put her off no matter how polite and sincere they seemed.

She had known hippies in her old Lower East Side neighborhood in New York. She marched with many of them at anti-Vietnam War protests. They were always friendly and happy. Mildred figured they were all on drugs. She also knew that her prejudice towards them was something to overcome.

"Is Albert around?" Neil asked. Albert was Stanley's brother and business partner who also followed Stanley to the island.

"I haven't seen him this morning. His car's not here so he must have gone somewhere."

"I guess we'll drive down there ourselves," Neil said. "Would you like to come with us, Mrs. Meyers?"

"No… No thanks. I have work to do around here."

Neil and Annie said their goodbyes. A few minutes

later Mildred watched them drive past the house on their way to the main road, once again the wild chickens squawked and scattered in a panic.

CHAPTER 2

Early afternoon, Mildred and Mrs. Watanabe prepared dinner in the spacious kitchen. The kitchen took up the entire back of the house. It had many windows that made it bright and airy with a pleasantly warm breeze wafting through.

Mrs. Watanabe was the cook at the Hollywood house. In this new house, she and Mildred shared cooking duties.

Sue Watanabe was in her early sixties. Her Japanese name was *Mio* (meaning a beautiful cherry blossom on a beautiful thread). She was a short woman, a little overweight with an unwrinkled, sweet looking face, and a pretty smile. She was born on Oahu but moved with her family to Los Angeles at a young age. For her, living on Kauai was a return to the islands she loved and remembered as a child.

Mildred and Mrs. Watanabe stood at the center island preparing food. They watched Clark Watanabe, Sue's husband, set down a large assortment of fruits and vegetables on one of the countertops.

Clark was in his late sixties. He wore khaki work pants and shirts, a beat-up, sweat-stained, straw hat. He was just a few inches taller than his wife. He had a little bit of a potbelly but looked in good shape for his years.

Clark's Japanese name was *Ryu* (meaning dragon spirit). Friends and family started calling him Clark because as he grew older, he grew a mustache and he resembled an Asian Clark Gable. The name stuck. He was born on the island of Maui where his parents worked on the sugar plantations. His family relocated to Los Angeles when he was five-years-old. Mildred had gotten fond of Sue and Clark since they all moved to Kauai and lived together. The Watanabes shared the bedroom adjacent to the kitchen.

Clark said, "They had some beautiful lettuce—I couldn't resist. We won't have to buy it soon. Neil said we'll have a lettuce crop in a few weeks."

"You buy too much," his wife scolded, but she knew he enjoyed shopping for produce. "We can't eat it fast enough."

Clark smiled and watched his wife and Mildred put away everything while he unpacked more from his shopping bag.

Before moving to Kauai, Clark retired and turned over his gardening business in Los Angeles to his oldest son John. Since the move, he was enjoying retirement. He found plenty of things to keep him occupied around the property, especially tinkering in the fields, and nurturing the flowers and trees on the property.

"We can always make soup," Mildred suggested.

"I guess we could," Mrs. Watanabe said as she stuffed more produce into the refrigerator.

The Watanabes were victims of Japanese internment during the Second World War. The U.S. government had relocated them from their home in Los Angeles to Manzanar in California's Owens Valley in the high desert north of Los Angeles. After the war, they returned to Los Angeles to rebuild their lives.

Mr. Watanabe asked, "Where's Arthur?"

Mildred looked up at the wall clock and said, "I don't know what happened to him. He's not back yet." She was a little worried.

I saw him going out with his board when I was going to the farmers' market," Clark said.

Mildred answered, "I know. That was after breakfast. He's been gone ever since. I hope he's alright. I'll see if he's upstairs. Maybe, he's taking a nap."

CHAPTER 3

Later that afternoon, Stanley was back from the airport, sitting with Karen and her mother on the porch. Stanley and Karen's mother sipped *mai-tais*. Karen with an iced tea in her hands looked beautiful dressed in a white pants suit, her blond hair pulled back in a ponytail. She was tall and thin with the long legs of a ballet dancer. Karen's eyes were sparkling blue.

Irene Eichel, Karen's mother, was in her late sixties. It was obvious where Karen got her good looks. Irene was slim and tall like her daughter. Her blue eyes were crystal-clear, and her salt-and-pepper hair was short and looked recently coiffed. She wore a white flowery dress and Italian made white sandals on her feet.

Neil and Annie drove up the drive and stopped the car. Annie waved to the folks on the porch. "Stanley, we wanted to go to Lihue with you," Annie said.

"Sorry, I guess I forgot."

Mildred came out on the porch and said to Annie, "Come to dinner, later."

"Oh, thanks. What can we bring?"

"Just Jason." She was talking about their ten-year-old. "We'll see you later," Annie waved, and the car pulled away.

Mildred looked at Karen and her mother, and said, "I forgot to ask, how was your flight?"

"It was long. We had to make two stops before we got here, Chicago and San Francisco. And we couldn't get a seat in first class," Karen answered. "It's so nice to be here."

Clark stepped onto the porch. Stanley introduced Clark to Karen's mother. Clark already knew Karen from when they all lived in Los Angeles.

Mildred glanced out to the road, then asked, "Has anyone seen Arthur?"

Stanley looked concerned. "Why? He's not here?"

Mildred's face turned pale and she looked worried. "He's been gone since this morning. Something must have happened to him. He should have been back a long time ago," Mildred exclaimed.

"You think he's still on the water?" Mr. Watanabe asked.

Mildred said, "I checked upstairs earlier and he wasn't there. I'm gonna go look again."

"I'll go see how my wife is doing in the kitchen," Mr. Watanabe said.

Mildred started for the door. "Tell her I'll be right back."

Mr. Watanabe said, "I'll tell her. Mildred don't worry about Arthur. It is such a beautiful day. He's probably still at the beach." He was talking about the bright blue skies and gentle winds that were blowing over the farm.

Mildred hoped he was right about Arthur Kulak still being at the beach. She headed upstairs to see if he was there.

Mr. Watanabe turned to Mrs. Eichel and said, "Nice to meet you, Irene."

"Thank you. It's nice to meet you, too," she said as she smiled.

Mr. Watanabe went inside.

After a while, Mildred returned, panic-stricken. "Stanley, he's not up there. We better look for him."

Stanley said, "We'll take a walk down to the beach. See if we can find him. Mrs. Eichel, would you like to see the beach? Mrs. Meyers, do you want to come along?" Stanley asked.

Mildred was confused and upset. "No, no, I better stay here in case he comes back.

Mrs. Eichel rose from her chair. She had to steady herself a moment. "I hope I can walk after that drink you made me, Stanley."

Karen stood and took her mother's arm. Mildred said, "I'll be in the kitchen."

Mrs. Eichel asked, "Can I be of any help?"

"Thank you, but we can manage. If you can find Arthur and bring him back that would be a load off my mind."

Karen looked at Mildred, and said, "I'm sure we'll find him."

Mildred watched them leave then reluctantly went inside.

An hour later, Stanley walked into the kitchen where Mildred was putting chickens in the oven to roast. He asked, "Did he come back yet?"

Mildred closed the oven door. She straightened up with a little effort and turned to look at Stanley. Her face turned pale, she even felt faint, made it over to the center island, and gripped it tightly. "You didn't find him?" she asked.

Noticing how pale Mildred looked, Stanley asked, "You okay? You want to sit down?"

"I'm alright. Something must have happened to him. I hope he didn't get thrown off his board in some big wave."

"I'll go check upstairs," Stanley said and left the room.

Mildred said, "I hope he didn't get in trouble for taking his clothes off somewhere."

Mr. Watanabe, trying to put Mildred at ease said, "People walked these islands naked and free for hundreds of years."

"Well it's not that way anymore, dear," Mrs. Watanabe said.

Stanley returned and said, "I'm going out with the van to see if I can find him."

"I'll come with you," Mildred offered.

He was concerned about the way Mildred looked, and said, "No, you better stay here."

Stanley rushed out the back door. The weather had changed drastically. He looked up at dark threatening storm clouds. That worried him. Stanley started the van and pulled away. This time the ever-present chickens were gone, a bad sign of impending weather.

"I'm so worried about him," Mildred said.

Mrs. Watanabe tried to reassure her. "Oh, I'm sure he is fine. Maybe, he just lost track of the time."

Mrs. Watanabe stood at the stove sautéing vegetables. Mildred opened the oven and basted chickens.

CHAPTER 4

A short while later, heavy rain fell as Stanley drove up the drive, splashing mud and dirty red clay water; he jumped out, dashed to the back door and into the kitchen. Mildred and Mrs. Watanabe looked at him expectantly. "I couldn't find him."

"We better do something quick. I don't like this weather," Mildred said.

"I'm going to call the police." Stanley left the kitchen to go to his office.

Mildred called after him, "What about the Coast Guard? Maybe, you should call them too. He could have been washed out to sea." She walked over to close some of the windows where rain was splashing off the sill. Mildred looked out the window and frowned.

After a while, the rain slowed but the sun was sinking. Mildred knew it would be dark soon, and it troubled her.

The rain stopped by the time the police arrived, Stanley and Mildred met them on the front porch. They were young guys; one was tall with broad shoulders with a fixed smile across his wide face. The other police officer must have just made the height requirement, but despite his short stature, he didn't look like the type of guy you would mess with. Unlike his partner, he seemed incapable of smiling.

Following Mildred and Stanley's description of Kulak, they promised to find him—unless he met with foul play or something worse. Mildred didn't like the sound of that and returned to the comfort of the kitchen.

Dinner had temporarily been on hold, so the Benson's, Stanley, Karen, Karen's mother, and Mr. Watanabe sat on the front porch, sipping cocktails. Mr. Benson tried to calm everyone's nerves by entertaining them strumming his ukulele, playing some Hawaiian tunes he learned since being on the island.

When they heard a car coming, everyone anxiously turned their attention towards the road. They watched intently until Stanley said, "It's Albert!"

Mrs. Benson said, "Maybe, Arthur's with him. They were disappointed when the car came to a stop at the side of the house.

Stanley shouted, "You didn't see Mr. Kulak, did you?"

Albert Cutler said, "No," as he stretched his long legs getting out of the car. He was still athletic looking. Only his slightly graying hair and a hint of crow's feet showed the possibility of age on his handsome face.

Stanley's brother, Albert, a lawyer by trade had taken over the task of remodeling the cottages and starting a tourist business.

Albert was three years older than Stanley. He had been a star basketball and soccer player in high school. When he was in college at Berkeley, he made a name for himself on the basketball team. His accomplishments on the court drew lots of attention in his junior and senior year from NBA scouts who tried to recruit him to play professionally, but he chose to go to the University of North Carolina School of Law instead.

After a successful legal career and a divorce from his wife of five years, Albert decided he needed a big change and followed his brother to Kauai.

Albert helped Stanley with the details of a partnership for the property with Neil and Annie. He was also instrumental in handling the sale of the Hollywood house that Stanley sold to Calvin Daniels Development Corporation; they slated the house and neighboring houses for demolition and planned to replace them with a new condominium building, a sore point for Mildred who had opposed the project.

As Albert stepped onto the porch, he said, "I was in Lihue all day, trying to get all our paperwork filed for the bed and breakfast. There are so many applications and permits you have to submit."

"I was wondering where you went this morning," Stanley said.

"I wanted to get there early so I wouldn't have to spend the whole day down there. And I did anyway." He frowned, shaking his head.

Stanley introduced Mrs. Eichel to his brother, then said, "We can't find Mr. Kulak. The police are out looking for him."

Mildred came out the front door. This time she looked beside herself. "Stanley, what should we do about dinner? Everything is just about ready."

Stanley glanced out to the road. "I don't know. Is everybody hungry?" He looked at the others in the dim evening light. No one answered.

Finally, Mr. Benson stopped strumming and said, "I think we can wait a little while longer until Arthur is safely home. We're all concerned, Mildred." He looked at the others who seemed to agree.

"Can I get anyone another drink?" Mr. Benson asked with a smile.

After another half-hour, there was still no sign of Arthur Kulak or the police, Stanley said, "Maybe, we should eat."

Mildred standing next to him said, "Stanley's right. You should all eat," But the concerned look on her face told a different story. They all got up to go inside. Mildred said, "I'll stay out here and wait."

Then, they heard a car approaching. When they looked towards the road, they saw the police car turning into the drive. Everyone stopped and held their breath. The car came to a stop after splashing through the muddy potholes. At first, Mildred looked relieved. The taller, broader policeman got out, but Mildred noticed Kulak wasn't with them. Now, she was convinced something terrible happened. Stanley quickly asked, "Did you find him?"

"We found him in the hippie camp."

"Did he have his clothes on?" Mildred asked.

The officer looked curiously at her and said, "I believe he did, ma'am."

Mildred impatiently asked, "Well, where is he?"

"Oh, he's on his way. Two of the hippies are driving him."

"Thank you, officer—for your help," Stanley said.

The cop answered, "You're welcome."

Even though Mildred was somewhat relieved, she had to sit down to steady herself.

The policeman got back in the car and drove away, passing an old beat-up Chevy pickup truck, partially green and partially rust-colored, as it pulled up the drive.

A hippie chick in her twenties opened the passenger door and stepped out. She was short, had dirty-blond hair hanging in two braided ponytails, Birkenstocks on her feet, and a flowing tie-dyed dress.

Mr. Kulak stepped out after her. The driver's side door opened and a young man about the same age as the girl got out. He had long stringy black hair and a beard. Tony Santos was short and stocky, his arms were covered in tattoos, one of the most prominent being an eagle holding the earth in its claws with a banner below it that read, U S M C. He wore a tie-dyed tee-shirt, blue jeans with torn legs, and sandals.

Mildred darted to Kulak and hugged him. "Arthur, where have you been? I've been so worried." Mildred was angry at him but happy that he was safe. She couldn't bear losing someone else in her life.

Arthur Kulak was in his eighties though he looked younger. He was tall, lanky and mostly bald, a self-proclaimed nudist, former teacher, school principal, author, and historian.

The incident surprised Mildred about how attached she had become to Kulak. She hadn't been in a serious relationship in many years. The last was with one of her late daughter Nancy's ballet teachers. She didn't know if at this age she could sustain a relationship or love—let alone sex, which she felt guilty about enjoying after so many years of abstinence.

Mr. Kulak pulled his board and paddle out of the truck bed. As they walked up the steps, Kulak said, "I met these two lovely people. They took me to their camp. I forgot to look at the time. I learned a lot about riptides today. I'll tell you all about my little adventure over dinner."

Kulak noticed Karen and her mother for the first time. He walked over to them, still wearing his bathing trunks, sandals on his feet, and a torn denim shirt. He took Karen's hand, kissed the back of it, and said, "It's so nice to see you again my dear." He turned to her mother and said, "And this lovely woman must be your mother." He took Mrs. Eichel's hand and gave it a gentle kiss as well.

Karen said, "Yes, this is my mother Irene."

"I can see where your daughter gets her good looks."

Even in the semi-darkness, Mrs. Eichel's blush was obvious. Everybody stood around awkwardly, until Mildred said, "Well, I'm glad you're alright. Now, go get cleaned up everybody is starving, waiting for you." She poked him playfully in the ribs.

"Please accept my apologies." He kissed Mildred on the lips, then stepped towards the door. He turned around, looked at his new hippie friends and said, "Why don't you join us?" Then, he looked at Mildred for approval.

"Sure, we have plenty of food. Please stay for dinner!" Mildred urged. "And thanks for bringing him home." Looking at these kids, Mildred felt like they needed a good meal.

Tony and the girl looked from one to the other. "Thank you!" Tony said.

Glo said, "Thank you. That's so nice of you."

Mildred looked at the group still milling around and said, "Well what are we waiting for? Let's get moving!" She clapped her hands to motivate them.

Everyone jumped up. As they walked inside, Kulak said, "This young man has quite a story about his time in

Vietnam. I'm going to freshen up a bit. See you all in a few minutes."

CHAPTER 5

They served dinner on the lanai behind the house. Everyone sat around a large wooden table with a flowery tropical tablecloth. The table sat under a covered, wooden structure with rough-hewn beams, and vertical posts supporting a waxy *pili-grass* roof that kept the rain out. The structure was open on all sides. Tall *tiki* torches surrounded it, giving off a golden glow.

Mildred and Mrs. Watanabe came out the kitchen door. Mildred carried a platter of chicken. Mrs. Watanabe carried a salad bowl.

"Start passing the salad around," Mildred said.

Mildred placed the chicken on the table. While they passed the salad, Mildred and Mrs. Watanabe went back inside.

Mr. Kulak dressed in a black tee-shirt and jeans came out the back door and sat at the table. "Well look at you," Glo said with a smile.

"I feel a lot better now," Mr. Kulak said.

Mrs. Watanabe and Mildred returned with hot biscuits and butter. They placed them on the table and sat down. Mildred sat next to Kulak; Mrs. Watanabe sat alongside her husband.

Mildred looked at Kulak and asked, "So where were you all day?"

"I had a wonderful lesson, and then, after my lesson, I was practicing, and I came upon a large sea turtle. I was enjoying my ride until I got caught in a riptide. I didn't panic. But I had to paddle a long way to get out of it before I could get to shore. It exhausted me. I wound up on the beach where I met Glo and Tony. We got to talking. Tony related some of the hardships he endured in Vietnam. We went back to their camp, had lunch, and passed the afternoon talking. I forgot about the time of day. Do you know? He's a decorated war hero with a Purple Heart, and Silver and Bronze Stars. People spit at him when he returned home."

Tony hung his head as though he was ashamed of the time he served.

"What branch of service were you in?" Albert asked.

"The marines. I did two tours over there, man."

"Thank you for serving our country," Mildred said, "but I hated that war and protested it."

"I'm with you, Mrs. Meyers," Tony said. "I've had a change of heart since then."

The others listened with interest. He continued, "I was so brain-washed by the industrial-military complex, and I was just seventeen when I joined. Now, I see the real injustice of it all."

"I'm glad to hear that," Mildred said.

Kulak stopped eating for a moment. "This is delicious. You ladies deserve a toast." He put down his fork picked up his *mai-tai* and raised it. "Here's to Mildred and Sue. Oh yes, and a toast to the soon to be newlyweds." He motioned towards Stanley and Karen.

Everyone raised and clinked glasses, reiterating Kulak's good wishes for the soon-to-be newlyweds.

Mildred turned to him, and said, "Thank you, Arthur.

"You're welcome," he said.

Glo looked at Stanley and Karen, and asked, "You guys are getting married?"

"Yes," Stanley said, smiling at Karen who smiled back.

"Oh, congratulations, man," Tony said enthusiastically.

Mildred turned to Tony and Glo, and asked, "Have you heard anything about them building on that land where you live?"

"There have been rumors about a condo development," Tony answered.

Glo added, "I'm sure they're going to push us off the land eventually."

Tony said, "The local authorities have been harassing us—threatening to burn down the camp. We think somebody else has bought the land."

"Do you know who the developer is?" Mildred asked.

"No." Tony continued, "We live off-the-grid and tread carefully on the land. These rich developers destroy the environment and the powers that be bend over backward to get their tax dollars."

Albert said, "I don't know how they get away with the kinds of things they do. I was at the county offices all day. They had me jumping through more hoops than a circus act."

"They say they're going to widen the road," Tony offered.

Stanley responded, "That's a good thing. You can barely get two cars wide."

Mr. Benson looked over at Neil's son and asked, "Jason how's the pitching arm?"

"Good."

Jason French had dark brown hair that hung over his bright, blue eyes. He was tall for a ten-year-old, almost five feet, and lean like his father.

"He's getting ready to try out for the little league team," Neil mentioned.

"That should be exciting," Mrs. Benson said.

"We have to go shopping for a new baseball glove this week," Annie told them.

Jason stopped eating, looked up and said, "Yeah, I saw the mitt I want—the Hank Aaron one."

"You like Hank Aaron?" Albert asked.

"Yeah."

"I met him once," Albert said.

"Yeah?" Jason asked with wide eyes.

"He came to a basketball game I played in college."

"That's so cool. Did you get his autograph?"

"I did. When I get the rest of my stuff unpacked, if I find it, I'll show you."

The salad bowl and biscuits were still circulating, and people began digging into their food.

Mrs. Eichel, after her first bite of chicken, said, "This chicken is delicious."

"It's an old Hawaiian recipe," Mrs. Watanabe answered. "I'm glad you like it."

There were more raves as others started to eat.

"You two cooked another delicious meal," Mrs. Benson said.

"Thanks to both of you," Mr. Benson said. "We had an interesting walk today. There was an open house—we went to see what they were selling. We met a very nice realtor and after relating to him our real estate experience, he offered us a job—selling condos."

"Can you imagine that?" Mrs. Benson said.

"You're not thinking about doing it, are you?" Mildred asked.

"It's very tempting, Mildred," Mr. Benson answered, "to get back into the action again."

Mrs. Benson said, "Who knows if we would have the energy."

"It sounds like you'd be helping the enemy," Mildred complained.

"Now Mildred, if they care to work, who are we to put the kibosh on it?" Kulak asked.

"Condos! Everywhere you look around here—they're putting them up. I heard Princeville is going to be mostly condos," Mildred claimed.

"That's exactly why it would be a good opportunity for Pauline and me," Mr. Benson said. "There are eleven-thousand acres up there they're going to develop."

"Mrs. Meyers, I agree with you," Tony said.

"I'm with you, too, Mrs. Meyers," Glo admitted.

"I don't like them either," Mrs. Eichel added. "They're gutting buildings all over the Upper West Side, where I live, and turning them into condominiums. Sometimes they call them co-ops. I don't know what the difference is."

"It's just how they market it. It's marketing bullshit," Neil said with a smirk.

Karen looked concerned and said, "I didn't realize that was going on Ma."

"Oh, yeah, it's so noisy all day long with big trucks coming and going constantly. Then, they dump all the refuse down these long shoots into dumpsters at the curbside. It scares the heck out of me sometimes."

"Wow!" Stanley uttered.

Mildred looked around the table. She was pleased everyone was enjoying dinner, and said, "Make sure you save room for dessert."

"Yes, Mildred made her delicious strudel," Mrs. Watanabe told them.

"That sounds wonderful," Karen said. "Stanley and Nancy told me how scrumptious it is."

"You never had my strudel?" Mildred looked surprised.

"No. I can't wait."

Tony and Glo wondered who Nancy was. Mildred noticed their curious looks and clarified for them. "Nancy's my daughter. She passed away last year."

Karen added, "And my best friend."

Tony and Glo offered their condolences.

A quiet moment ensued. There was only the sound of forks and knives clinking on plates.

"How are the wedding plans coming?" Mr. Kulak asked, looking at Stanley and Karen.

"We're excited about it," Stanley said, smiling at Karen.

Karen smiled pleasantly at her fiancé. "My dress is beautiful. We have the guest list."

"We ordered the pig," Neil said.

"And I have a crew to help prepare and cook it," Albert explained.

Neil added, "And Stanley, we were looking for you earlier. They're giving us the larger pig for the same price as the two suckling ones. They don't have any of those right now."

Stanley and Karen thanked him for taking care of that.

"We have all the food and drinks ordered," Albert told them. He looked at Tony and asked, "Do you do any carpentry?"

"Yes," Tony said.

"He's very good," Glo said, proudly. "He built the place we live in."

"We need help remodeling the cottages in the back," Albert said. "Would you be interested in helping? I can pay you."

"Yeah, man. I can use the work."

"Albert, that's a good idea," Kulak said between bites of food. "I saw the place Tony built. Quite impressive!"

For the second time, a quiet fell over the table as everyone continued to enjoy their food.

CHAPTER 6

The next morning before they finished breakfast, they heard a vehicle pull up the drive. The dining room had a large table, three windows on one side of the room made it bright and airy. On the opposite wall and behind the table, there was an antique credenza. An old crystal chandelier hung over the table. The front of the room had an archway to the living room. On the opposite end of the room, a door led to the kitchen.

Tony walked into the dining room, and said, "*Aloha*, and good morning!"

Everyone greeted him in return.

"You're here to work?" Albert asked.

"I'm ready to get started, man."

Mildred asked, "Do you want some breakfast or coffee?"

"No thank you, Mrs. Meyers. I already had breakfast. I don't drink coffee anymore; it makes me too hyper and keeps me up at night."

Albert stood up with his dish and cup. "Why don't you follow me, Tony? I can show you what needs to be done."

"I'll probably see you all around," Tony said.

Everyone wished him well and he followed Albert into the kitchen. Albert put his things in the dishwasher, and they went out the back door.

Albert and Tony walked to the cottages behind the big house. They were also in need of a paint job—their green and white paint was chipping or in some cases gone completely. Some of the rooftops looked like they needed patching or replacement. "I'll show you the farm, and then, I'll show you inside."

They walked past the last cottage. Before them, a path led through the fields of which both sides had rows of produce growing. Albert pointed out the various crops that were flourishing. "So, we have lettuce, green beans, and different kinds of herbs over here." He pointed over to the other side, where Neil and Annie were clearing weeds from around carnations, orchids, birds-of-paradise, and hibiscus. They waved. Albert and Tony walked over to them.

Neil said, "Hey that's great that you can help us."

"Yeah thanks," Annie added.

"No problem, man." Tony smiled.

Albert said, "I'm just going to show him the rest of the farm."

"Let us know if you need anything," Neil told Tony.

"Yeah, thanks, man."

At the end of the planted rows, there was a somewhat larger green cottage with white trim. Originally, it served as the plantation manager's home. Albert said, "That's where Neil, Annie, and Jason live. It's all remodeled inside. They did a nice job."

They continued around the back of the property, passing, rows of coconut palms, banana, mango, noni, and papaya trees. Then, several large marijuana bushes shot up from the ground. As they got closer, there was a strong skunk smelling odor. Tony smiled, and said, "*Pakalolo!* That's what they call it around here."

"Neil and Annie take special care of these. I'm sure they wouldn't mind you helping yourself. But please be discreet about where you got it. We don't want the authorities back here snooping around."

"Smells pretty potent, man."

"Let me show you the inside of the cottages." They walked back to the first one and stopped. "I'll show you what we've done to this one. Let's go inside."

The cottage sat above ground to allow water to flow under in case of a *tsunami*, or flooding. Four steps took you up to a wooden porch. A cedar door opened into a living room/dining room. There was a high ceiling also made of cedar. There were enough windows in both rooms to bring in lots of sunshine. The updated kitchen had new appliances and cabinets, and a high counter with four bar stools in front of it. The dining and living room furniture had a tropical appearance and looked new. Albert explained, "As you can see this one just needs to be painted outside."

Albert walked him through the rest of the house, showing him the two bedrooms that were also furnished and a remodeled bathroom as well. "You can start working on the next one. Right now, that one needs to be gutted just like we did here."

They left the cottage and walked a few steps to the next one. Upon entering, its rundown condition was obvious. The kitchen looked old, the porcelain sink had green-stains, and the linoleum floor was worn. The dining room and living room carpeting had threads showing through. The rooms had old decrepit pre-war furniture.

As they came back into the main room, Albert said, "You can start in here. There's a dumpster outside. All the furniture, carpeting, the kitchen cabinets can go in there. When you're ready, we'll help you take out the refrigerator and any other large items. There's a pile of junk already out there. We'll have it taken away when we have enough for a pickup."

"Maybe, we can use some of that out at the camp."

"You're welcome to take whatever you want."

"Thanks. I'll look through it… I'll get my tools and get started."

The two men walked outside. "I'll be in the house if you need me," Albert said.

Tony walked over to his pickup, got in, drove it over to the cottage, got out, took some tools out of the back, and went inside. He put his tools down on the floor, and before he started to work, pulled out a joint, lit it, and inhaled. As he gazed around the room, he could envision this place looking as nice as the one Albert had just shown him. He was glad to have the work.

CHAPTER 7

Stanley, Albert, and Karen were in Stanley's office. Albert sat in front of the desk. Karen sat behind it counting names on the wedding guest list and said, "There are forty-two people confirmed."

Stanley was taking toy soldiers out of a small box, unwrapping the tissue paper, and wiping them with a cleaning rag. "We should have enough food and drinks," Stanley said. He placed one of the soldiers carefully into a glass cabinet mounted on the wall. It contained a small army of these little guys. Several intricate model ships and airplanes sat on bookcases, and shelves around the office.

"Sounds like we are in good shape," Albert indicated.

"Miss Louise and her friend will be here today. I'm picking them up at the airport this afternoon," Stanley told them.

"Her friend?" Karen questioned.

"Yeah, she said she's coming with someone named Harry, an old friend of hers."

Karen and Albert smiled mischievously. "I'm going to come with you," Albert said. "We need to pick up some materials for the cottage Tony's working on."

"When's Jeff coming?" Stanley asked, Karen.

"I spoke to him before I left L.A. He said he would probably be here tomorrow. He has a place to stay and will rent a car."

"Tomorrow he's coming?" Stanley asked. "Mrs. Bennetti is coming then, too. I wonder if they're on the same flight. I was going to go pick her up, but maybe, she can come with Jeff."

"I'm sure they're on the same flight. There's only that one afternoon flight coming in these days," Albert said.

Karen said, "I'll give him a call later."

Stanley stopped what he was doing. Something in the pile of mail on his desk caught his attention. He picked up the envelope on top, opened it, removed a small piece of beige colored stationary, unfolded it, and read it. "Oh, no!" he uttered.

"What's the matter, sweetheart?"

Stanley looked up, tears forming in his eyes. "It's from Robert Bennetti, Mrs. Bennetti's son."

Karen and Albert sensed something wrong. With tearful eyes, Stanley said, "Mrs. Bennetti passed away."

"Oh," Karen sighed.

"He wishes us well with our wedding plans. He's mailing her wedding present."

Stanley stood slowly and said, "I'm going to go tell the others." He left the office. Albert and Karen followed with their eyes. They knew he was upset.

Stanley went out to the porch where Mildred and Kulak were sitting. "Can you come inside a minute? I have to tell everyone something."

Mildred and Kulak wondered what it was. They got up and followed him to where the Bensons sat in the living room reading *The Garden Island* newspaper. The

Bensons looked up as Stanley, Mildred, and Kulak stepped into the room followed by Albert and Karen. "Please stay here. I have to get the Watanabes." Stanley still held the piece of stationery in his hand. They looked at Albert and Karen for an explanation but neither one of them wanted to break the news.

Stanley returned with the Watanabes. The Watanabes sat, and Stanley stood next to Albert and Karen. When everyone settled with curious and anxious looks on their faces, Stanley held up the letter and said, "This is from Mrs. Bennetti's son..." Stanley couldn't help choking with emotion.

Stanley said with a controlled effort, "Mrs. Bennetti won't be coming to the wedding." The others suspected something terrible. "She passed away last week."

"Anna? Oh, no!" Mrs. Benson gasped.

"She was so excited about seeing everyone and coming to the wedding," Mildred said. "What happened?"

Karen put her arm around Stanley's waist as he tried to compose himself. Finally, he said, "She won a lot of money at the track. They found her sitting on a bus stop bench. She had all her winnings in her purse. Mrs. Bennetti suffered a heart attack."

A pall fell over the group. Mr. Kulak broke the silence and said, "Anna was a good woman. She loved her gambling. Her husband was worse. But I think the man had more winners than poor old Anna. She'd lose her whole Social Security check sometimes."

They all agreed.

"And she did have a bad heart," Mrs. Benson reminded.

"Remember how obsessed she was with that Rubik Cube?" Mr. Benson said.

"And then, she lost it," Stanley added.

"Did he say anything about funeral arrangements?" Mr. Benson asked.

"No, he didn't. I think they probably had one already."

"We should send flowers or something," Mr. Kulak suggested.

"We could send him and his family some fruit from the island," Mildred added.

"Yes, that's a good idea," Karen agreed.

"There's that fruit stand in Kapa'a that ships. I can stop there on my way to the airport and order something," Stanley said.

"Good idea," Kulak responded.

Mr. Benson offered, "Let us know what it costs. We can all chip in."

The mood in the room was glum.

Mrs. Watanabe said, sympathetically, "We all have to go some time."

Her husband shook his head in agreement. They all sat with sad expressions.

"That's it!" Stanley said. "Sorry to be the bearer of bad news." He was not good with death, especially when it was one of his residents.

CHAPTER 8

In the late afternoon, Stanley and Albert returned with Miss Louise Hart, and her friend Harry Leonard. As they stepped out of the van, the residents stood side-by-side as though they were a reception line, waiting to greet the new arrivals.

Miss Louise, a tall, still attractive eighty-year-old, wore an expensive-looking white pants suit, a white straw hat over her blue-gray hair, and big black sunglasses. She smiled at her old friends. "I'm so glad to be here. It looks lovely."

Harry her companion was a few inches shorter than Louise, also in his eighties. Despite the wrinkles, he was still dashing with thinning white hair, slightly overweight with a bit of a paunch. He wore a white Panama hat, white linen suit, over a white and black pinstriped open collar shirt. The thickness of his glasses and the cautious way he took steps suggested failing eyesight.

Miss Louise introduced Harry to the others. Harry looked at all the chickens running around the property and said, "Are these guys tonight's dinner?"

Everyone laughed.

Mrs. Benson asked, "Stanley, did you get the fruit?"

"Yes, they were sending it out today—a basket of tropical fruit."

"Did Stanley tell you about Anna?" Mrs. Benson asked.

"Yes. I'm so sad. I was so looking forward to seeing her."

"We all were," Mildred said.

"We tried to have lunch several times, but I had to cancel. My schedule was so crazy working on the show. It was hard to plan anything. Now, I'm so sorry we didn't. Oh gosh! I feel awful."

While everyone chatted, Albert asked Stanley, "Should we take their luggage out, now?"

"We can drive it over to the cottage."

Miss Louise overheard them and asked, "What we can't stay here?"

"You're going to be in one of our cottages in the back," Stanley said.

"Oh!" Miss Louise looked surprised.

"They just remodeled it," Mildred added. "It's lovely. Wait till you see it."

"That sounds nice," Harry said with a wide smile.

"Maybe, you want to freshen up a little?" Stanley asked.

"We've been traveling all day. I could use a nice shower and a change of clothes," Miss Louise said.

"I can use a drink," Harry said.

"We'll have cocktails on the porch," Karen suggested, "when you're ready."

"We want to hear all about your TV show," Mrs. Benson said.

"It's not on the air here," Mr. Benson claimed.

"It might not be on the air anywhere, soon," Miss Louise said with a disappointed look on her face.

The others looked at her with interest.

"We're waiting to hear its fate," she clarified.

Stanley looked around and said, "Let's get them settled, and then, we can all sit and catch up."

They went to the van. Stanley said, "I guess we can just walk over."

Stanley and Albert took out the luggage and led Miss Louise and Harry to the cottage.

As they walked inside, Miss Louise saw the kitchen and said to Harry, "Don't expect me to do any cooking."

Harry laughed, dramatically put his hand to his heart, and said, "Oh, I'm so disappointed," as he shook his head from side-to-side.

"There are two bedrooms," Stanley said.

Albert and Stanley set the suitcases down on the living room floor. "I have some stuff in the van for Tony." He explained to Miss Louise and Harry that Tony was working on the other cottages. "It was nice meeting both of you. I'll see you later."

Miss Louise and Harry thanked him for picking them up and for their accommodations. Albert left.

Stanley said, "Let me show you the rooms." He picked up their luggage and carried it down the hall. Miss Louise and Harry picked up two small carry-ons.

As they got to the first bedroom, Stanley felt uncomfortable asking, "Do you both want to stay in here?"

"Oh gosh, no," Miss Louise exclaimed. "He'll keep me up all night with his snoring." Then, something seemed to come to mind, and she said, "Anna was the best roommate."

Stanley looked at her sadly. Mrs. Bennetti and Miss Louise had shared a room in the Hollywood house.

"She was such a great friend. I loved the time we had together. At least, she died doing what she loved." She turned to Harry who looked a little confused. "She loved to gamble."

"The horses?" Harry asked.

"The horses, cards—she enjoyed the excitement gambling gave her," Stanley exclaimed with a slight smile.

"Well I guess I'll be in the other bedroom," Harry said.

Stanley got them settled and left.

Later that evening, everyone sat around the outdoor dining table. Soiled dinner plates and leftover food sat on the table.

Miss Louise dressed in a flowery muumuu. Harry wore Bermuda shorts, a colorful Hawaiian shirt, and sandals on his feet.

"It is so nice to be here with you. I've missed you all," Miss Louise said.

Almost simultaneously, they all responded about how much they missed her.

"I don't know how long my TV series is going to last, but I told Stanley to save a room for me."

"That sounds wonderful Louise," Mrs. Benson said.

Mr. Kulak asked, "So how do you two know each other?"

"We're old friends," Miss Louise answered. "We hadn't seen each other for years until one day we met in the lobby and found out we were both living at the Chateau Marmont."

Harry said, "We reunited after what," he stopped to think, "some twenty-five or thirty years?" Harry looked to Miss Louise for verification.

"Who could remember back that far?" she said and waved her hand at him.

"So, what's the story on your TV show?" Mr. Kulak asked.

"We're waiting to hear if it's going to get picked up for another season. Jeff thinks it will."

"Are you enjoying it?" Mildred asked.

"Oh, yes. I missed the work. I have to admit I'm a lot slower to learn lines than some of the younger ones on the show."

"And what about you Harry… What do you do?" Mr. Benson asked.

"I've been retired over twenty years."

Miss Louise added, "Harry's an award-winning writer."

Back in the day, Harry and Louise had a very sensual relationship, but now, they enjoy each other's company, sharing memories, meals, drinks, and conversations. They loved talking about old Hollywood, their friends, and acquaintances. Who was still alive and who wasn't?

"What did you write?" Mrs. Benson asked.

"Broadway plays, TV shows, and movies. I dabbled at writing several novels, but they always fizzled out after a hundred pages or so."

Mrs. Watanabe started to pick up dishes. Her husband helped and Mildred did too. The three of them carried everything into the kitchen. Karen and her mother pitched in, too.

CHAPTER 9

The day before Stanley and Karen's wedding was a busy one for Mildred and Mrs. Eichel. Starting early that morning, there were deliveries of food, liquor, beer, wine, soft drinks, a large white tent, *tiki* torches, tables, chairs, lights, dinnerware, silverware, serving plates, and linens. Later that evening, there was a rehearsal and dinner.

Mildred had prepared lists of to do's and deliveries they expected. She and Mrs. Eichel carried their lists like commandants in a military operation. Like Mildred, Karen's mother possessed excellent organizational skills, a result of her many years of helping New York City non-profits with fundraisers. She had no problem keeping up with Mildred.

Stanley was a nervous wreck. He kept checking with the two women every time a truck pulled up the drive. "Did the tent come, yet?" he asked.

Mildred said, "Stanley, it's best if you just let us take care of everything."

Nevertheless, as the three of them stood in the yard and watched the deliverymen unloading the truck, Stanley continued pacing, almost as if Mildred hadn't said anything. He looked around for something, and then asked, "Where are the tables and chairs? Did they come yet?"

"Stanley, please!" Mildred scolded.

"We have everything under control, dear," Mrs. Eichel told him. "Why don't you and Karen take a nice walk on the beach or something?"

Mrs. Watanabe, with an apron wrapped around her waist, came out the back door. "Can I help with anything?" she asked.

"Yes, give Stanley something to do," Mildred said.

Stanley looked a little miffed.

"I need help finding my cake pans." Looking at Stanley she said, "There are still some things we haven't unpacked. Can you see if you can find them? Maybe, they're in that room with all the boxes."

"Sure." He looked at Mildred and Mrs. Eichel and said, "You ladies seem to have everything under control. Call me if you need help."

The women looked at each other and sighed simultaneously. Stanley and Mrs. Watanabe turned towards the house, then stopped when they noticed dust flying behind Tony Santos's pickup as it quickly came down the drive and pulled to a stop. Tony jumped out and asked, "Is Glo here?"

Stanley said, "No. We haven't seen her. What's going on?"

"The cops came this morning and told everybody to get out of the camp, man."

"Why?" Mildred asked.

"They say that the property was sold. The new owner wants everyone off his land. I just wondered how come the current owner didn't tell us he was selling."

"Who's the new owner?" Mildred asked impatiently.

"We don't know. A bunch of kids left right after the cops came."

"Where did they go?" Stanley asked.

"I don't know."

"What did the cops say?" Mildred inquired.

"'You people better pack up and get out of here.'"

"That's what they told you?" Stanley asked.

"Yeah, man."

Mrs. Watanabe started up the stairs, turned around, and said, "Stanley, come on. I need your help."

"I'm sure everyone will be all right," Stanley told Tony.

"I hope so. I just wish I could find Glo."

Stanley followed Mrs. Watanabe into the kitchen.

Stanley looked in the room with all the unpacked boxes and decided the only way he would find anything was to empty the boxes and clean out the room. Karen noticed him in there and said, "I'll help you."

"Thanks. I haven't found Mrs. Watanabe's cake pans yet."

Karen started emptying boxes, too. Then, Stanley found Mrs. Watanabe's pans. When he returned from the kitchen, Karen stood over an opened box. She held out her hand and said to Stanley, "Look what I found."

Stanley stared at the Rubik's Cube in her hand. She gave it to him. Stanley rolled it around in his hand. "It's Mrs. Bennetti's." He held it out for Karen to see. "She had only one more on each of these two sides."

With Stanley out of their hair, Mildred and Mrs. Eichel turned their attention back to the deliverymen who were almost finished unloading their truck. Tony walked over and asked, "What's going on?"

"Stanley and Karen are getting married tomorrow," Mildred said.

"Oh, I didn't know the wedding was tomorrow. "Maybe, I shouldn't come to work tomorrow?"

"You'll have to talk to Albert about that," Mildred said."

"Is he around?"

"No, he's out running errands. He'll be back later. You and Glo should come to the wedding."

"Thank you. What time is it?"

"Come at four o'clock for the ceremony," Mrs. Eichel said. "The reception will be around five."

"Thank you! We'd love to. What should we wear?"

"Something nice," Mildred said. "And comb that hair!"

"Yes, ma'am!" He clicked his heels, saluted them, and then grabbed his tools from the truck.

"If we see Glo, we'll send her back there," Mildred said.

"Thanks!" He headed to the cottage where he was working.

Mildred said to Mrs. Eichel, "He's a nice young man... for a hippie."

"Yes, he is."

"I wish he'd cut that hair and shave."

The deliverymen finished unloading the truck. The guy in-charge carried his clipboard over to Mildred and Mrs. Eichel. They compared lists and verified the delivery. "It looks like it's all here," Mildred said to Mrs. Eichel. Karen's mother nodded in agreement and Mildred signed the invoice. The man ripped off a pink copy and gave it to her. "Just call us when you want us to pick everything up."

The women smiled and Mildred told him they would.

A little later in the morning, Albert drove up and got out with four native-looking young men that he hired to help. Albert said to Mildred and Mrs. Eichel, "They're going to put up the tent, assemble a wooden dance floor, set up tables and chairs, and dig the *imu*."

"What's that?" Mrs. Eichel asked.

"That's the hole for the pig roast."

Albert took the men over to the area on which the tent would sit, then they walked about fifty yards from there to a beautiful green lush area in a grove of kukui trees sitting beside a tributary of the Waioli River whose gentle waters lapped at the shore. Albert instructed them to clean up all the fallen leaves and debris, lay the rolled-up carpet of fake grass for the bride and groom to walk and stand on, and to set up a trellis under which the wedding ceremony would take place.

After Stanley finished cleaning the room, he looked tired and wandered into the living room where Karen and Mr. Kulak were playing chess. Kulak looked up as Stanley entered. "She's beating the pants off of me, Stanley."

"I bet you don't mind that," Stanley said with a sly smile on his face.

Karen smiled at Kulak just before she moved her knight and said, "Checkmate!"

Stanley laughed and said to Karen, "At least he's not beating your pants off."

"Damn! I must be slipping because I didn't see that move coming. I think Stanley distracted me."

"Hey, don't blame it on me," Stanley pleaded.

While Kulak stared at the chessboard, trying to figure out where he went wrong, Stanley looked dolefully at his fiancée.

Karen asked, "What's the matter, sweetheart?"

"Your mother and Mrs. Meyers suggested earlier we take a walk on the beach."

"Sure."

"Hey, that's a grand idea," Mr. Kulak said. "You kids go and enjoy yourselves. It's a beautiful day out there. I'm going to get my board and get out on the water. Maybe, I can walk to the beach with you."

"Sounds good. Let's go," Stanley said.

Stanley and Karen walked hand and hand towards the beach. Kulak walked alongside carrying his board and paddle. When they got there, Kulak headed out on the water. Stanley and Karen kicked off their shoes. For a few minutes, they watched Kulak paddle out. Then, they walked along the surf's edge, the water dancing at their feet. "We haven't had much time alone together since I got here," Karen said.

"I know. I'm sorry. It has been so busy. I still have a ton of boxes to unpack. And the wedding is tomorrow."

Karen had a curious smile on her face. "I hope you aren't getting cold feet," she said.

He looked down and said with a mischievous smile, "No just wet feet."

"Hah, hah!" She poked him playfully.

"I'm just a little nervous. I've never been married before."

"Ah… Stanley, I haven't been either. How do you think I feel?"

"Nervous, too?"

"A little."

"But you're used to performing in front of large audiences."

"That doesn't make it any easier." Karen seemed to remember something, and said, "I keep thinking about Nancy. I wish she was here. I miss her so much. We always said we would be each other's maid of honor."

Stanley felt her remorse as they walked along quietly, until Karen said, "Mrs. Meyers seems to be doing alright."

"I know. She doesn't talk much about Nancy. I wish she would."

"Maybe she talks to Mr. Kulak about her."

"I hope so."

"She got pretty upset when we couldn't find Mr. Kulak."

That night, Mildred and Mrs. Watanabe prepared a delicious lasagna dinner, with meatballs on the side, to follow the wedding rehearsal. The table was set on the lanai.

Jeff Kress had arrived earlier in the day and sat at the table along with the others. Jeff was the Hollywood producer of Miss Louise's TV show. He was also Nancy Meyers' boyfriend. The two lived together for three years until she passed away. Nancy spent her final days at Stanley's retirement home. During that time, Jeff bonded with Stanley and his residents and even helped Miss Louise to get the role in his show.

Jeff felt honored that Karen had asked him to take her down the aisle. Karen and Jeff remained friends after Nancy's death, and she and her mom, Irene Eichel, felt comfortable with Jeff filling in for her dad who had passed away ten years earlier.

Everyone sat around the table and watched Albert carry out a large pan of lasagna.

Mildred and Mrs. Watanabe came out with a dish of meatballs and a large salad bowl.

Mrs. Watanabe turned to her husband and said, "Clark! Can you please cut the lasagna?"

Mr. Watanabe picked up a knife and spatula He began cutting squares of lasagna; they passed him dishes and he placed servings on them.

"Jeff, how was your trip?" Miss Louise asked.

"Good. We even got in early."

"You've been here, before?" Mildred asked.

"One other time."

Harry said, "I've been here quite a few times. Kauai is my favorite island. Every time I come, there's more building going on."

There was a flurry of conversation about the condominium developments around the island.

Mr. Benson said, "They tell us these new condos in the area are selling like hotcakes."

"And the prices…" Mrs. Benson said as she shook her head in disapproval. "You won't believe what they're asking."

"And I heard they have monthly fees too," Stanley added.

"Those are called H-O-As," Mr. Benson clarified.

"What the hell's an H-O-A?" Mr. Kulak asked.

While he picked a forkful of the pasta, Neil said, "Homeowner association fees."

"And just what does that get you?" Mr. Kulak asked.

Albert explained, "They pay for maintaining common areas, landscaping, elevators, swimming pools, clubhouses, parking garages, fitness centers, and stuff like that."

"Sounds like another way to grab your money," Mr. Kulak said. He looked at Karen and Stanley and said, "So are you kids ready for the big day tomorrow?"

"I am," Karen, answered. "I don't know about Stanley. She squeezed Stanley's hand and smiled at him. He looked at odds with the situation.

In-between bites, Stanley said, "I'm ready too—just a little nervous."

"Ah, nerves. That's understandable," Mr. Benson said. "The day we got married there was an accident and we were caught in a massive traffic jam. We got to the church a half-hour late."

"And on top of that the best man, who was more nervous than us, left the rings at home," Mrs. Benson added. "We had to borrow some rings at the ceremony from wedding guests."

"There's something for you to remember, Albert," Mr. Watanabe said. "Don't forget the rings."

Albert was Stanley's best man.

Miss Louise said, "Everyone has a funny story or two about their wedding day."

Karen leaned over and whispered something in Stanley's ear. He turned to her, shook his head, stood up, and walked to the back door. He returned a few minutes later and placed the Rubik's Cube on the table, and sat down. The others stared at it with interest. Mildred was the first to speak, "Where'd you get that?"

"Oh, my gracious," Mrs. Benson said, "is it Anna's?"

Stanley picked it up and pointed out the two sides that were nearly complete. "I'm pretty sure it is. She said she had it almost done."

"Where did you find it?" Mrs. Watanabe asked.

"I found it… in a box I opened," Karen told them.

"How did it get in there?" Mr. Benson asked.

"I don't know. Maybe someone put it in the box when we were packing up," Stanley said.

They looked around the table to see if anyone could verify that.

"I don't think anyone would have done that," Mildred said.

"I miss Anna," Mrs. Watanabe said.

"We all do," Stanley second it.

"I never liked that she gambled," Mildred said, "but she was a good person."

"She was a lovely woman," Mrs. Benson said.

After dinner, the men took Stanley out to get him drunk at the Tahiti Nui. The women stayed behind and played games, sang, and danced behind the house to Hawaiian music, rock and roll, and old classics.

CHAPTER 10

The morning of the wedding was a bright, sunny day. The sky resembled the surrounding blue waters and a light trade wind blew from the west.

After breakfast, Mildred went out the back door to watch them prepare the pig. The table where they ate the night before had chicken wire over it, banana leaves, and a large, uncooked pig, split down the middle. The Watanabes were seasoning the pig with soy sauce, brandy, and rock salt. Mildred joined the Bensons, Miss Louise, Albert, Stanley, and Harry as they looked on.

Just a few feet away the young men who dug the *imu* the day before were stoking ironwood burning in the hole. Black river rocks sat atop the burning ironwood. The men started the fire a couple of hours earlier to properly heat the rocks. Mildred stood next to Albert and Stanley watching, she said, "That's a big pig!"

"Two-hundred-sixty-pounds. Born and raised right here on Kauai at Yamashiro's Farm," Albert said,

One of the workers said, "Let me know when you want rocks."

Mrs. Watanabe looked at her husband. He said, "As soon as we get the leaves in."

He and Mrs. Watanabe placed banana leaves inside the cavity. When they finished lining the pig, she said, "Start bringing them over."

"Why do you put the rocks inside?" Miss Louise asked.

"That way the inside cooks too," Mr. Watanabe explained.

The men carried over shovels filled with white-hot rocks and used them to cover the cavity. The pig sizzled, steam and smoke rose from the carcass. When the rocks completely covered the inside, the men tossed their shovels aside. The Watanabes and the others stepped back from the table.

The workers tending the fire raked the glowing coals and spread them out, making a flat surface for the pig to rest on, and then, they placed banana and ti leaves over the smoking fire.

At the table, two of the men wrapped the pig in the chicken wire. With wire ties, they secured the chicken wire in several places and covered it with more leaves. When they were finished, it looked like a big green bundle.

The other two workers came over and the four men carried the pig and set it down on the bed of leaves and hot rocks. They covered it with more leaves. Wherever steam poured out, they sealed it with leaves. Following that, they placed wet folded burlap over the pig, covering the entire hole.

Mr. Watanabe went to get the shovels by the table and handed them to the workers. He and the men shoveled dirt around the edges of the tarp. One of the men said, "We no want steam come out." He looked at Stanley and smiled, "In little while, it blows up like big balloon—like wife two-months afta wedding." He laughed heartily and his friends joined in.

Mr. Kulak said, "Stanley! I hope you are as fruitful as that."

Stanley shifted uncomfortably. Albert patted him on the back and smiled.

"How long does it have to cook?" Mildred asked.

"The longer the better," Mr. Watanabe said.

"The lead workman said, "Maybe, seven, eight hours—mo bettah."

At four o'clock that afternoon, all the wedding preparations seemed in-place. They had the trellis decorated with white and yellow flowers from the gardens. White folding chairs were set up in rows. At the ends of each row, tall white ceramic vases containing colorful bouquets of birds of paradise, white carnations, and orchids.

Under the big white tent with its sides rolled up, tables and chairs were set with white linen tablecloths, dinnerware, and glasses. There were two bars with bartenders to serve drinks. Several young people arrived dressed in white tops and dark pants—they were the servers.

One of the servers lit the many torches around the yard. The pig was still in the ground. Tantalizing aromas rose from the pit and wafted through the air.

There was a designated parking area and Neil, dressed in a white flowery Hawaiian shirt and dark pants, directed arriving guests into spaces. As they exited their vehicles, he told them, "Drinks and appetizers are being served in the tent. The ceremony will be over in the lush green area to the left of the tent. Get a drink and something to eat and find a seat."

People mingled in and around the tent as they sipped *mai-tais,* wine, champagne, and munched on Mrs. Watanabe's appetizers: bite-size *teriyaki* spareribs, miniature eggrolls, *teriyaki* beef skewers, *poke* and miniature grilled vegetables from the farm. Some curious folks wandered over to where the pig still roasted in the ground. They inhaled the fragrant aromas coming out of the *imu.*

Miss Louise wore a white hat with a big floppy brim and dressed in a tight print dress that revealed her thin and still attractive figure. Mrs. Benson wore a yellow pantsuit and her white hair looked recently styled. She and Miss Louise walked among the guests. They placed flower *leis* made of white and purple orchids around the necks of the guests and greeted them with *"Aloha!"*

As the time drew closer, guests wandered over to the ceremony area and found seats. Before too long, the preacher from the Waioli Hui'ia Church in Hanalei arrived. He was a middle-aged Hawaiian man with a round friendly face and a huge smile that matched his size. Just off to the side of the gathering, a three-piece band with a keyboard, ukulele, and slack key guitar, played soothing Hawaiian music.

The wedding party gathered in the yard. A female photographer snapped photos of the group.

Karen's bridesmaids were fellow ballet dancers. One of them, a pretty girl with dark hair piled high in Grecian curls, called Adrienne, the other bridesmaid was a very attractive tall blonde named Maureen.

Their partners were also male dancers from Karen's company. They wore a white shirt and pants. Adrienne and Michael were partners. Michael was an Italian dancer in the company and a former lover of Nancy

Meyers' while she and Jeff were living together. The well-built young man had a swatch of black hair over his eyes and looked more like a weightlifter than a ballet dancer. The other man had blond hair, very thin, and athletic looking. His name was Grant.

Mildred was matron of honor; she didn't want to be but when Karen asked her, she couldn't refuse. Mr. Kulak admired Mildred when he saw her approaching with the bridal party. She wore her hair up and had on the same long light green flowery dress that the bridesmaids wore. They had a tropical look and hung like a muumuu. Mildred carried a bouquet of colorful flowers as she walked down the aisle.

The wedding party marched down the aisle behind Mildred. The female photographer stood up front, her camera clicked away. Stanley and Albert stood next to the preacher. They dressed in white with Stanley wearing a traditional Hawaiian red wedding sash around his waist. The bridal party stood to the side awaiting the bride.

Karen appeared with Jeff Kress at the edge of the seating area. A collective sigh erupted when the guests noticed how beautiful she looked. Jeff also wore a white shirt and pants. Everyone stood awaiting their walk down the aisle. The photographer continued to move around and take pictures.

For a moment, Karen experienced an emotional emptiness because her best friend, Nancy, wasn't there. She wore a simple but elegant white, straight ankle-length dress. Around her head, she had a crown of white flowers, and around her neck a *lei* of white marriage flowers. Stanley wore a similar *lei* around his neck.

As Jeff and the bride started down the aisle, the band played the wedding march. In her nervousness, Karen almost tripped on the uneven ground. The audience gasped but Jeff steadied her. Karen looked embarrassed. They reached the front without any further mishaps. Jeff handed Karen to her husband-to-be and stepped aside.

The preacher began by saying, "*Aloha!*" He wore a white suit and an open-collared white shirt.

The guests and wedding party responded with, "*Aloha!*"

The cleric continued, "The *lei* is a love symbol, fragile and temporary as it may be, a *lei* may last only one day, but your love for each other will last until eternity. You may now exchange *leis* to recognize the love you have for one another."

Stanley and Karen took off their *leis*. Stanley's hands trembled as he placed his *lei* around Karen's neck. Karen smiled as she lifted her's over his head and let it fall around Stanley's neck. She took his hands and squeezed them. Stanley took a deep breath and seemed to relax a little.

The preacher continued, "On this beautiful day, in this gorgeous setting, we have come together to join Karen Eichel and Stanley Cutler in holy matrimony. Marriage is one of life's most sacred institutions. It's a commitment by two people who love each other and meant to bring out the best in one another."

He looked out at the guests, then, the bride and groom, and continued, "A wife and husband are each other's best friend. Marriage is a journey. Not always a smooth and joyful one, but the love you hold in your heart for each other will carry you through difficult times as well as those not so difficult ones. For a marriage to succeed, you must understand and forgive the mistakes life throws in your path. It encourages you to nurture new life, new experiences, and new ways to express the love you have for one another. When you pledge to love and care for each other, it will bind you closer than ever before. This ceremony is a promise to love each other and that will take a lifetime to fulfill."

A strong breeze blew and the leaves rattled; some of the guests shifted in their seats.

The minister continued, "Please repeat after me. I Stanley, take you, Karen, to be my wife. I promise to love, cherish and adore you for better and for worse for richer and for poorer in sickness and in health for as long as you both shall live."

Stanley repeated; his voice shaky.

The preacher turned to Karen and asked her to repeat after him. When he was through, Karen said, "I Karen take you Stanley to be my husband. I promise to love, cherish and adore you for better and for worse for richer and for poorer in sickness and in health for as long as we both shall live."

The preacher turned to Albert and asked, "Do you have the wedding rings?"

Albert handed over the rings.

The cleric held them up for everyone to see. He said, "These rings symbolize your love for one another as well as longevity. The ring is a never-ending circle of love and commitment. When you look at your rings, they will remind you that the love you have for one another is forever."

Looking at Stanley, he said, "Stanley please repeat after me."

Stanley accepted the ring from the preacher and took hold of Karen's left hand. He repeated the minister's words, "With this ring, I thee wed. I give myself to be your husband from this day forward. I seal it with this ring." He slipped the ring on Karen's finger. She smiled at him.

When Stanley was through reciting the pledge, the preacher turned to Karen, handed her the ring, and said, "Repeat after me."

Karen took hold of Stanley's shaking hand. She felt his hand relax as she said, following the preacher's words, "With this ring, I thee wed. I give myself to be your wife from this day forward. I seal it with this ring." She slipped the ring on Stanley's finger. He stared at it, then looked at Karen and smiled.

The preacher once again continued, "Your friends and family are witnesses to this blessed event. They will honor you as husband and wife from this day forward."

At this point, the cleric recited a Hawaiian prayer that loosely translated brought God's blessing upon the newlyweds, then he said, "Stanley and Karen, it is my pleasure to join you in holy matrimony as husband and wife. What God has joined together, let no man put asunder. I now pronounce you man and wife. You may kiss the bride."

They kissed for what seemed like a long time as the guests applauded. When they separated and smiled, Stanley looked relieved. The band began to play the *Hawaiian Wedding* song. The newlyweds turned and walked down the aisle followed by the wedding party. They stopped behind the seating area to greet their guests.

Shortly after, the guests went into the tent; the wedding party disappeared with the photographer for more pictures.

When it was time to remove the pig, a crowd gathered around to watch. The men from earlier, now dressed in finer clothes, and wearing work gloves, aprons, and rubber boots, lifted the smoking bundle and brought it to a nearby table.

They untied the chicken wire, removed the leaves and rocks. Steam, smoke, and a fragrant slightly sweet vanilla aroma rose from the carcass. There were oohs and aahs when the crowd saw the golden-brown pig. The crowd parted, clearing a path, and the men carried the pig into the tent to the serving area.

When the bride and groom returned, the band played soothing Hawaiian music. The bandleader introduced the members of the wedding party as they entered. Then, he introduced the bride and groom. The guests applauded. When the bridal party sat at the dais, everyone else took their seats.

Mr. Watanabe carved the pig, and they served dinner buffet style. Along with the roasted pig, there was *poi*, chicken long rice, stir-fried noodles, pork *laulau*, salmon, salads, and tropical fruits.

Albert toasted the newlyweds, "I wish our mom and dad were here today. They would be so proud to see my little brother, Stanley, married to his beautiful bride, Karen. Karen, I'm proud to have you as my sister-in-law. You're the sister I never had."

Karen smiled up at Albert.

"Stanley and Karen may your lives together have much happiness, and may it be a fruitful one." Albert raised his glass. Everyone clinked glasses, Albert clinked Stanley and Karen's glasses.

Later in the evening, Mrs. Watanabe's wedding cake made its entrance. It had five layers with a pineapple and cream filling. Guests stood up to see it carried into the tent. Mildred said to Mrs. Watanabe, "Sue, it's so beautiful we shouldn't eat it."

By nightfall, the lit *tiki* torches gave off their golden glow. Guests danced to Hawaiian music, rock and roll, and old standards.

However, there was another glow in the air that evening that went unnoticed and it came from down the road.

The band turned out to be quite versatile, and for the rest of the evening, the guests filled the dance floor. The band played Joe Cocker's *Leave Your Hat On*. The singer's voice was rough and gravelly, a lot like Joe Cocker's. Mr. Kulak joined a group of young men in an impromptu striptease on the dance floor. He stripped down to his boxer shorts and tee-shirt. A crowd surrounded the dancers and cheered them on.

Mildred refused to watch and sat at the dais. She thought about Kulak out there and smiled to herself. He was quite a guy in her mind, much freer with his body than she was.

CHAPTER 11

The reception was winding down when someone shouted, "There's a fire at the hippie camp."

Wedding guests streamed out of the tent and looked in the direction of the flames and smoke. The air had a noxious smell. A beat-up old Chevy raced up the drive and pulled to a stop at the side of the house. A bedraggled young man with long hair and beard jumped out. He walked quickly towards the tent and ran into Stanley, "I'm looking for Tony Santos and Glo! Are they here?"

Stanley pointed inside the tent where Tony and Glo were standing paralyzed on the dance floor staring out at the fire. Tony wore an ill-fitting white suit over a bright orange, flowery Hawaiian shirt. His long hair hung in a ponytail down his back. Glo wore a long flowing orange-colored flowery dress, with her hair swept on top of her head. The young man rushed over to Tony and Glo and said, "You gotta come right away. They're burning down the camp."

"I see it," Tony said.

"They're burning everything."

"See, I told you they were going through with it. They're not fooling around. We better get back there," Glo said.

As they rushed out of the tent, Tony said to Stanley, "We're leaving. Thanks for inviting us, man."

"Tell your friends to come here if there's nowhere else to go. We'll see what we can do."

"Thanks." Tony, Glo, and the young man got in their vehicles and sped away.

By the time they reached the main road, they saw residents of the camp wandering through the smoke and noxious air. They looked around as though in a bad dream, while others stood watching the destruction of their homes. Tony and Glo directed them to the Hanalei House.

The band had stopped playing. Folks stood on the dance floor and were concerned about the inferno.

When Stanley peered down the drive, he saw people walking towards the house. Some carried backpacks; others carried duffel bags and sacks filled with belongings. A few young children tagged along or were in the arms of adults. Karen stood next to Stanley. "Are the children from the camp?" she asked.

"Yeah, I think so."

"We have to help these people," Karen said.

Stanley and Karen, still in their wedding clothes, waved to the arrivals. The group coming up the driveway waved back. Mildred and Kulak came up beside Stanley and Karen. Mildred said, "We better make sure no one is hurt or burned."

Mildred stepped forward to meet them. Stanley, Karen, and Kulak followed. The hippies all had black smudges on their faces; their clothes were filthy and smelled of smoke. "What's going on?" Stanley asked.

One of the young men, a tall skinny guy said, "The cops and guys from the county's engineering department came. They warned us to get our belongings together and get the hell out. With flame throwers, some of the cops and the engineering guys went around setting the whole place on fire."

A girl with dreadlocks held the hand of a scared little girl who was crying. The dreadlocked girl said, "We tried to stop them. Anyone who got in the way, they hit with their clubs and arrested them. They took my boyfriend away." She started to cry.

Mildred, Karen, and Kulak helped them with their things and checked to see if anyone was hurt. Mildred asked, "Are any of you hungry?"

Some of them nodded that they were. Stanley said, "Follow me." He led them into the tent where there were still plenty of leftovers.

Mrs. Watanabe noticed the condition of the new arrivals and asked, "Are the *keiki* (children) alright?" She walked over to some of the young children to check.

Mrs. Watanabe turned to her husband, and said, "Go in the house and get some towels, soap, and water. There are basins under the sink."

Mr. Watanabe rushed into the house. The rest of the residents gathered around to help and make everyone comfortable. Some of the wedding guests hung around to help, too. Mr. Benson went inside to give Mr. Watanabe a hand. The two men returned with basins of water, soap, washcloths, and towels.

Mildred, Miss Louise, Mrs. Benson, Karen, and her mother helped clean the children. Stanley and the men filled plates of food for everyone. After some time passed, Tony and Glo returned with several more friends. Looking down the road, the flames and smoke were billowing above the trees. The air smelled of burning wood and rubber.

"It's a mess out there, man," Tony said. He was almost in tears. "All our hard work, gone, gone, gone..." He sat down on the ground with his hands over his face. "All our things are gone. It's all rubble now."

The ones who came back with Tony grabbed plates of food. Stanley told them, "You can all stay here in the tent tonight. In the morning, we'll figure out what else we can do."

They were grateful and thanked Stanley profusely.

That night, Stanley and Karen went to stay at the Coco Palms Hotel on the east side of the island, compliments of Jeff. Stanley felt anxious over what happened to the people from the camp, so he and Karen returned early the next morning in Albert's car. When they drove past the camp, they stopped to look at the still-smoldering devastation. There were piles of charred and still burning rubble where tree houses used to stand.

They turned into the Hanalei House drive but couldn't get close to the house because pickups, jeeps, and vans were parked haphazardly so he stopped the car and parked in the first place he could.

Stanley and Karen approached the big white tent and noticed the number of people had more than doubled from the night before. Mildred, Kulak, and the Watanabes were in the tent helping to feed everyone some breakfast.

When Stanley and Karen went into the tent, Tony noticed them and rushed over.

"There are a lot more people today," Stanley said.

Tony answered, "Yeah, I know. I'm sorry about all this, man. A lot of them are leaving later today."

"To where?" Stanley asked.

"Some are staying with friends in Lihue and on the south shore. Some who have money are leaving for the mainland. We'll have to figure out what to do with the rest."

Mildred came over and said, "You two didn't have to come back so early."

"We were concerned," Stanley said.

"We couldn't sleep anyway," Karen added.

Kulak wandered over and mischievously asked, "Did you have a nice evening?"

Karen smiled at him and said, "We had a lovely night, and this morning after our room service breakfast, we went for a swim in the pool."

"Just lovely," Kulak said.

Mr. Benson was busy giving the small children piggyback rides.

By the afternoon, the group had dwindled to a handful of people. Most of their vehicles were gone too. Stanley packed a bunch of hippies in his van and drove them to Lihue.

Later that day, Tony and Glo wanted to return to the campsite to see if there was anything, they could recover. Stanley suggested he take his van so they could put things into it. As the two couples approached the site, their nostrils filled with that acrid smell of smoke, burned wood, and rubber. Stanley pulled the van forward into the camp and stopped. They got out. There was a security guard on duty. He approached them aggressively and said, "This is private property. You're trespassing!"

Tony seemed to go into a trance as he looked around at the smoldering rubble. The smell and devastation made him flashback to burned villages he had been to in

Vietnam. His body shook for a second. His eyes bulged as he angrily faced the security guard who was at least a head taller. "We're here to look for our stuff!" he shouted.

Stanley said, "We don't want any trouble."

The guard backed away. "Yeah, yeah, yeah, sure, it's okay... Get whatever you need. Some other people are in there looking for stuff, too."

Tony with fists still clenched continued to scowl at the man for a long moment, and then, slowly backed away.

They looked around the camp with all its houses leveled and smoke rising from piles of rubble that were once homes. A few hippies were wandering around half-dazed, while others sifted through rubble searching for precious belongings.

Stanley and his group walked among the ruins. Tony pointed over to the left, and said, "That's our place over there. I mean that was our place." They walked towards a big heap of remains where embers still glowed.

As Glo got closer, she noticed something in the mess. "Look! Tony, it's my sewing machine." Under a pile of charred wood, and almost untouched, stood an old peddle-drive black Singer sewing machine. Part of the table burned, and its edges were charred black, but the machine itself looked all right. "See if you can get it out," Glo said.

Tony and Stanley pulled and pushed debris out of the way until they reached it.

Karen shouted, "Stanley, look at your feet!"

Stanley looked down at his high-top sneakers, they felt hot and smoke rose from under them. He jumped out of the space he was in and went into an awkward dance in which he tried to stomp out his smoldering shoes. It was somewhat amusing and made Karen and Glo laugh.

While Stanley continued to stomp his feet, the two women made their way into the rubble to help Tony who was struggling to free the machine. Tony said, "Keep pulling and pushing. I think it's coming free." He looked over at Stanley and asked, "Are you okay, man?"

Stanley was still rubbing his shoe on the ground and dancing around. "Yeah, I think it went out. Boy! Was that hot."

"You got a hot foot, man." Tony laughed.

Stanley jumped back in to help. Through everyone's efforts, the sewing machine came free. Their hands were black, and they had black smudges on their clothes. They carried it out of the rubble. Glo looked pleased as she assessed the damage. Karen asked, "How old is that?"

"Old, it was my grandmother's. It was perfect here because it doesn't need electricity. It operates with that peddle on the bottom."

Dusting off his hands, Tony asked, "How does it look?"

"All the rubber burned, but I think we can replace them."

"That's good," Stanley said. They gazed at the recovered machine. Stanley looked around the property. He felt a connection to the hippies that lived there. Nothing was standing. Many trees were charred or burned completely. Stanley felt bad for Tony who had built the house. With a sad look on his face he said, "What a mess."

Karen took his arm and felt a pang of sadness. "What a terrible thing to do to these people," she said.

"I know. We didn't do anything to hurt anyone. We were just trying to live peaceful lives in this serene place," Tony said.

Glo was rummaging around while Tony and Stanley carried the sewing machine to the van.

The security guard saw them and said, "Can I help you?"

"Thanks. I think we got it," Stanley said.

Tony looked at the man with the same contempt he had earlier. To Tony, this guy was the enemy. The marines trained Tony to kill his enemies.

Karen stood sadly watching Glo who looked frustrated as she picked up one burned object after another. "I don't see anything else that doesn't look ruined."

When Tony and Stanley returned, Tony had the same disgusted look on his face as Glo. He said, "Glo! Come on! Let's get out of here. There's nothing else to save."

Standing in the middle of all that rubble, Glo looked around and tears began to slide down her cheeks. Tony put his arm around her and led her away. Karen and Stanley watched and sympathized with the couple as they got back into the van.

CHAPTER 12

Several days later, only a few of the hippies remained at the farm. The little children, the wedding reception tent, and all the supplies were gone, too.

Three of the remaining hippie men and their girlfriends stayed in the cottages. They received room and board in exchange for helping Tony with the remodels. Their female partners helped in the kitchen and on the farm with Neil and Annie.

It pleased Albert to see how much progress they made on the cottages in just a few days. He had to order more lumber, appliances, paint, and supplies. They started painting the outside of the cottages. Albert was jubilant because it meant an early opening of his tourist business.

Mildred called the county offices and found out the new owner of the camp land was none other than her nemesis Calvin Daniels. She wasn't surprised. Mildred had already had confrontations with Daniels in her old neighborhood in New York City and again in Los Angeles.

She put it in her mind that she would stop him this time. Mildred heard through what the locals called the coconut wireless (word-of-mouth that passes news quickly around the island) that there would be a demonstration at the county offices in Lihue. She planned to be there. It was her first protest on the island, as well as the first one since the protests she organized in Los Angeles over a year ago. The rally was to coincide with Daniels' arrival on the island where he would meet with local officials to finalize the permitting process for the new project.

Miss Louise and Harry were still in their cottage, but Mrs. Eichel had returned to New York and Jeff to Los Angeles. Karen would have to return to Los Angeles for her final performance in a short while. Stanley planned to go with her. Following that, the two would head to Europe for a honeymoon. Then, Karen would retire with plans to start a family.

Miss Louise waited to hear if her show would have another season. Ratings had been so-so, not stellar. During its run, she made lots of money. She felt that she socked away enough to last her until the end of her life. She and Harry enjoyed their days on the beach and evenings with the other residents.

One afternoon, Karen and Miss Louise talked about starting a dance and acting school. "I don't know how much more work I can get in Hollywood. I enjoyed teaching when I did it in the past," Miss Louise said.

"I'm sure we can find a place in town to open our school," Karen said optimistically.

"That would be lovely," Miss Louise said. "Let's just see what the next few months are like. I may be back here before you know it.

With all the excitement over the fire at the hippie camp, Karen and Stanley never opened their wedding presents.

One afternoon, they sat in the living room with everyone to open their gifts.

There were many cards with cash, checks and even a U.S. savings bond. Mildred sat next to them collecting all the cards. Several opened boxes sat around the room. Some with silver plates, wine glasses, a wine decanter, towels, and more.

Mrs. Benson asked, "Where's Anna's present?"

They waited patiently to see what Mrs. Bennetti had sent. Her present came in a large padded envelope. They opened and unwrapped a picture in a dark wood frame. It was a younger, very attractive version of Mrs. Bennetti. She was sitting on a thoroughbred that had a horseshoe-shaped wreath of beautiful flowers around its neck.

Mr. Kulak said, "Now that looks like the kind of gift Anna would send." He laughed.

"Did they say anything about the picture?" Miss Louise wanted to know.

Stanley passed it around to everyone. The questions persisted until Karen opened an envelope with a wedding card and read out loud: "Dear Stanley and Karen, my mother wanted you to have this as a remembrance of her. This was at Belmont Park years ago. For a short time, my father owned a piece of this horse. It didn't win many races but somehow, it finished first in this big race. Wishing you a long and loving life, Robert Bennetti."

CHAPTER 13

A large crowd of protestors gathered outside the county office building in Lihue chanting, "NO MORE CONDOS! NO MORE CONDOS!" Among the crowd of locals, were hippies and the residents of the Hanalei House: Stanley, Karen, Albert, Annie, Neil, Miss Louise, and Harry. The demonstration was a peaceful one.

People stood on the top step of the building and addressed the crowd. Mildred got her turn and said, "I've seen firsthand what Daniels Development can do to deplete neighborhoods of their uniqueness and charm. These developments while satisfying short-term demands have long-term implications for the community. I say let's stop them now!"

The crowd cheered in response.

A stretch limo pulled in front of the building. The driver got out and opened the curbside back door. Calvin Daniels, the fifty-nine-year-old business executive, responsible for the protestors' anguish stepped out. The short, squat tycoon was slightly bald with a bad comb-over. He looked at the crowd in front of him and arrogantly marched toward them. Some folks recognized him and began booing; the others joined in when they realized it was Daniels.

Before he could reach the front door, the crowd encircled him. He tried to force his way through while the protestors continued to chant, "NO MORE CONDOS!"

With help from the limo driver who cleared a path, Daniels made his way to the edge of the crowd closer to the entrance. As they emerged from the throng of people, Daniels came face-to-face with Mildred. She stood between him and the door. She looked at Daniels with contempt and said, "So we meet again Mr. Daniels."

He frowned trying to recall who the woman in front of him was. Just then, a pineapple sailed through the air, narrowly missing Daniels. Mildred had to dodge it, too. Daniels' eyes darted around the crowd trying to determine where it came from. Mildred looked at the smashed pineapple on the ground. When she looked up, Daniels had a smirk on his face and they locked eyes. Apologetically and with a smile, she said, "I had nothing to do with that."

Suddenly, a spark of recognition came over him, "You're that woman—from New York. What are you doing here?"

"You do remember me. I'm trying to save this beautiful island from your greedy hands."

"And I'm trying to figure out how you got here. Because of you, I had to discard a suit badly stained by your rotten produce."

"I see you haven't changed your ways either. You're just out to destroy another place but this ain't the Lower East Side. It's a beautiful island with people who love it."

"You have some nerve talking to me like that."

Mildred shook her head and laughed. "Oh, why? You somebody special?"

"I know a troublemaker when I see one. You should be behind bars," he shouted angrily at her. "I don't know why you aren't."

The crowd that had been watching the altercation didn't like Daniels' tone and reacted. Besides booing louder and louder, people started shouting epithets and another pineapple flew out of the crowd, just missing Daniels again.

Inside the building, a couple of security guards observed the incident; they came out to rescue Daniels. He continued his tirade, this time turning and speaking directly to the protestors. "This woman has whipped you people into a frenzy. She's a convicted criminal who should be behind bars and I'm going to see that she's put there."

The crowd kept chanting. Daniels had to shout over the noise. The security guards tried to push the crowd back with little effect.

Daniels said, "Don't let this unstable woman influence you. She's a troublemaker and a professional agitator from New York—probably a communist."

Mildred took offense—she felt her anger rising.

Daniels continued, "She should be in an institution... Our condominium developments have won multiple awards for their design and environmental considerations. In every community we've built, property values have soared. You people are damn lucky to have this quality of residence on Kauai. We will build a place here that we can all be proud of."

The crowd booed him.

Mildred got in his face again, and shouted, "Not if I can help it!"

He ignored her and continued, "And it will create good-paying jobs for the people of this island."

The crowd was not buying it and booed louder. Daniels turned red with anger and addressed Mildred again, "I will be in touch with the New York authorities and report your behavior here today. I'm sure they will be very interested in how you got here." With that as his final remark, he pushed Mildred aside almost knocking her off-balance.

"You go right ahead and do that Mr. Daniels," she shouted after him.

With the help of the security guards, Daniels and his driver made it to the front door with the crowd right at their heels. The guards ushered Daniels inside: the people outside continued chanting, "NO MORE CONDOS! NO MORE CONDOS!"

Mildred held her hands high in the air to silence the crowd. She said, "That's our enemy. Now, you see what we're up against."

In the background, a TV news crew recorded the demonstration. The reporter, a thirtyish looking man with blond hair, tall and athletic-looking approached Mildred. With cameras rolling, he asked, "Calvin Daniels mentioned a previous confrontation you had with him?"

"Yes, he tore down my tenement and several others on my street on the Lower Eastside of Manhattan sending people who lived in those buildings for years and years into the street. I organized a protest to stop him. We were unsuccessful and we lost our homes."

"How did you wind up here on Kauai?"

"Well, that's a long story that I don't want to get into right now but I was surprised when I recently found out

Calvin Daniels is behind the development in Hanalei. This is the third time I've battled with him."

"You had other encounters."

"Yes, in Los Angeles. That's why I live here now."

"Well, that's an incredible story. Why are you so against this development?"

"Because once again, he's using his wealth to take advantage of another community. God knows the beautiful people that live on these islands have been taken advantage of enough. His development will have a detrimental impact on the locals and the environment, with traffic and overcrowding."

"And what's your name?"

"Mildred Meyers."

"Well, thank you for your input, Mrs. Meyers." He swiped his finger across his neck, indicating to the camera operator to cut.

The crowd started dispersing. Mildred and Stanley gathered their group together and headed away from the building.

That evening at the Hanalei House, everyone sat in the living room hoping to see Mildred on the news. As they watched, the anchor said, "As part of this year's bicentennial celebration, Kawika Kapahulehua with a fifteen-man crew on a double-hulled canoe with sails departed Hawaii today for Tahiti. Ben Finney the organizer of the adventure wants to prove the trip is still possible."

"I'd like to travel around the world on a sailboat," Tony said.

"Not with me," Glo claimed.

They noticed the picture changing and the protest came on TV. Stanley said, "Shh, here it is."

After the camera panned the crowd, Mildred appeared on screen talking to the reporter.

After the story, Mildred said to her fellow residents, "I wasn't prepared. He surprised me. I didn't expect to be interviewed."

"Well you did a good job," Miss Louise said.

"It depends on how Daniels' meeting went today with the land use people," Mildred answered.

"If they granted him the permits, construction will begin soon. You can bet on that." Neil said.

CHAPTER 14

Mildred was in the kitchen with Mrs. Watanabe helping prepare dinner. Annie and Neil came in. They looked as though there was something on their mind. "Is everything all right?" Mildred asked.

"Oh yeah," Annie said. "We're going to the community meeting this afternoon. We were wondering if Stanley and Albert are coming."

"Stanley and Karen didn't know if they would be back in time. They went shopping in Kapa'a. I don't know about Albert."

"Are you going, Mrs. Meyers?" Annie asked.

"Yes. Maybe, we can go over with you, Arthur and me. What time is the meeting?"

"Three o'clock," Neil said. "We'll come and get you when it's time"

Later in the afternoon, the Watanabes and Mildred were busy in the kitchen. Mrs. Watanabe was rinsing a big head of kale at the sink when Annie entered. "Mrs. Meyers, are you ready to go?" Annie asked.

"Yes. I don't know where Arthur is. He hasn't come back from the beach. He said he wanted to go."

"What time is the meeting?" Clark asked.

Mildred replied, "Three o'clock…"

"Why during the day?"

"I don't know. Maybe, they always have them during the day," Mildred wondered aloud.

Sue looked up at the wall clock. "It's almost that now."

"I'd like to go," Clark said.

"I'll stay here. You go," Mrs. Watanabe told her husband

The back door opened, and they turned to look, thinking it might be Kulak. To their disappointment, it was Miss Louise and Harry. Neil followed them in and impatiently said, "It's almost three—let's get going."

"We're ready," Mildred said.

"I'll stay and finish the cooking," Mrs. Watanabe told Mildred.

Annie asked, "What about Stanley?"

"They're not back yet," Mildred said. "Neither is Arthur."

Neil said, "Well maybe they can meet us there. Can you tell them we left, Mrs. Watanabe?"

"I will."

"We should go," Neil insisted.

"Sue, is it alright if I leave you?" Mildred asked.

"Go. I'll manage."

"I'll get back to help you as soon as I can."

"Let's go," Neil said.

"Alright, alright," Annie replied impatiently.

They all went out the door.

People packed the meeting room on the Waioli Hui'ia Church grounds. There were a few seats still available when Mildred and her group arrived. Some people stood on the sides and back of the room. Mildred and her companions took seats near the rear.

A long table with chairs behind it was set at the front of the room. A local male facilitator, two representatives of the condominium development company sat alongside the mayor of Kauai and two members of the land commission.

An elderly man, who looked like a longtime local, was standing at the podium in the center of the room facing the group seated at the table. He waited to be recognized. Finally, the mayor picked up the microphone and said, "Yes?"

"Why is this meeting being held during the day? People can't come because of work or they've had to take off from work just to be here. Why aren't we having this in the evening when more people can attend?"

The mayor, a short, middle-aged man with dark features said, "Thank you for your concern but there were scheduling issues between the parties involved. And this place is booked solid in the evenings, so we had no choice but to have it now."

"Well, I would suggest that in the future we find another venue where we can have this type of meeting at night—so that everyone can participate."

The mayor responded, "Thank you! We'll consider that."

The audience applauded and the man sat down with a still-troubled look on his face. The facilitator, a tall, middle-aged, Hawaiian man stood up and said, "As you all know, we are here to present and review the plans for the Daniels Development condominiums in Hanalei. Mr. Hodges from the company will speak first, then the architect, Mr. Jones. We'll open it up for questions following their presentations."

Mr. Hodges, a man in his forties, dressed in an expensive-looking, silk, Hawaiian shirt stood and turned on a slide projector. "I'm the construction manager. This is our latest rendition of the community." With a pointer in his hands, he circled the buildings with the pointer and said, "We took the communities' concerns about density and cut back the number of units from eighty to fifty."

The crowd grumbled and didn't seem appeased by this small token. "We also cut back the square footage of each unit by five-percent." There was more displeasure expressed. "Once all the applications and permits are in place, we estimate that the construction process will take about twelve months before we can open for business." Hands popped up all over the room.

"Please hold your questions and comments following Mr. Jones, the architect's discussion. Are you through Mr. Jones?" the facilitator asked.

The man sat and nodded that he was. "Mr. Jones would you like to speak now?" the facilitator asked.

The architect wore glasses, a white short-sleeved shirt, and a tie. He stood slowly and said, "I like to point out that we also scrapped the ten two-story homes from the project and we plan to widen the road leading to the property."

He displayed a slide showing a similar development. "As you can see from one of our completed projects, we've used landscaping, palm trees, and shrubbery for a more appealing appearance. This new plan is low-keyed compared to the earlier plans, which you may have seen in the newspaper. You probably still have unanswered questions and concerns." He sat down.

The facilitator stood up. "Let's do this in an orderly fashion." There was already a man at the podium. "You're first, sir," the facilitator instructed.

The man was short, Asian looking in his late fifties. "I've lived in this village all my life. I've witnessed so many changes. It's changing the way people live and work here. Why do we need this development?"

The audience applauded enthusiastically.

The man continued, "What will it add to our community? I see it as nothing but an inconvenience and trouble. I'm against it."

The room erupted in applause again.

Mr. Jones said, "This is our business. We build communities. We've built award-winning condominium complexes all over the United States. This project will reflect the good taste and excellent planning and land use of your community."

The room erupted in boos. Hodges continued, "It will also create jobs."

The man still at the podium interrupted, "We've heard that before. What kind of jobs—low paying jobs? Gardeners, caretakers, bellhops? Those aren't the kind of jobs we need on this island." The man turned his back and walked away from the podium before anyone on the dais could respond.

The next man stepped up to the microphone. "This land that we live on is sacred and holy. Houses, hotels, and condos are built all over sacred spots. It's got to stop. I want to see it stopped in my lifetime."

The crowd cheered. A little elderly Asian woman wearing a colorful muumuu spoke next. She had fuzzy white hair and bad teeth. "My name is Lucy Kapana. I live here a long time. I see a lot of changes all the time.

This is my home and you are messing with it. This is my community and you're trying to change it. I don't like it!" She stepped away from the mic.

Mildred stood up and got in line behind the last person.

A young man in his twenties, probably a surfer, stood at the microphone. "I've lived here since I was twelve. The numbers of people you're talking about coming here and buying condos…. and staying in them is way more than this small town can handle."

The speakers continued. No one spoke in favor of the project. Finally, Mildred got her turn. "My name is Mildred Meyers." People recognized her and started clapping. When they stopped, Mildred asked, "Where is Mr. Daniels? Why isn't he here?"

The facilitator answered, "Mr. Daniels couldn't be here because of another commitment on the other side of the island."

His answer didn't appease Mildred. She said, "I've only been living here a few months. I used to live on the Lower East Side of Manhattan. The tenement that I lived in for over thirty-years was torn down by this same company. Calvin Daniels, the owner, is a despicable human being."

The men on the dais shifted uncomfortably.

Mildred continued, "He's illegally evicted people from homes they lived in their entire lives. I was arrested in New York for starting a riot to save our homes. That's why I'm here today. To warn you about this man. To see that he is stopped. He's doing the same thing wherever he can get away with it. He has no concern for people whose lives it affects. It needs to stop here and now or else Calvin Daniels will continue to ruin people's lives. I'm here to fight this development with you."

Mildred touched a nerve. People stood and cheered.

At the end of the meeting, people congregated around Mildred asking questions and recruiting her and her companions' help. A tall, young man, in his early-thirties with blond-sandy hair wearing a press pass that said *Joe Thomas, The Garden Island* approached Mildred, and said, "I heard what you said about Mr. Daniels. Those are pretty strong words."

Mildred looked wearily at him. "Like I said. He's despicable."

"I'd like to interview you about your experiences with Mr. Daniels for my newspaper. Would that be alright?"

"Yes, but not right now. I have to get back home to cook dinner."

"When would be a good time?"

"How about tomorrow morning?"

"Ten o'clock?"

Mildred thought for a few seconds. "Yes."

"I can come to you. Where do you live?"

Mildred gave him the information.

"I'll see you tomorrow at ten."

Mildred nodded and as she walked away, she noticed a small man at the back of the room staring at her. Something about him seemed familiar.

CHAPTER 15

The next morning from her seat on the front porch, Mildred watched an old gray Volkswagen bug come up the road and turn into the driveway. The car came to a stop and Joe Thomas got out carrying a black leather attaché case. He said, "*Aloha*, Mrs. Meyers."

"Good morning!"

He climbed the stairs onto the porch.

Mildred asked, "Would you like coffee?"

"No thank you. I've already had too much this morning." He sat down next to Mildred, unsnapped his case, and took out a recording device, yellow legal pad, and pen. "Do you mind if I just ask you questions?"

"Not at all. Go ahead."

"Is it okay if I record it?" he asked, pointing to his recorder.

"Sure."

He switched on the recorder. "You're from New York?"

"Yes."

"How do you like it here?"

"Well, I'm still getting used to it. But I think I'm going to like it. It's so beautiful and green. I've never lived in a place like this. I lived in concrete and brick all my life."

"I'm glad to hear that. You know many people call this place paradise."

"I can see that."

"What brought you here?"

"I was living in this house in Hollywood—"

Joe interrupted, "I thought you said you came from New York."

"I do come from there, but after I was arrested, they made me leave New York and go to Los Angeles where my daughter lived."

"So, you were living with your daughter in L.A.?"

"No, she found a place for me to live… a nice place with people my age. Most of them are here as well."

"What were you arrested for?"

"Inciting a riot and some other things. Calvin Daniels and his company wanted to knock my tenement down so we protested. We lost the battle and eventually they demolished my home and several other neighboring tenements."

"So, you took on the city of New York?"

"That's right."

He wrote some notes on his pad. "Tell me about the riot?"

"We blocked off my street with barricades at both ends. We threw rotten fruit and vegetables at the police and sprayed them with whipped cream and shaving cream."

"Where did you get the rotten produce?"

"I used to work in the New York produce market until I retired. I had connections."

"Was Mr. Daniels there?"

"Oh, yeah. He didn't like it one bit. But in the end, we got arrested. They dropped the charges against most of the people. They wanted to make an example of me because I was the organizer."

"How long were you in jail?"

"It was about a day and a half."

"Had you lived there long?"

"Over thirty years. I grew up only a few blocks away."

"What about your daughter—how did she feel about what happened to you?"

"God bless her. She came to my rescue. I didn't like the place she moved me into at first; my room smelled funny and needed a thorough cleaning. But the people were so nice to me, especially, when Nancy—that's my daughter—got sick."

"Is she alright?"

"Oh no, she passed away… last year." Mildred choked up saying that.

"I'm sorry to hear that. What happened?"

"She had a very aggressive cancer that started in her liver. It advanced quickly. We lost her in two-weeks. They couldn't do anything else for her. We just tried to make her comfortable."

"What about chemo, radiation?"

"It didn't help. They ran out of options and the cancer spread quickly."

You must have been devastated."

"I was. Still, am."

"What about your husband?"

"He left us right after Nancy was born."

"Oh… You never heard from him again?"

"Never. He's probably dead by now."

"What an interesting life you've had. You must have had a hard time after your husband left."

"Fortunately, I was able to go back to work. My sister took care of Nancy along with her own two kids. I don't know what I would have done without her. I was a bookkeeper working for one of the vendors in the produce market."

"Trying to raise a child in New York City on one income must have been difficult."

"It was, but she turned out to be gifted."

"In what way?"

"Dancing. She became a prima ballerina and danced all over the world."

"How old was she when she passed away?"

"Thirty-three."

"That's awful. What about your family? You said you grew up on the Lower East Side."

"I did. My father was a bookkeeper, too, on Wall Street. He never made a lot of money. Not enough to support five kids. Mom helped by taking in sewing, laundry, and ironing. All of us kids tried to help out. She wasn't well either. She had Asthma. The New York winters were rough on her. When I was ten, she had a miscarriage. There were complications and then she developed pneumonia. She recovered eventually but she was never the same after that. I took over most of the household duties. Mom couldn't do the sewing, ironing, and laundry jobs anymore. Sometimes she coughed so much she would just collapse in a chair. I did most of the cooking and cleaning in the house."

"You were just ten?"

"Yes. My mother had another setback in 1919. My father died from the flu epidemic which was bad that year. Then, my brothers and I quit school to work and help out."

"Did you ever finish school?"

"Eventually, I did. I even went to Brooklyn College where I studied accounting."

"How did you go from all that to being an activist?

The day after the interview, the residents sat around the dining room table eating breakfast. Mr. Kulak read to them the article about Mildred in the newspaper. *I met Jane Jacobs at a community meeting. She was one of the speakers who were trying to save their neighborhood from the grasps of Robert Moses. He wanted to put a roadway under Washington Square Park in the Greenwich Village section of Manhattan. We got to talking afterward and I became involved in the effort to stop the proposed project. After that, we stopped construction of an expressway that would have destroyed neighborhoods along its route in Lower Manhattan.*

Eleanor Roosevelt was a friend of mine, too. She was involved in human rights and the civil rights movement. I marched with her for civil rights.

Mr. Kulak stopped reading when Albert asked, "Mrs. Meyers were you arrested other times?"

"Yes, I was. It's a good thing Nancy traveled a lot, even as a teenager. It gave me time to get involved."

Kulak started reading again. *I never thought that someday I would be fighting to save my neighborhood. This time Calvin Daniels was the enemy, not Robert Moses. Now, Daniels and his company are here on Kauai doing the same things they've done everywhere else. I'm prepared to take him and his company on again.*

Kulak finished reading and looked up. "Very nice article about you Mildred."

"Thank you. I just told him how I feel about condominiums and how they change communities."

CHAPTER 16

Several days later, Mildred sat on the porch drinking her morning coffee and reading *Newsweek*. Miss Louise and Albert came out the front door. He carried Miss Louise's suitcases, and Harry carried his. "Mildred, I have to say goodbye," Miss Louise said. "It was so nice to see you, again."

"Oh, I didn't know you were leaving today," Mildred said. "I thought you were waiting to hear about the show."

"I did. The show has been canceled."

"Oh, that's too bad. Well, why don't you stay, then?"

"My agent got me an audition for a role in a feature film. So, I have to get back for that."

"Oh, I hope you get the part."

"Me, too."

"And I hope you can come back for good," Mildred said.

"I'm thinking about it."

"Well don't think about it too long. You're not getting any younger. How about you Harry?"

"I'm seriously thinking about living here, too. I have nothing holding me in Los Angeles," Harry said.

"It so beautiful and peaceful here," Miss Louise said.

Mildred frowned. "If we can only get rid of Daniels and his damn condominiums…"

"Well don't let it get you down." Miss Louise smiled and hugged Mildred.

Harry hugged Mildred too. They got in Albert's car to drive to the airport.

Mildred sat back down. Miss Louise was right about not letting Daniels get the best of her, but she couldn't help the condominium project frustrating her. She wanted to do something to stop it. Something more than just protests. They needed to take drastic action.

Mildred looked up from her *Newsweek* magazine when a man's voice softly said, "*Aloha*, Mildred!"

The voice startled her. Somewhere in the deep recesses of her mind it sounded familiar. She stared at the man looking up at her but couldn't place him. He was short, wore a beat-up, sweat-stained, navy-blue sea captain's hat with a shiny black brim, a white tee-shirt, and plaid Bermuda shorts. Frail varicose-veined, bowlegs, poked out from his shorts. He didn't look healthy. Something with his left eye was awry because it sat lazily in its socket. That side of his face looked like he had suffered a paralysis. He stood stooped forward a little and his bushy white mustache twitched when he said, "Mildred, it's me, Vic!"

Mildred felt her heart stop for a moment and restart, beating even faster. She could feel her cheeks burning and making her face flush. As she looked closer, she couldn't believe her eyes. Different scenarios spun furiously in her mind but she couldn't emit a single word.

"Yeah, I'm sure this is a surprise. Yeah!" Vic Meyers continued.

Finally, Mildred, wide-eyed, responded, "A surprise is putting it lightly!"

"I saw you on the news, then at the meeting, and read about you in the paper. It took me a while to find out where you lived."

Then, she remembered seeing him at the meeting, staring at her when she was leaving. Mildred continued looking for some sign of the man she once knew. She couldn't believe this was who she married over thirty years ago. *What happened to his dashing good looks?* She wondered.

"Can I come up?" he asked.

He took Mildred's unconscious nod as permission to step up on the porch. As he did, she saw in those pale blue eyes something that looked familiar. *He has Nancy's eyes,* she thought to herself. *Or was it—Nancy had his?*

Mildred felt vulnerable and wanted to call out to someone, but just sat motionlessly. She could feel her anger rising but said, "Have a seat," then she wondered why she even said that. Did she really want him to sit near her?

Vic sat cautiously, less than a foot away from the woman he knew he still loved.

Mildred said in a not-so-friendly tone, "All these years I thought you were dead."

He looked at her and wondered why he'd come. "I'm still alive," he tried saying light-heartedly. "Yeah! We would probably have been married... thirty-four or thirty-five years by now."

Mildred knew exactly how many years it was. She didn't want to tell him she had never filed for a divorce.

Instead, she said, "I don't know what to say to somebody I haven't seen in over thirty years."

"I'm having the same trouble, yeah."

"I have a million questions. I don't even know where to begin," Mildred said.

"I'm sure you do."

"Where'd you go? Why'd you leave?"

He sighed and then said, "Yeah, I was in trouble with some guys in Little Italy. I owed them money—see—gambling debts. Yeah, they would have killed me and maybe even you and the baby. I was scared. So, I skipped town, yeah, that was it."

Mildred didn't want to believe him.

He continued, "I had a merchant marine card so I got work on the next freighter leaving New York. Yeah! I could see them searching the docks for me. Fortunately, the ship I signed on with left before they could find me. I've never been back to New York. Yeah!"

Mildred wondered why he kept saying "yeah," then she remembered he reminded her of the actor James Cagney. It was one of the things that appealed to her. "What are you doing here?"

"I retired after I had a stroke out at sea."

That explained the paralysis that Mildred noticed.

"We had a good doc on board, and he kept me alive till we got to Oahu. They got me back on my feet in the hospital. I had to do a lot of rehab. I lived on Oahu until two years ago. Yeah! I moved here because it's not as crowded."

Mildred wanted to say *not now it isn't*. She was thinking about the impact of the new condominium development down the road, and other developments elsewhere around the island but she was still reeling from the shock of his presence.

What are you doing here?" Vic asked.

Mildred related to him the entire story about why she moved to Kauai. She avoided telling him about Nancy, until he asked, "I don't even know if we had a boy or a girl."

Mildred told him about Nancy, her life, her career, her cancer, and her death. He looked saddened by the news. He hung his head, tears filled his eyes and poured down his cheeks. His body shook a little.

"I'm sorry. She... must have been... beautiful," he stuttered.

"Very," Mildred answered indignantly. She wondered why he would even care at this point.

He seemed a little put off by Mildred's bitterness. "I wish I knew her, yeah."

Mildred just shook her head in agreement. "She always wanted to know who her father was and why she didn't have one."

He put his head into his hands and shook with emotion. When he finally spoke again, he said in a shaky voice, "I never imagined I would see you again."

"I bet!" She laughed.

"I didn't think this would be easy. I wanted to write many times but feared the men who were looking for me would find you and the baby and harm you."

Mildred still didn't know if she believed his story. Her attention turned to Mr. Kulak who came out the front door and looked curiously at the man sitting next to Mildred.

"Oh, Mildred I was looking for you." He waited for Mildred to introduce the stranger.

Vic wiped his eyes with a handkerchief. Kulak noticed and wondered about the man. Vic looked up at Kulak. He said, to Kulak, "Vic Meyers." He reached out to shake hands. Kulak took it and shook the man's hand. Because of his stroke, Vic's hand felt limp in Kulak's still strong grip.

"Arthur Kulak," he responded, thinking this was one of Mildred's relatives. She hesitated to say anything else, but then, said, "This is my…" She stopped again, trying to decide how to introduce Vic, and said, "He's my ex-husband." She knew that was a lie but couldn't imagine how else to handle the situation.

Kulak gazed at her, confusion written all over his face. He said, "I thought…"

Mildred said, "Yeah, I thought he was dead, too."

Vic shifted uncomfortably, hearing her talking about him in the third person and saying that he was dead. He didn't know what Mildred's relationship to Kulak was. He wondered if they were married but he observed that neither one of them wore wedding bands.

Noticing Kulak's confusion, she said, "I was just as surprised as you."

Mr. Kulak felt his indignation rising, he asked, "What are you doing here after all these years?"

"As I told Mildred, I've been living here about two years. Yeah!"

"You've got a lot of nerve coming around after all this time," Kulak said indignantly.

"I didn't go looking for her. She was on the news. I couldn't help coming."

Mildred trying to avoid a confrontation suggested, "Arthur, why don't you leave us alone for a little while?"

Kulak looked at her and then at Vic. "You sure this guy's not going to be any trouble?"

One look at Vic, Mildred thought it humorous that Kulak would think Vic possessed the strength to do anything violent. She nodded to Kulak that it was all right.

"Okay, if you say so. I'm going paddleboarding. I'll be back in a couple of hours."

"Be careful out there," Mildred warned. "And don't get in any riptides."

Once again, Vic wondered what Mildred's relationship was with Kulak. He figured they had an intimate one. Kulak walked down the steps and a short time later, he walked away carrying his board and paddle, but once or twice, with a frown, he turned back to look at the porch.

When Kulak was out of earshot, Mildred asked, "Where do you live?"

"Oh, not far from here. I have a little house I bought when I first came to Kauai. We have a lot of catching up to do."

Mildred wasn't sure about that. Did she want to see him again? Let alone catch up with him. Somehow, he presumed that he could just walk back into her life and continue where they left off. She wanted to tell him to go away but something kept her from saying anything. She was as curious about his life after he left her and Nancy as he must have been about her's.

He smiled and then asked, "Do you still make that delicious apple strudel?"

"It's not apple…"

"That's right, I remember, it was… apricot, yeah… apricot preserve and not apples. Right?"

Mildred laughed. "You remembered."

"How can someone forget something so delicious? Mildred, I've traveled the world. I've never tasted another strudel as good as yours."

Mildred didn't believe him and figured he was just trying to get on her good side.

Stanley and Karen came out on the porch. She wore a man's white shirt over her white bikini. Stanley was in his bathing suit over which he wore a tie-dyed, colorful tee-shirt with a big peace sign emblazoned on the front. They stopped when they saw Mildred and the stranger. Mildred didn't want to introduce Vic but she said, "This is Nancy's father."

Stanley's eyes widened behind his thick glasses, and both he and Karen looked stunned and surprised. Karen was having a hard time accepting that this little man was her best friend's father. Stanley didn't know where Vic had come from and what he wanted from Mildred after all these years. Stanley was suspicious of the little man and felt protective of Mildred. After some small talk, Stanley said to Karen, "If we're going to the beach, we better get going."

They said their goodbyes. As they went down the stairs, Stanley turned around and said, "Why don't you come to dinner tonight?"

Stanley didn't notice the look that Karen gave him. Mildred wished he hadn't said that but Vic jumped at the opportunity and responded, "I'd love to."

"We usually eat around seven," Stanley said.

"Can I bring anything?"

"No! Just come."

"Thank you for the invitation. Yeah!" However, when he looked at Mildred's icy glare, he realized he was unwelcome.

Mildred watched Stanley and Karen walk down the lane. Vic stared after them, too. Karen whispered something to Stanley about Vic's appearance.

Vic removed a folded check from his shirt pocket. He unfolded it and extended it to Mildred. She took it, looked at it, and asked, "What's this?"

"It's the money I took when I left."

"But it's for, ten-thousand dollars."

"I'm sorry that's all I can give back to you."

"But... you didn't... we didn't have that much."

"I added interest for all the years. Yeah! I hope it's all right."

Mildred's hand shot out with the check extended to return it.

"No, it's yours," Vic said.

"I don't want your money!" She got up abruptly and tossed the check at him. "And I don't want to see you around here again." She left him sitting there, tears forming in her eyes and rushed into the house.

CHAPTER 17

From inside the house, Mildred peeked out through the front window. Vic sat in the chair where she left him. She still couldn't believe that he was the husband who disappeared so many years earlier. Finally, he got up, stepped off the porch, and walked down the lane with a slight limp. Mildred watched until he turned onto the road and disappeared from her sight. She felt like she had just awakened from a bad dream.

Still shaken, Mildred walked out the back door towards the gardens. She stopped when she saw Mr. Watanabe sitting cross-legged on the ground. The post of a small umbrella was stuck into the earth and the umbrella top sat over his head. He was pulling weeds from around the base of some orchids. He looked up when he saw Mildred. "Mildred, what's the matter. You all right? You look like you've seen a ghost."

Mildred felt light-headed and didn't realize the color had drained from her face. "I just had a big shock."

"Oh!" Mr. Watanabe sighed.

Mr. Watanabe took his pruning knife and cut three white orchids, stood, and handed them to Mildred. She looked at them and put them to her nose. The fragrant scent put a smile on her face. "Thank you, Clark. They're beautiful."

"I can see they are already changing your mood."

He looked up at the sky, which had been growing overcast for some time, "It looks like rain. These plants can use the water. They're a lot like young children. With proper care, they start to grow at their own pace. Careful watering, the right nutrients keep them healthy, wealthy and wise." He smiled. "You know what's so funny, Mildred?"

She looked at him with interest.

"I was a gardener all my life, and I'm still learning." He held up his coarse hands. "These hands are happiest when they're in the soil."

"I know what you mean. I wanted to get out here and help, but with the wedding and everything else going on…"

"Well, maybe, now you can."

Neil and Annie noticed them from where they were picking lettuce. They waved to Mildred. With several heads of lettuce in her arms, Annie walked over to Clark and Mildred. "Hey, how ya'll doing?" she asked.

"Good," Mildred lied.

Clark smiled at the lettuce. "Nice lettuce. Now we won't have to buy it anymore."

Annie looked past Clark at the orchids growing in the row. "Those orchids look beautiful," she said. "When we get enough, we can start making *leis.*"

"That would be fun," Mildred responded.

"Yep, nothing says *Aloha* more than a *lei* of Hawaiian orchids," Mr. Watanabe said.

"Neil talked to the management at one of the hotels and they want us to provide flower arrangements for their lobby," Annie said.

"They're going to pay you, aren't they?" Mildred asked.

"We sure hope so," Annie answered. "And we have enough produce now to sell at the farmers' market."

"That's good news," Mildred said.

"We haven't seen you out here at all, Mrs. Meyers."

"I know. I was just telling Clark—I want to start coming out to help."

"We can always use the help. Maybe you can help at our stand."

"You know I worked in the produce market in New York for over thirty years?"

Annie's eyes widened, "Oh, well then, you have to come work at the stand."

Just then, the sky opened in a sudden torrent of rain, sending them all running for cover.

At dinner that evening, the rain continued to come down heavily. Mildred was nervous—uncertain whether Vic would take Stanley up on his invitation. She hoped she had been emphatic enough to discourage him from accepting the invite. Mildred felt relieved when he never showed up.

CHAPTER 18

The next morning at breakfast, with everyone gathered around the dining table, Albert walked in with the newspaper. He sat down at the table and said, "When I was coming up the road there was a big crowd at the construction site. I stopped to see what was going on. Some people chained themselves to the construction equipment."

"When was this?" Mildred asked.

"Now," Albert said.

"We should have done that!" Mildred griped.

"I don't think so. I don't want anyone getting arrested," Stanley said.

"That should slow them down some," Mr. Kulak speculated.

"Are the police there?" Stanley asked.

"I didn't see any," Albert said. "They may be on their way."

"We should go take a look," Mr. Benson suggested.

"I read about protests where they did stuff like that. Tied themselves to trees, too," Mildred said. "They call them tree-huggers."

"It does have a negative effect on construction and will slow things down. If they can delay the construction process, it drives up costs and can result in the project going belly-up," Albert explained. "It happens a lot."

"We should go see what's going on," Mr. Kulak said.

"Yes, let's take a look," Mildred agreed.

A short while later, Mildred, Kulak, the Bensons, Albert, Stanley, Karen, Tony, and Glo walked to the construction site. There was a large crowd of people jeering the police who tried to disperse the crowd.

Mildred and her group pushed their way to the front where they could see a young Hawaiian looking man with his arms chained and locked around the tread of a bulldozer.

A man dressed in Carhartt work clothes and wearing a welder's helmet and a face shield was delicately working on cutting through the chains with an acetylene torch. The chained man also wore a similar helmet and protection for his hands and arms.

Several yards away, a young hippie woman had chained herself to a dump truck's bumper. Across from her by about ten- or fifteen-yards, a middle-aged man was locked inside the cab of a large grader with chains wrapped tightly around his waist and the steering column.

One of the police officers walked over to the construction supervisor and asked, "Don't you have another torch?"

With a disgusted look on his face, the supervisor shook his head no and said, "This won't take long to get them free. We're getting another set of keys to unlock the grader and get that guy out."

It didn't take much time to free the people and arrest them, but the incident delayed productive work that day.

Among the crowd, Mildred noticed Joe Thomas from the local newspaper. Mildred grabbed Albert and said, "Let's go talk to the guy from the paper."

Albert looked a little puzzled but followed Mildred. They approached Joe. He immediately recognized Mildred. "*Aloha,* Mrs. Meyers!"

"*Aloha,*" Mildred responded. She still felt a little awkward about saying *Aloha.*" Mildred introduced Joe to Albert.

"I thought I'd see you chained to something," Joe said.

"Oh, I wish I had thought of it. Can you come back to our house? Albert and I would like to talk to you about something."

Joe agreed and they went back to the house and sat on the porch. "So, what is it?"

"We wanted to see if you would do an exposé on Calvin Daniels?" Mildred asked. "Something that would bring to light for the people of Kauai his corrupt business practices. He and his family have used them over the years to dislodge people from their homes."

"And how their developments have hurt the communities they are in," Albert added.

Joe smiled. "It's funny that you suggest that—I've been researching Calvin Daniels and his family. I have a file filled with derogatory information."

Mildred said, "I've heard from friends in New York that there are many lawsuits in the courts because they used asbestos in their construction projects. People are getting sick."

"I have uncovered some similar information in Miami. Right now, I have enough to do an article about him, his father and his company."

"When do you think you can have something in the paper?" Albert asked.

"I can probably get it in next week's paper. When I get back to the office, I'll discuss it with my editor."

"Excellent," Mildred said.

"I'll give you a call as soon as I get the okay."

Joe departed and called later that day to tell them that he got the go-ahead and was proceeding with the story.

The people chained to the equipment inspired Mildred. She knew she had to do something more aggressive; non-violence wasn't getting the desired result. *But, what?*

Later that night, Mildred, Kulak, and Tony met secretly in the back of the property in a grove where the marijuana grew. Mildred said, "I don't think we can stop them. We can make it more difficult for them and slow them down like those people did today."

"I'm thinking the same thing," Tony said. "I'd like to get even with that Daniels for burning down our camp."

Mildred sniffed the air around them, and said, "I hope I'm not getting high."

Mr. Kulak smiled and said, "I like the aroma."

Mildred continued, "I just read in *Newsweek* about a group of environmentalists in Oregon. They drove a logging truck filled with logs over a cliff into the Pacific Ocean."

Tony said, "Oh, I like that. We can drive one of their bulldozers into the bay."

"A bulldozer will make too much noise trying to move it," Kulak said.

"Yeah, you're right," Tony agreed. "But we need to do more than passive protests."

"They have trucks," Mildred said.

They looked at each other as they thought about the possibilities.

Mildred said, "We can drive one of their dump trucks into the water. I can't drive, though," Mildred claimed.

"I'll drive it," Kulak said.

"No, no... I'll drive it in. You two stand guard," Tony said.

They all agreed to the plan.

The following night, the three conspirators dressed in black crept to the construction site. While Mildred and Kulak stood lookout, Tony broke into what looked like a new dump truck. He hotwired it then picked up Kulak and Mildred on the way out to the road.

They drove it to the beach where Mildred and Kulak got out and stood on the sand watching the surrounding area.

Tony steered the truck towards the water. He rolled down the driver's side window, revved the engine, popped the clutch, and drove the truck straight into the bay until it got bogged down in the waves and soft bottom. The water was up to the window when the truck engine sputtered, stalled, and stopped dead.

Tony tried to push the door open. It wouldn't budge as he had figured so he dove out the window. When he reached the shore, he was soaking wet, the three conspirators hugged each other enthusiastically. Tony said, "Come on let's get out of here before somebody sees us."

CHAPTER 19

The next morning, the authorities found the dump truck in the bay. The tide came in and the truck was almost completely underwater. The police talked to everyone in the area to see if they had seen anything. They came to the farm and questioned Stanley who had no information to give them.

That day, they put a fence around the property to prevent any further vandalism. But that didn't stop Mildred and her cohorts. They went back that night. Tony cut an opening in the chain-link fence and they slipped into the site. Tony and Kulak removed rotors from the distributors of several trucks and earth-moving machines while Mildred stood lookout. They also poured sand in the gas tanks.

Following that, Daniels hired a night watchman for the site. Mildred, Kulak, and Tony decided they'd done enough damage and it would be too dangerous to continue their vandalism with a night watchman on duty.

Because the burned-out hippies had an ax to grind about the demise of their camp, the police came to question Tony and his friends working on the cottages. Their answers were hostile, and for the most part, they remained uncooperative. The police said they would be back if there was more trouble.

Stanley questioned Tony, "You sure none of your friends are behind this?"

"Not at all. Why would we do something like that, man?"

"I don't know. Just asking."

"Hey man, there are lots of people on this rock that don't like that guy and his developments. Not just us."

CHAPTER 20

With all the help from Tony and his hippie friends, the remodeling of the cottages moved quickly towards completion. It thrilled Albert to see them transformed into attractive living quarters.

Albert gathered everyone at the cottages. Tony and his three friends stood proudly next to Albert on the porch of one of the cottages. The Hanalei House residents gathered at the foot of the porch.

Albert said, "I got you out here this morning for the unveiling of our bed and breakfast units. In a few minutes, we will take a tour of the cottages. You'll see firsthand the improvements we made. "I have to thank Tony, Marco, Snake, and Poncho for the great work they did."

Marco a tall skinny guy wore denim cut-offs. He had long hairy legs and a dirty looking tie-dyed wife-beater shirt. His beard and thinning brown hair were both long.

Snake had beady eyes, a thin build, and curly black hair. He got the nickname Snake when he worked at an alligator farm where he wrestled gators and handled snakes.

Poncho didn't look Mexican or Spanish. He had long blond hair and blue eyes. He was a surfer with strong looking legs, arms, and shoulders. Besides Tony, he was the only one who looked like he could do construction work. The ragtag group of hippies smiled at the folks standing in front of them.

Albert removed some checks from his shirt pocket. He handed each of the workers two checks and he explained, "One is for your hours and the other is a bonus for helping us get these finished sooner than expected."

The onlookers clapped and uttered their appreciation of a job well done. The hippies stared at their checks as though they were a million dollars. "Thanks, man, for the work, and a place to live," Tony said. His friends seconded Tony's sentiments. They whispered among themselves praising Albert's generosity.

"As a result of the hard work these gentlemen provided, we have started to take reservations. Our first guests will arrive in two weeks," Albert said. "There will be a grand opening celebration tomorrow."

Stanley waved to his brother to remind him of something else. Albert took the signal and said, "Stanley and I have spoken with Tony and Glo, and they will be staying on with us. Tony as our maintenance man and Glo will handle housekeeping duties in the cottages. They'll be moving into the downstairs bedroom in the house."

Everyone applauded the decision. "Marco, Snake, Poncho, and the girls will be leaving," Albert continued. "I've helped them obtain work and housing at Poipu Gardens on the south shore. Now, let's go inside and take a look."

As everyone filed inside, they oohed and aahed. The front room had an open look with its living room, dining room, and kitchen. The ceiling was high and made of red cedar with two sets of track lights, and two ceiling fans, one over the living room the other over the dining room and kitchen. The refinished bamboo-wood floors shined. There was a waist-high white Formica countertop with light-colored wooden stools facing it. It separated the kitchen from the dining area. They replaced the old kitchen appliances with new white ones.

Mr. Benson said, "Albert, this is magnificent."

"Yes, it certainly is," Mr. Kulak agreed.

"These are superb living accommodations," Mrs. Benson said. "I could easily stay in one."

The living room had a blue sectional couch, light-colored blond end tables with modern-looking lamps and shades, and a coffee table in front of the couch. A TV console with a built-in turntable and stereo receiver stood against the wall opposite the couch.

Mildred asked, "So how much are you going to charge for these?"

"It will be based on the season," Albert answered. "And depending on whether they want us to provide breakfast, or not... So, rates will run from seventy-five dollars a night to a hundred."

Mr. Kulak whistled at that.

"Like I said, we're starting to get reservations."

Albert led them through the rest of the house. The bedrooms had new furniture in the same style as the living room. The bathroom had a whirlpool tub and a shower stall with smoked glass. There was a large mirror over the sink and a beige Formica countertop over a light-colored wood cabinet. It also had a chrome towel warmer on the opposite wall. Everyone poked their head in the room and gave their approval.

When they returned to the living room, Albert and Stanley opened champagne and sparkling apple cider.

Karen pulled glasses from one of the cabinets. They poured glasses of champagne and cider as they toasted the new places.

CHAPTER 21

A week later, Mr. Kulak walked into the dining room; everyone sat at the table eating breakfast. He had the *Garden Island* newspaper open. He looked up from the paper and said, "I'm reading the article about Calvin Daniels and his company."

Mildred asked, "What does it say? Read it to us."

Mr. Kulak read. *The controversial condo development planned for the North Shore is the brainchild of Calvin Daniels and his company. Daniels and his family have been at the forefront of housing development starting in New York City with his father John Daniels.*

In the nineteen-forties and fifties, John Daniels got rich building single-family homes and apartments in the New York metropolitan area. Over the years, he exploited tenants with unfair housing practices, discriminating against black and Hispanic, and minority prospective buyers. This resulted in an investigation by the U.S. Senate. In the same year, New York State launched an investigation into his business for profiteering.

Mr. Kulak looked up from the newspaper, and said, "In other words, he probably took advantage when housing was in short supply and made excessive profits."

"That shows you the kind of people we're dealing with," Albert said.

"Yes! They're not very nice," Mildred added.

Mr. Kulak looked down at the paper and started reading, again. *After his death in nineteen-fifty-nine, his son Calvin picked up the mantle of his father's business, centering its operations in Manhattan, where he constructed skyscrapers.*

He wanted to follow in his father's successful footsteps but lacked the business acumen of the old man. What he lacked in business savvy, he made up for with a total disregard for anyone that got in his way.

"They just step all over people," Mr. Benson said.

"That's right, no regard for anyone else," Mrs. Benson added.

Mr. Kulak continued. *Daniels' enterprises and his personal life have been plagued with numerous lawsuits. There has been a slew of bankruptcies as he attempted to create new companies to avoid taxes and to take advantage of government funding opportunities.*

Currently, many of their properties are under investigation for the use of asbestos, resulting in numerous lawsuits.

"I'm glad this has come out about him," Albert said.

No one else had anything to say, so Kulak began again. *He has relied upon enormous bank loans and secret investors to overcome financial setbacks. Over the years, there have been accusations of mob-related connections, which led to investigations by the New York City District Attorney's office as well as the Attorney General of New York State.*

"That's interesting," Karen said.

Kulak began reading again. *In recent years, he has gotten into condominium development in New York, Los Angeles, Miami, and Honolulu. Several of these projects went belly-up and into bankruptcy. Others sold for pennies-on-the-dollar to other investors to complete, and some remain entirely abandoned, leaving behind blighted unfinished construction sites. Many of Daniels' projects have left the most-needy individuals without a home.*

"That's what happened in my neighborhood," Mildred claimed.

"I wonder if they completed the condos they knocked our houses down to put up," Stanley said.

"Well, they certainly have a poor track record," Albert speculated.

Kulak started again. *Because he uses Chapter 11 bankruptcy laws, Daniels has been able to continue the operation of his company. He says, "My attorneys and I understand the bankruptcy laws so completely and I use them to my advantage."*

"See how arrogant he is?" Mildred complained.

"He's going to fall on his face someday," Stanley said.

Kulak began reading again. *Whether his controversial Hanalei condominium development is completed, remains a question that the people of Kauai may have to live with for years to come.*

Mr. Kulak looked up from the paper and said, "So, that's it."

"It's a good article. It certainly shows him for what he is," Mildred said.

"Well it certainly sounds like—he's not a very nice man," Mrs. Watanabe claimed.

"It is a good reveal about him and his family," Albert told them. "I hope it has the effect we are looking for."

"It should make the people of Kauai aware of what they are up against," Mildred said. "We'll have to call Joe and thank him."

CHAPTER 22

Albert's dream of owning a bed and breakfast finally became a reality with the completion of the cottages. Stanley and his residents shared Albert's enthusiasm.

Invitations to the opening day party went out to travel agencies, airline management, rental car offices, restaurants, recreation companies, and local government officials. It would be an opportunity to show off the new cottages and the farm.

Mrs. Watanabe and Mildred prepared food for the event. Albert had champagne on ice, wine, beer, cocktails, and soft drinks. There was a bartender to serve drinks and two servers to make the rounds with appetizers.

Everyone gathered behind the main house. The table under the lanai had a colorful Hawaiian-looking tablecloth on top with a variety of delicious-looking food. The bar was set up next to the food table.

Mildred asked Albert, "How many people are you expecting?"

"I don't know. We got about twenty-five RSVP's but I think there might be a few more people."

Mrs. Watanabe standing near-by overheard and said, "I hope we made enough food."

"It looks like plenty to me," Albert said.

Just then, several vehicles drove up the driveway and people got out. Albert greeted them. "Get yourself a drink and there's plenty of food. I can take you on a tour of our guest cottages whenever you like."

More cars and people arrived. Mr. Benson entertained the guest on his ukulele and Tony accompanied on his guitar, playing mellow Hawaiian tunes. The realtor the Bensons befriended arrived with several associates. He was middle-aged, tall and thin with white hair and a well-trimmed white beard. He had on a white silk suit over a colorful Hawaiian shirt. The man waved to Mr. Benson and approached Mrs. Benson. "*Aloha!* How are you, Pauline?"

"Very well. Thank you for asking," Mrs. Benson answered. Albert was standing nearby and she called, "Albert!" He turned in her direction, and Mrs. Benson said, "Albert, I'd like you to meet David Zimmer." As Albert and Mr. Zimmer shook hands, Mrs. Benson told Albert, "He's the realtor we were telling you about."

"I'd like to get Pauline and Jim working with me."

"You'd be lucky to get them," Albert said.

"What do you say, Pauline? Are you and Jim ready to make some money?" Mr. Zimmer asked.

"Well, I don't know. We're still considering it. We'll have to study-up to get our license."

"With your background, you won't have any trouble doing that. You always have a place with me."

Stanley and Karen walked over and joined the group. "Some of the folks would like to see the cottages," Stanley said to Albert.

"Well let's get them together and show our new accommodations," Albert answered. He introduced

Stanley and Karen to Mr. Zimmer, then gathered a group of people and led them to the cottages.

It became quite an event with more and more people showing up. Everyone was having a nice time. Mildred and Mrs. Watanabe took away empty dishes and replaced them with new ones with more fresh food. She said to Mildred, "I hope we have enough."

"I think we're okay, Sue," Mildred assured her.

Mr. Kulak joined the women. He asked, "Did you see that limo that just pulled in?"

"No," Mildred answered. She looked towards the driveway and saw Calvin Daniels dressed in a Hawaiian shirt over white pants with a white Panama hat on his head and wearing dark sunglasses. Mildred felt a little uneasy seeing him. "It's Daniels," she said in a quiet voice."

"Who?" Kulak asked.

"Calvin Daniels!"

"Oh. That Daniels—the son-of-a-bitch."

Daniels looked surprised to see Mildred. However, it didn't stop him from walking right up to her and saying, "Well Mrs. Meyers I'm surprised to see you here."

"Likewise, Mr. Daniels."

Kulak, standing next to Mildred, gave Daniels an unfriendly look.

"I didn't think you'd like this type of thing," Daniels said.

"What do you mean?" Mildred asked arrogantly.

"I don't know. You seem to be against condominiums. I didn't expect to see you here promoting tourism."

"She lives here with the rest of us," Mr. Kulak said indignantly.

"Oh… You live here, in this house?"

"Yes," Mildred answered.

"I thought this was a bed and breakfast establishment."

"It's both," Mildred said, "a bed and breakfast and senior housing. Several of us live in the big house. The cottages are rented to vacationers."

"That's an interesting concept," Daniels said.

Albert returned from his tour and noticed Daniels talking with Mildred and the others. Mildred said, "Oh, Albert, this is Mr. Daniels."

"Yeah, I know who he is," Albert said in an unfriendly tone.

Daniels stuck out his hand. Albert shook it reluctantly.

"I wanted to see this place that's a neighbor to my development," Daniels said.

"I suppose you would be interested in what we are doing," Albert speculated.

Daniels scanned the surroundings. "This is a pretty nice piece of property. It would make a nice addition to mine. How much would you want for it?" Daniels asked.

"It's not for sale, Mr. Daniels," Albert told him.

"Well maybe not now, but when your little venture fails, you'll probably reconsider. And then, it will be worth a lot less."

Albert laughed and said, "I don't think so."

"I hope you and your people don't have anything to do with the vandalism that has taken place at my site."

"There are a lot of angry people around the island that don't like you or your project," Mildred told him.

"And I wonder about that fake article about me in the newspaper," he said in an accusatory tone.

"Like I said there are a lot of angry people that don't like you," Mildred repeated.

"If I can prove that you had something to do with that slanderous piece of garbage or any of the damage done at my property, there'll be a price to pay."

That rubbed Albert the wrong way. He moved closer to the little man who backed away.

"Are you threatening us?" Mildred asked

"I'm not threatening anyone. I came here as a good neighbor with good intentions." With that, he turned and walked away.

Albert shouted after him, "Don't you want to see our cottages?"

Daniels ignored the question, got in his limousine and drove off leaving Albert, Mrs. Meyers, and Mr. Kulak staring after him.

Tony had been watching from where he was playing guitar. He stopped playing, put down his guitar, and walked over to Mildred, Kulak, and Albert. "What did he want?" Tony asked.

"He was just snooping around," Mildred said.

CHAPTER 23

The following morning, the police arrived early to question Stanley about the shack that went up in flames the night before at the building site. Stanley was in the kitchen fiddling with the coffee pot. Mrs. Watanabe was fixing breakfast. Stanley was already familiar with the two police officers; they had been to the farm before questioning him about the vandalism at the construction site.

"Mr. Cutler, we found your van down the road by the site. Where were you last night?" the police officer asked.

"I drove back from Lihue and my van stalled as I turned onto the road and it wouldn't start. I thought I was out of gas but the needle was well above empty."

"And you just left it there?"

"I tried to get it started. I'm going to get it towed to the shop this morning if it won't start."

"What time did you come back?"

"Around nine."

"From where?"

"I went to the airport to pick someone up but she wasn't on the plane."

"Can someone corroborate that?"

"I'm sure someone can. My wife…"

"Hmm," the police officer sighed. The cops looked doubtfully at Stanley. "Someone with long hair fitting your description was seen running away from that van last night in this direction."

"Well, it wasn't me."

Mrs. Watanabe listened from across the room. She didn't appreciate the officer's interrogation.

The cop said, "Let's go down and see if your van will start."

An annoyed Stanley went along reluctantly. It felt like a charade to him. He got into the back of the police car and they drove to the van.

When they got out, one of the police officers said, "Why don't you see if it will start?"

Stanley got in the van, pumped the gas pedal, and turned the key. To his surprise, the engine turned over immediately and purred—no rough start, no sputtering. The cops looked at him suspiciously. "I thought it wouldn't run?" the policeman asked.

"It just died on me last night," Stanley pleaded innocently.

The other policeman said, "You're going to have to come to the station house. You're under arrest for suspicion of arson."

"What? But I didn't do anything."

The policeman began to read Stanley his rights, "You have the right to remain silent. Anything you say can and will be used against you in a court of law..."

The other police officer pulled out handcuffs and approached Stanley who looked panic-stricken. Stanley, in self-defense, pushed the cop away. The officer grabbed Stanley roughly from behind, pulling Stanley's arms forcibly behind his back.

"Hey, come on that hurts! Let me go. I'm innocent."

The policeman handcuffed Stanley and said, "You've just added assaulting an officer and resisting arrest."

The other cop continued to read Stanley his rights.

"I had nothing to do with the fire."

"You can plead your case to the judge."

Stanley didn't like feeling trapped. "I have to tell my wife, my brother—he's an attorney."

Not even listening, they roughly pushed him towards their car. "You can call them from the station."

They forced him into the back seat and slammed the door. Stanley said, "Oh come on. This is ridiculous."

As the two cops got into the car, one of them said, "Goddamn hippies!" They drove away with a forlorn Stanley sitting in the back.

Later that morning, Karen sat in the office wondering where Stanley was. She worried because Mrs. Watanabe told her that he left with the police earlier. By mid-morning, everyone in the house knew about the fire, especially Mildred, Kulak, and Tony, but no one knew the police had taken Stanley away as the prime suspect.

Karen just thought Stanley must have gone with the tow truck to the mechanic and that's why it was taking so long until the phone on the desk rang, startling her. She picked up and answered, "*Aloha!*"

"Karen, it's me."

"Where are you?"

"I've been arrested."

"What? Why?"

"They think I started the fire down the road last night."

"Did you tell them you were here with me?"

"I did. But I wasn't home all the time. They're frustrated and grasping at straws. Is Albert there?"

"No, he went out."

"When he gets back, tell him to get here right away."

"I will. Are you going to be all right?"

"I'm okay. Just a little shaken up."

"I'll come there with Albert as soon as he gets back."

"I just hope he can get me out on bail. I'll see you later." They said goodbye and Karen hung up with a troubled look on her face.

Unfortunately, Albert didn't return until late afternoon. Mildred and Kulak knew Stanley hadn't set the shack on fire and felt terrible that he was taking the blame. However, they hadn't done it either. Mildred questioned Tony and he said, "It wasn't me. Glo and I were home all night."

Mildred and her coconspirators had mixed emotions. On one hand, they were happy the construction project hit another snag but didn't like Stanley's arrest.

Albert, Karen, Mildred, and Mr. Kulak piled into Albert's car and rushed to the jailhouse. By early evening, Albert had Stanley bailed out.

CHAPTER 24

Mrs. Watanabe was in the kitchen cleaning. She heard a car coming up the drive. Figuring Stanley and the others returned from Lihue, she looked out the window and saw Miss Louise get out of the car and stand at the back with a handsome looking elderly man. He removed quite a bit of luggage from the trunk.

Mrs. Watanabe dried her hands on a kitchen towel and went outside. "What are you doing here?" she asked.

Miss Louise said, "It's supposed to be a surprise."

The two women hugged. "Stanley knew I was coming. I was supposed to get here last night but missed my flight." Turning to the man, Miss Louise said, "This is Carl Hanson. He's a producer friend of mine."

Carl Hanson was in his sixties, average build, graying with thinning hair. He was well dressed in a blue blazer, white silk shirt, and khaki pants.

Carl reached out and shook Mrs. Watanabe's hand. "Nice to meet you," he said.

"Yes, thank you," Mrs. Watanabe returned. She turned to Miss Louise and said, "Nobody's here."

Miss Louise looked curious.

"They all went to Lihue to get Stanley out of jail."
"What?"

"Well except for the Bensons. I think they're doing some real estate thing today with their friend." Mrs.

Watanabe went on to explain that the police took Stanley away in the morning.

"I sure hope it doesn't turn into anything serious," Miss Louise worried.

"I think it has something to do with the fire last night."

"What fire?"

Mrs. Watanabe told her about the shack. She made a sad face. "Oh, it's been one thing after another since we got here."

"What's going on?"

"It's that darn condo development down the road. Nobody around here wants it... We should get you settled in."

"Stanley said I would be in that empty room upstairs."

Carl picked up some of the luggage. The two women grabbed the rest. Miss Louise said, "Just put it up on the porch, Carl. We can manage from there."

"Are you sure?"

Miss Louise said, "Yes, you've done enough. Thank you so much!"

Mrs. Watanabe and Miss Louise carried the remaining luggage to the porch.

Carl hugged Miss Louise, said goodbye to her and Mrs. Watanabe, then drove off.

As they carried luggage upstairs, Miss Louise said, "I met Carl in the lobby of the Marmont last night when I returned from the airport. I was so frustrated about missing my flight. He said he was coming here today. We came in his private plane. He has a place on the beach."

"Oh, that must have been nice," Mrs. Watanabe said, "flying in a private plane."

A little while later, Stanley, Albert, Karen, Mildred, and Kulak returned. Stanley looked haggard from the ordeal. Miss Louise surprised them when she walked out on the front porch. There were lots of hugs and kisses.

Stanley said, "I thought you were coming last night."

"I tried calling but couldn't get through to tell you about missing the flight."

"I wondered what happened. They would only tell me there was nobody with your name on the plane."

"It's so nice to be back. I'm sorry about your being arrested. I'm sure you will be vindicated."

"I thought you were doing a movie?" Mildred asked.

"I did it already."

"Well that was fast," Mildred said. "I thought it took a long time to make a movie."

"Yes, it does but I did my work in two days and I was through. It was a delightful experience. It has been a long time since I was in a feature film."

Miss Louise asked, "Karen are you ready to open that dance and acting school?"

"Yes, I am but I have to leave for L.A. in a couple of days. I found a space we can rent."

Stanley looked sullen. Karen said, "The only thing—Stanley can't leave the island now."

Miss Louise looked at Stanley for an explanation.

"I'm out on bail, until the trial."

"Oh, that's too bad. Weren't you going to Europe for your honeymoon?"

Karen and Stanley nodded.

"Don't worry. I'll get you cleared of the charges. They don't have a case," Albert declared.

"I hope you're right," Stanley said.

Albert continued, "They're just looking for a scapegoat. Who knows...? Maybe Daniels is pressuring them."

"We have to postpone our honeymoon until I'm cleared."

"I'm sure you're both very disappointed," Mr. Kulak said sympathetically. Even though they weren't responsible for the fire, a heavy burden of guilt weighed on Kulak and Mildred.

Several days later, Stanley reluctantly drove Karen to the Lihue Airport for her flight to L.A. They kissed goodbye at the gate and Stanley hung around until the plane took off. All the while, he was hoping for some unforeseen event that would return the plane to the gate.

CHAPTER 25

It was a beautifully sunny afternoon with the warm, trade wind breezes blowing from the west. It looked like an ideal day for selling produce at the farmers' market. Stanley, Annie, Neil, Mr. Watanabe, Mildred, and Kulak loaded just picked produce into Stanley's van. With the back of the van filled, they all got in and drove to the market area in an empty field just outside of Hanalei with large mountains in the background.

When they got there, they set up their table and tent. They loaded the table with heads of lettuce, spinach, strawberries, tomatoes, herbs, and flower bouquets. When it looked like they were ready for business, Stanley and Neil got in the van and drove away, leaving the others to operate the stand.

Many farmers were selling produce but there were also plenty of buyers to go around.

A local woman approached the stand when she saw Mildred. She wasn't too much younger than Mildred. She said, "*Aloha,* Mrs. Meyers!"

"*Aloha,*" Mildred returned.

"Glad to see you here. Thank you for what you have done for the community."

Mildred wracked her brain trying to remember where she met this little Asian woman with bad teeth and fuzzy white hair. Finally, she said, "I'm so sorry. I can't remember your name."

The woman extended her hand and said, "Lucy Kapana."

Mildred smiled and said, "Nice to see you again Lucy. How can I help you?"

"Did you hear the news?"

"What news?"

"They stopped construction. They found bones," Lucy said triumphantly.

Mildred wondered what that meant. Lucy continued, "They dug up some bones. It's probably a sacred site, maybe Menehunes."

"Who?" Mildred asked.

"They were an ancient little people, two or three feet tall, that populated this island a long time ago," Mr. Kulak said. "They were a very industrious group."

"That's right," Lucy said with a smile.

"What will they do now?" Mildred asked.

Lucy laughed and said, "Oh, they're not around anymore."

"No, I mean the construction people," Mildred reiterated.

"Oh, two guys are diggin' around."

"They're probably anthropologist," Mr. Kulak mentioned.

Lucy smiled at Kulak, looked at Mildred and said, "He's a smart one. You bettah hang on to this one... They're trying to find out if it's a burial place or no. The bones they found are from a little person. Maybe more there."

"You think it is a burial ground?" Mildred asked.

"It might be. There are sacred sites all over these islands," Lucy claimed.

"You think it will put a stop to the project?" Mildred asked.

"I'm sure it will," Lucy said.

But Mildred looked at Lucy. Her cohorts heard the woman. Mildred said to them. "Did you hear that?"

"Nothing was going on when we passed," Mr. Kulak said.

"Let's pray this puts an end to the construction," Lucy said and hoped.

Mildred and her friends felt optimistic but also doubtful about the demise of the project.

"You have such lovely stuff," Lucy said.

"Yes, we'll be out here every Tuesday from now on," Mildred told her."

The woman picked up lettuce, then strawberries, and tomatoes. More people gathered in front of the stand. Mr. Kulak, Annie, and Mr. Watanabe helped the folks with their purchases. Their inventory diminished quickly.

Mildred helped another woman pick out produce, then she noticed Vic Meyers approaching. Kulak saw him too. He wasn't happy to see Vic and braced himself. Vic smiled at Mildred, who stiffened with anxiety. He stopped in front of her and nodded to Kulak who returned a disgruntled, unfriendly look. Vic said, *"Aloha,* Mildred!"

Mildred didn't respond. Kulak stared at Vic with contempt and said, "What do you want?"

Vic looked a little put off by Kulak. He said, smiling, "I need some lettuce, some strawberries, and want to talk to Mildred—alone."

Mildred wanted to avoid an argument so she smiled at Vic and asked, "Can we talk some other time?"

"Actually, what I want to talk to you about won't take long. Can we just do it now? Yeah. And get it out of the way." He glanced over at Kulak and shifted uncomfortably under Kulak's unfriendly gaze.

"Why don't you just go away and leave her alone. You're good at that," Mr. Kulak said, indignantly.

Vic didn't like the inference. He looked up at the much taller Kulak and said, "See, unless you're her husband, you should mind your own business. Yeah."

Mr. Kulak wanted to leap over the table and crush the little man. Mildred touched Kulak's arm gently. To change the subject and avert an unpleasant situation Mildred said, "Let's get your order first."

Vic picked up several items. Mildred placed them in a bag. He handed her a ten-dollar bill and Mildred gave him change.

The whole time, Kulak stared at the man. Noticing, Mildred said, "Arthur, why don't you take over while I go talk to Victor."

Kulak nodded reluctantly as Mildred and Vic walked away. Kulak followed with his eyes until someone else approached the table and needed help.

Mildred and Vic walked until they reached a quiet spot off to the side where they sat down on a bench. Vic began, "It's nice to see you again." Mildred half-smiled. Vic continued, "I thought a lot about our first meeting. Something didn't seem right to me."

"What do you mean?"

"Yeah… Well, something about our marriage didn't seem right."

"Yes, you leaving me and our baby and taking all our money. That's what wasn't right."

"I offered to pay you back, generously."

"It's a little late for that. Don't you think?"

Vic shifted in his seat. "I talked to a lawyer. He couldn't find any record of our divorce."

Mildred was uncomfortable anticipating what would come next.

"He said, maybe you went before a judge and had me declared dead."

Mildred shook her head, indicating she had not.

"So, it seems to me that we're still married."

Mildred looked unusually perplexed.

"Yeah, what do you say, Mildred. Are we still married or not?"

Mildred thought to herself, *I should probably talk to Albert about this,* but she shriveled under Victor's intense gaze. "Alright, you want to know the truth. I didn't do anything when you left. I thought about calling the police. I didn't. I thought you'd come back. Then as the years passed, I thought about a divorce. Nancy always wanted to know why she didn't have a father like all her friends. So now, you have it. I guess we're still married."

They both sat in silence. Vic finally said, "How about getting back together?"

Mildred looked at him incredulously.

"You're not married to that Kulak guy? 'Cause that would make you a bigamist, yeah."

Annoyed, Mildred said, "No, I'm not married to him nor did I ever marry anyone else. I think we should just go ahead and file for divorce now."

Vic looked disappointed. "How about moving in with me? I have a nice house. I think you would like it."

"Thank you for the offer, but I'm very happy where I am."

"I want to make amends for what I did. It's a nice little house with a nice yard. Right around here, closer to the beach, yeah. You should think it over."

"Victor, there is nothing to think about. Absolutely not! It was over the day you walked out on Nancy and me."

"What if I don't want to give you a divorce?"

"Then life will just go on like it has for the past thirty-five years. As if you didn't exist..." She let that hang in the air indefinitely.

"Yeah, it's because of that Kulak guy? What's going on between you two?"

"I don't think that's any of your business."

"It is my business because you're still my wife. That's adultery."

Mildred laughed. "Then divorce me!" She got up and walked away.

Vic shouted after her, "Think it over, Mildred! Maybe, you can come over for dinner some night. I'll be in touch."

Shaken by the conversation, Mildred re-joined the others at the stand. Kulak asked, "What did he want?"

"He just wanted to talk."

On the ride home that afternoon, Stanley stopped the van in front of the construction site. They all got out and peered into the area. Two men wearing plastic gloves crouched over a shallow grave. They worked with small brushes, dusting the dirt off and around what looked like a skeleton.

"So, it's true," Mildred said.

"I'm glad it put a stop to construction," Stanley added.

"They think there may be more bones. It may be a sacred burial site," Mr. Kulak said.

"I think it's creepy," Annie responded. It's like; we have a cemetery right down the road."

"Even that would be better than condominiums," Mildred responded.

CHAPTER 26

A few weeks later, Karen returned and was prepared to defend her husband when Stanley's trial came up. The trial was presided over by Judge Henry Paumakua. He was a large man in his fifties with a big round face and black hair that contrasted with his brilliantly white teeth.

The prosecutor, a short balding man with glasses in his fifties presented the evidence against Stanley, accusing him of assaulting an officer, resisting arrest, and suspicion of arson.

In his opening statement, Albert pointed out that the vandalism at the construction site continued following Stanley's arrest. He argued that other parties were involved, and Stanley was completely innocent of the charges.

For some unexplained reason, the two arresting officers could not appear in court that day. Albert was surprised that the prosecutor didn't ask for a continuance. Instead, he dropped the charges of assaulting an officer and resisting arrest. The prosecutor went on with the trial on just the arson charge. His only witness was the night watchmen who claimed he saw Stanley running from the construction site. Albert cross-examined the watchman and asked, "What time did you allegedly see the man running away from the site?"

"It was about ten-thirty."

"Are you certain, Mr. Cutler is that man? I will remind you that you are under oath. Please take a good look at Mr. Cutler. Is he the one you saw?"

The man appeared nervous. He looked carefully at Stanley and then admitted, "I can't say for sure. It was very dark that night."

Albert called on Karen to take the stand. He asked her, "What time did Mr. Cutler come home that night?"

"A little before nine o'clock."

"What did Mr. Cutler say when he came home?"

"He said his van stopped running and he left it down the road."

On the witness stand, the Bensons and Mr. Kulak corroborated that Stanley was at home at ten-thirty. Albert also put into the court record a document from an auto mechanic stating Stanley's vehicle had a vapor lock problem and he presented the court an invoice for the necessary repairs.

At the close of the prosecution's case and following Albert's closing remarks, the judge said, "Let's take a ten-minute recess."

Upon returning to the court, Judge Paumakua declared that based on the evidence Albert presented, the testimony of the witnesses, and lack of a positive ID, he declared Stanley not guilty.

Back at the house that afternoon, there was a small celebration. Everyone sat on the porch drinking tropical drinks concocted by Mr. Kulak and Mr. Benson. The weather was perfect—just the right temperature that gently caressed your skin.

In reference to the weather, Mr. Kulak said, "This is why they call it paradise. It makes me want to take my clothes off."

His fellow residents told him if he was going to do that to go somewhere else on the property. He settled back in his chair. Kulak wanted to be with his friends more than he wanted to be bare-assed. Everyone felt relieved about Stanley's innocence.

Neil's ten-year-old son, Jason, came along carrying his new Hank Aaron baseball glove, and a bat and ball. "Hey! Anyone want to play catch with me? I want to try out my new mitt. Somebody can use my old one." He held out his old baseball glove hoping for takers.

"I'd be happy to toss the ball with you young man," Mr. Benson said. He bounded down the stairs with the pep of a younger person. At the bottom, he limped a little, favoring his right knee.

For the porch dwellers, this was a new source of entertainment. Mrs. Benson shouted, "Don't throw your arm out," to Mr. Benson.

Jason asked, "What's she mean?"

"You have to be careful you don't throw the ball with too much force. You want to condition your arm with proper training. If you don't, you can strain muscles, ligaments, all sorts of things." Mr. Benson caught the ball and was careful throwing it back.

As they tossed the ball back and forth, Jason asked, "What about baseball pitchers who throw the ball ninety miles an hour? How 'bout that?" Jason smiled.

"Well, that's why they train—to build up their muscles. Conditioning. That's what they call it."

"Are you conditioned?"

"Oh, not at all. I used to be when I played football."

A surprised look came over Jason's face and he blurted, "You played in the NFL?"

"Oh, no nothing like that. I just played high school. and college ball. I hurt my knee in college that's why I have this limp today." Mr. Benson smiled at the boy. "That ended my football playing days before I finished my senior year."

Mr. Kulak stepped off the porch and picked up the bat. "Maybe, I could hit a few?"

"Yeah," Jason said excitedly, "Let's start a game."

Mr. Benson laughed and said, "Let's see if he can hit it first."

Mr. Kulak boasted, "Better get ready to run, Jim."

Jason pitched and Mr. Benson played the field. Mr. Kulak completely whiffed the first few pitches and they went right by him. This was a bit of a problem because without a catcher it took a while to retrieve the ball. "We need a catcher!" Mr. Benson yelled up to the porch.

Karen quickly sprang off the porch. "I can catch." She went behind Mr. Kulak, and Jason threw one in the strike zone. Without a glove, Karen caught it mostly in her belly.

Stanley went into the house and returned with several baseball gloves. He tossed one to Karen. With the next pitch, Mr. Kulak slammed it over Mr. Benson's head. "See I told you," Mr. Kulak said as Mr. Benson hobbled after the ball. The spectators cheered from the porch.

Mr. Watanabe must have been watching from inside. He came out with a mitt on his hand and an L.A. Dodger hat on his head. "I've been waiting for a nice ball game since I came to the island." He jogged out to where an outfield would be.

In a matter of minutes, Albert and Stanley were on the field, too. Jason kept insisting they needed to play a game. Instead, everyone took turns at-bat. The entire event played well to those sitting on the porch sipping their drinks.

At one point, Mildred wanted a turn at bat claiming, "I used to play stickball with my brothers in the street." From her swing, it was obvious those days were a memory long gone.

They attempted to coerce Mrs. Benson to join them, but she wouldn't budge. They played until Mrs. Watanabe came out and informed them, "Dinner's ready! And make sure you all wash your hands before you come to the table. Jason, would you like to eat with us?"

He said, "Nah. I better not. Annie's cooking franks and beans tonight." From his smile, it was obviously one of his favorites. "Can I take a rain check?"

"Anytime you like," Mrs. Watanabe said.

In the kitchen, a line formed leading to the sink. Mildred handed out soap and towels.

At the dining room table, Mrs. Watanabe had made one of her specialties—Hawaiian meatloaf.

Mildred said, "Sue this is delicious. What's the sauce on top?"

"It's a pineapple chili glaze. You just put it over the top near the end and cook it another ten minutes."

Everyone agreed it was very good.

A week after Stanley's trial, the Hanalei Fire Department concluded that the shack fire started from a lit cigarette that ignited some rubbish and subsequently the shack went up in flames. The nightwatchman was a smoker;

they felt he was responsible so he was immediately dismissed. The newspaper claimed he was facing criminal charges as well.

CHAPTER 27

The first vacationers to arrive were friends of Neil from his days at the Los Alamos Lab in New Mexico. Their names were Carmen and Craig Lambert. Both were in their early fifties. They came to Kauai to celebrate their twenty-fifth wedding anniversary, and to see Neil and Annie.

The night before their arrival, a thunderous rainstorm knocked out power on the North Shore. It took out the well-pumps for the farm, so it left them without water. The power failure caused Neil to get up late but he still made it to the Lihue Airport to pick up the Lamberts on time. However, their plane arrived an hour late. Neil didn't know why. He thought it might have been a result of the storm and power outage. When the Lamberts disembarked, they looked travel weary.

Neil was happy to see them, and they felt the same. Neil hugged Carmen who was tall and thin with shoulder-length straight black hair and dark-rimmed glasses. She was a descendant of Spanish ancestry with deep-set dark sultry eyes and silky olive skin.

Neil and Craig shook hands and then hugged. Craig was about the same height as Neil. He looked older than Carmen and he wore thick glasses, had a salt-and-pepper beard that matched his thinning hair.

When they arrived at the farm, Neil hoped the power had returned. As soon as they stopped the car, Mrs. Watanabe came out the back door, ran over and said, "We still don't have water or power. Albert called the electric company and they told him they're working on it."

"On the way back, we saw them working along the road," Neil said.

"I sure hope they get it back soon. I can't do anything in the kitchen."

Neil introduced the Lamberts to Mrs. Watanabe. "I'm going to get them settled," Neil said.

"Take some candles with you. Stanley bought a whole box. They're in the kitchen."

Neil went into the house and returned with two hands full of candles. "I'm sorry about all this," Neil apologized to his friends as he led them to their vacation cottage. He had wanted everything to be perfect for his new guests.

At the cottage, they stepped onto the porch and got a big surprise—Mr. Kulak lying naked on a chaise lounge, basking in the sun. Neil shouted, "Mr. Kulak!"

It startled Kulak. He opened his eyes, sat up with his hand on his chest and noticed Neil and his guests. "Oh!" He grabbed a towel and covered his naked private parts. "I'm sorry. I was just getting a little sun. I didn't know anyone was around."

"Don't worry about us," Craig said. "We may strip down and join you."

"That's wonderful." Kulak smiled. "My kind of people. Well, maybe next time I'm out here. I'm about fried anyway."

Neil introduced the Lamberts while Mr. Kulak slipped on his Bermuda shorts and tee-shirt. He got up to leave and said, "Well I guess I'll be seeing you around."

They said goodbye and Kulak headed towards the house. Neil apologized to his friends about Kulak but they didn't seem to mind it at all. It reminded Neil of his days at the communes in New Mexico and San Francisco where he didn't wear clothes for days at a time.

Neil took the Lamberts inside and gave them a little tour of the place and said, "Mrs. Watanabe usually serves dinner around seven. I don't know what's happening since the power has been out. You can take some time to rest, walk around the farm, or go to the beach. Annie and I are in the last house in the back. Let us know if you need anything. You'll probably meet the rest of the people that live here later at dinner."

They thanked him and he left.

Stanley and Karen sat in Stanley's office. Karen said, "Since we missed going on our honeymoon, I wanted to talk to you about something else."

Stanley looked concerned. "What is it?"

She laughed. "Don't look so worried, sweetheart. They asked if I would like to dance in the *Nutcracker* over the holidays in Vienna. It's one of my favorite ballets and I've never danced it."

"What happened to retirement?" Stanley asked.

"It will be my last performance."

"You'll be away for the holidays?"

"And my mother has always wanted to go to Vienna." She looked at Stanley's frustrated expression. "I won't do it unless you come with me. We can travel around Europe after the run is complete."

"Oh." His face had a troubled look.

"Why? What's the matter?"

"I was just thinking about the holidays," Stanley said.

"We have a little time before I let them know."

"It's just that it is going to be a very busy time here around the holidays."

"I'm sure Albert can handle it."

"I'll have to talk to him."

"See what he thinks."

Miss Louise stuck her head in the door. She looked at Karen and Stanley and said, "Ooo, am I interrupting something?"

They looked at her and Karen said, "Oh no."

"I thought maybe we can go see that space you told me about."

"Yes, let's do that. I've talked to several parents who would love to enroll their children in our classes," Karen said.

Miss Louise looked pleased.

Karen turned to Stanley, "We're going to take the van."

"Sure, I'm not going to need it."

"Any word on when the power is going to be restored?" Miss Louise asked.

"They said they're working on it, and it should be back soon.

Karen got up. "We'll see you in a little while." As they were leaving, Karen said to Miss Louise, "I'm going to have to use the space to stay in shape. I may be doing one more performance…"

"Oh, that sounds lovely."

That evening they ate dinner on the lanai; the electricity was still out. Candles inside the house and cottages gave off an orange glow. Outside, *tiki* torches provided light for the residents who sat around the outdoor table with candles.

Mr. Watanabe and Tony built a makeshift barbeque out of stones. They grilled a delicious meal of spareribs, corn on the cob and Mrs. Watanabe prepared a salad with fresh ingredients from the farm. Earlier, several of the men filled buckets of water from the tributary that flowed past the property. They stored it in a big drum outside the back door.

"What's taking so long to get the electricity back on?" Mildred asked impatiently.

"I don't know," Stanley said.

"They think there's a problem at the generating station," Albert added.

"We can just build a little dam out there on the river and make our own generator," Craig Lambert suggested.

"It's just the way it goes on these islands," Tony offered.

"We found a place for our acting and dance classes," Karen said.

Miss Louise added, "And it's a lovely little space. Just perfect for our needs.".

"When are you opening the school?" Annie asked.

"We probably have to get a license and I don't know what else we'll need," Karen told her.

Albert said, "I can help you with that, having been through all the red tape for the cottages."

Miss Louise looked over at Jason who sat quietly, probably a little bored. "Jason, how about you? Would you like to learn to dance and act?"

"I don't know. I got little league."

"How is that going young man?" Mr. Benson asked.

"I... I don't know. Some of the kids call me *haole*."

"You getting to pitch?" Mr. Benson asked.

"Sometimes. Most of the time I play center field. They say because I have a good arm. But I really want to pitch."

"Don't worry about what they call you. You do a good job out on the mound—they'll be calling you 'champ,'" Mr. Benson advised.

"I just wish they wouldn't call me *haole*."

"Don't worry about it man," Tony injected.

Mr. Kulak said, "The Hawaiian people have had a tough time of it. They have their prejudices..."

To change the subject, Albert asked the Lamberts, "So what are you going to do while you're here?"

"Relax," Carmen said. "Celebrate our twenty-fifth anniversary."

"Yes, that's for sure," Craig, admitted. "We both have very stressful jobs."

"Deadlines to be met all the time," Carmen added.

"I don't know how you do it," Neil said. "I knew it was time to get out, and I'm glad I did."

"You did the right thing," Craig agreed.

"It's the industrial-military complex!" Tony ranted. "I was manipulated by it, too."

With that, a hush fell over the group, Mrs. Watanabe asked, "Any *keiki?* Oh, that means children."

"No, we never had time for kids," Carmen answered.

"What are your plans while you are here?" Stanley asked.

Craig said, "We want to do some hiking in Waimea Canyon and the Napali coast trail. We heard it's a beautiful hike. We'll go for a nice dinner on our anniversary."

"That sounds lovely," Karen said.

Albert said, "If we can do anything to make your stay more enjoyable, please let us know."

Just then, flashes of light burst into the semidarkness from the cottages and the house. Everyone cheered in delight. The power had returned.

CHAPTER 28

The next day, Albert and Mildred sat in Stanley's office. "What is it you want to talk about Mrs. Meyers?"

"Well, you heard the news that my husband lives here and wants to get back together."

"I did. How's that going?"

"Can you imagine that? After thirty-five years—he shows up and wants me to forgive him. Take him back into my life. And here, I thought he was dead."

"What are you going to do about it?"

"I want to divorce him, now that I know where he is. Can you help me?"

"You think he wants one?"

"I don't think so… And I don't care what he wants after what he did to me and his daughter," Mildred said with a hurt expression. "He says he wants me to move in with him."

"Here?"

"No, he says he has a house. He's probably looking for a nursemaid with a purse."

Albert laughed. "Why? Is he sick?"

"I don't think so. He did tell me he had a stroke. I think it was quite a few years ago. He's got some paralysis on one side of his face."

"He's looking for money?" Albert asked.

"I don't know. He says he lives in a small house that he bought a few years ago. He was in the merchant marines. So, he must be getting a pension from that."

"Maybe you don't want a divorce. If he should pass away, you might stand to inherit the house and other financial assets he may have."

"I don't want anything from him," Mildred snapped. "He already tried to offer me ten-thousand dollars for the money he stole when he left us." Mildred had a displeased look on her face.

"Well, I do know divorces are filed in Family Court."

"What if he doesn't want to cooperate?" Mildred asked.

"You can get a divorce even if the other party doesn't want one. As long as you believe the marriage is irretrievably broken and can't be fixed. I would say abandonment for thirty-five years is a good, strong case."

"Well that's a relief," Mildred sighed.

"I'll go ahead and find out about filing," Albert said.

"Oh, thank you."

"You want to talk to him before? Or, do you just want to spring it on him?"

"Let me think about that. The less I see him the better. Do you want a retainer or some money up-front?" Mildred asked.

"No. There are probably some filing fees. It shouldn't cost much. We'll deal with that later. Let me see what I find out."

"I want to pay you for your time."

"We'll talk about it later. In the meantime, you decide if you want to prepare him for it. I'll start on the process."

Stanley walked into the office. Mildred and Albert looked up at him. Something seemed to be troubling him. "I was down the road and construction has begun again."

"What?" Mildred asked.

Albert looked at his brother and inquired, "I thought it was a sacred site?"

"Apparently, it isn't. Somebody said the bones are those of a young boy who disappeared in the fifties," Stanley said with a frustrated look on his face.

"How do they know that?" Mildred wanted to know.

"They checked dental records. They think the boy must have been the victim of foul play."

"So, we're right back where we started," Mildred complained.

"I don't think we're going to stop them now," Albert said reluctantly.

Mildred didn't like the sound of that. "We'll see how the locals feel about it," Mildred said. "I don't know if more protests will help."

"I don't want you doing anything that'll get you in trouble, Albert warned, "both of you." He looked seriously at Mildred, then his brother.

"There's got to be some way to stop them," Mildred said.

"I don't see one right now," Albert answered. His words left them feeling glum.

CHAPTER 29

Karen and Miss Louise found a small building with a big enough room for a dance class, plus plenty of room for acting and improvisational theatre. It was right on the main road in Hanalei, making it easily accessible.

Stanley, Albert, and Tony helped them get the place open for business. They made some repairs, installed tall mirrors on one of the walls including ballet barres, built a slightly elevated platform for a stage and painted walls in blues, yellows, and pinks. The room had a delightfully pleasing whimsical appeal. They also built a small space at the front to serve as an office and dance apparel store.

At the opening day celebration, quite a few children and their parents showed up. The residents of the Hanalei House came to help celebrate the event. They served refreshments with ice cream and cake.

Karen and Miss Louise stood on the stage. Karen said, "I'm Karen Eichel. I'm a professional ballet dancer. My partner here," gesturing with her right hand to Miss Louise, "we call her Miss Louise. She's a professional actress with over sixty years' experience. She recently starred in the TV series *Life's a Treasure*, and she just completed a movie, but I'll let her tell you more. As for me, I've danced all over the world and performed in many different ballets. I just got married to Stanley Cutler." She pointed to Stanley in the back of the room;

everyone turned to see him. "And I have just moved here, recently."

The residents applauded and the crowd applauded too. Karen smiled at them. She turned to Miss Louise and said, "Would you like to tell them about your career, Miss Louise?"

"Thank you, Karen. Yes, I too have just moved to this beautiful paradise. As Karen said, I just completed a motion picture. It's a Christmas story, entitled *A Holiday Surprise*. It will be in theatres for the holidays. It's the first one I have done in many years. In my sixty-year career, I have acted on Broadway, in movies and television. I am more than happy to pass on my expertise in acting and improvisation to the lovely children of Kauai. I hope you young boys and girls will join us to have some fun. Who knows, we may even have a few budding stars."

The young people in the audience nodded and smiled.

Karen continued, "I will be teaching classical and modern ballet, jazz, and creative movement."

A woman raised her hand and asked, "Will you have any classes for adults?"

Karen looked at Miss Louise and said, "I don't know. We haven't thought about that. Are you interested?"

The woman said, "Yes."

"If there are more people, maybe we can after a while. We'll also be able to sell shoes and dance clothing if you need them. And someone has talked to us about using the space for yoga classes. We'll also have some recitals and maybe do some plays." She nodded to Miss

Louise who gave the guests a reassuring smile. Now, I'd like to perform a little dance routine for you."

Miss Louise stepped off the stage. Karen already in her dancing clothes prepared herself as Stanley turned on the music. It was upbeat and jazzy. Karen performed intricate steps across the stage with spins, kicks, and splits in time with the music. When the music came to a crescendo and stopped, Karen leaped into the air coming down into a split. The audience gasped, then applauded.

As Karen stepped off the stage, Miss Louise stepped back onto it. "I would like to introduce you to some improvisation." She invited three children of different ages up on stage, two boys and a little girl.

They shyly came on stage. Miss Louise asked, "Now, what are your names?"

The little girl of about six was the least shy and snapped back, "Maryann!"

She asked the first boy who was younger than the other two kids. "And what's your name?"

He answered with his eyes turned down and in barely a whisper, "Andy."

"What's your name?" she asked again. "And look out at these lovely people and tell them your name so they can hear it."

This time he mumbled even lower.

"Okay, here's acting lesson number one. As actors, we must project our voices so the audience can hear you in the last row of the theatre. So, try telling them your name again."

The young man looked terrified.

Miss Louise took his shoulders and turned him towards the audience. She gently raised his chin with her finger and said, "Now, let's do it together. Are you ready to tell these nice people your name?"

The little boy shook his head.

"Now together, what's your name?"

Together, they both said, "Andy!"

Miss Louise prompted him again, "Let's say it again." She pressed her hand on his diaphragm. "Okay, now say it as loud as you can."

And he projected, reaching the back of the room. Some people laughed and the audience applauded. The next boy seemed to have grasped the concept because when Miss Louise asked his name, he answered a little too loud, "Johnny!"

The room burst into laughter, then more applause. Miss Louise instructed them to sit on the floor, the girl in the middle with one boy in front and the other behind the girl. "Now, do you know what a roller coaster is?"

They shook their heads and the little girl said, "It's a ride that goes very fast and goes up and down hills."

"That's right," Miss Louise said, enthusiastically, "and it's fun and sometimes it can be scary too." They all shook their heads in agreement. "Now, I want you to pretend you're on a roller coaster and you're going up a big hill, slowly."

The kids looked up and when the boy in front leaned back, the other two did as well. "We're going up a big hill, getting to the top, over the top and down you go, faster and faster."

The children with big smiles on their faces reenacted the ride. "We turn right!" Miss Louise instructed. They all leaned to the right. "Now we quickly turn left!" They all leaned in that direction. "Down another hill!" Miss Louise guided them through dips, dip-see-doos, fast turns and up hills. The children laughed hysterically. When the improv concluded, the kids were all smiles and the people bestowed them with applause.

CHAPTER 30

Progress at the construction site was going slow. They seemed to be having many problems. The weather wasn't helping with several days of heavy rain that kept turning the site into a muddy quagmire. The locals helped slow things down with one protest after another.

Daniels showed up at several of the protests and he addressed the crowd on one occasion. He lost his cool when the protestors yelled so loud that they drowned him out. Out of frustration, he yelled back, "This project will continue until completion whether you like it or NOT!"

His outburst incited the crowd and they chanted, "STOP CONSTRUCTION NOW! STOP CONSTRUCTION NOW!" Each chant grew louder and louder.

Daniels scanned the crowd. He had seen many of the same people at some of the other protests. He was looking for Mildred. Daniels scowled when he spotted her standing alongside the other residents of the Hanalei House.

In recent days, the police came to the house several times to question Mildred and Stanley about more vandalism. They also inquired about the flags and markers used for staking out streets, sidewalks and building foundations that kept mysteriously disappearing. The property had a security guard at night, but it didn't stop the vandalism or keep the markers in place. Daniels fired several security people. It got so bad that one night, minus a guard, Daniels and his driver sat in his limo watching the property. It was the last time they did that.

It was a quiet night with not much moonlight. While Daniels read reports with the overhead light on, the chauffeur looked out the window. He couldn't believe his eyes when out of the dark he saw a sign propped up on a stick that read, NO MORE CONDOS. He strained his eyes to make sense of what he was seeing but he couldn't see anybody, only a stick about three feet off the ground with the sign attached.

He panicked and shouted, "Mr. Daniels!"

Daniels looked up from his reading and said, "What is it?" in an annoyed tone.

"Look out there!"

Daniels stared out the front window, but he could only see his reflection. He reached up and turned off the light and saw the sign almost dancing back and forth across the property. In a panic, he said, "Let's get out of here."

The driver started the limo and quickly drove off.

The next morning, the flags at the back of the site were gone.

Somehow, the story got out and made its rounds on the coconut wireless. The locals still claimed it was a sacred site, and that the Menehune spirits were responsible for the vandalism, the vanishing flags, and the dancing sign. They claimed the spirits were angry and retaliating.

However, Stanley suspected someone with a stealth-like ability was responsible, maybe an ex-marine. But he wouldn't ask Tony if it was his doing, because then he would have to lie to the cops if they questioned him. Besides, whoever it was, Stanley was glad to hear that every day there was another new delay. With each delay, building costs escalated.

CHAPTER 31

In the semi-darkness of Mildred's room, the sheets rustled, and the bed made a rhythmic sound. Lovemaking filled the air. "Ooo... Oh... Oh, yes... Oh, sweetheart... That's it... Oh... Nice..." Mildred's passion-filled utterances matched Mr. Kulak's pleasure-filled grunts, groans, and sighs.

Even the bed participated as it continued to squeak in a slow rhythm. Mildred sighed with delight. Kulak groaned... almost a moan. Mildred giggled softly. The bed stopped squeaking, followed by a long silence, and heavy breathing. After several minutes, Kulak rolled over on his back, his breathing slowing.

Mildred and Kulak were quiet, motionless until she turned on her side and kissed him on the lips. They held the kiss for a long moment. "Arthur, I haven't felt this good in years."

"Me too," Mr. Kulak said. "I never thought I would be doing this again at my age."

"I thought you had trouble getting it up?"

"I did until Tony told me about the fruit they call noni. It grows right here on the farm. I've been eating it. You can see the results." He turned on his side to face Mildred. "I feel lucky to have found you."

"I feel the same way, and we're lucky to be able to still do this," Mildred whispered. They held each other for a long while. Mildred said, "I have to tell you something."

"What is it?"

"Something's going on with that man you saw coming around."

"Oh, your ex-husband? What's he want anyway? Hasn't he done you enough harm?"

"Well, the truth is he isn't my ex."

Kulak raised his head, bent his elbow to his hand. Sounding a little confused, he said, "You said he was your ex-husband."

"I know. But the fact is I never divorced him."

"What?" Why?"

"I don't know I just never did. At first, I thought he might come back…"

"And you would have taken him back?"

"No, I don't think so. I was hurt and I had a daughter to raise all by myself. I didn't give it much thought. Then, I figured he must be dead. I felt sorry if he was."

"Mildred, I can't believe after what he did to you and Nancy, you never divorced him."

"I am now. Albert is working on it."

"Well, that's good. Will he consent to one?"

"Albert said it doesn't matter if he wants one or not. He'll probably be surprised when he finds out. He asked me to come live with him."

"What did you tell him?"

"Absolutely not!"

"He looks like he had a stroke or something," Mr. Kulak speculated.

"He did, out at sea… He told me it was a few years ago."

"How's this going to affect our relationship?" Mr. Kulak asked.

"I don't think it is going to change it one bit. That's how I feel. Do you feel differently?"

Mr. Kulak didn't answer right away. When he did, he said, "I wish this guy would stop coming around. Mildred, as long as you still want me, I'm here for you and will support you through anything."

Mildred kissed him and said, "I think we still have some fun years ahead of us."

CHAPTER 32

Miss Louise met with Stanley in his office to discuss Harry Leonard. "Harry would like to move here," she said. "He enjoyed meeting everyone and loves this area."

"I know. He called me. But we don't have an extra room," Stanley replied. "I don't know what your relationship is. Would you want to share a room with him?"

"No, absolutely not. We're close friends. We've had intimate relations but that was years ago." She shook her head from side-to-side in an odd sort of way. "Well, we did do it when he was here for the wedding. But that was the booze, and a little spurt of passion from each of us."

Stanley tried to look nonchalant, but his face gave away his embarrassment. He had been running the house since before his mom died and suspected hanky-panky from his residents but the hippie, liberal that he was, tried to ignore the fact the residents from time-to-time were having sex.

"What if Mildred and I share a room and he can have my room?" Miss Louise asked.

"I don't know if she would want to do that. I can ask her."

"Would you?"

"Of course! I liked Harry when he was here. I thought he fit in very well with everybody."

Miss Louise got up to leave. "Thank you, Stanley. Let me know what Mildred says."

Later in the afternoon, Mildred sat in front of Stanley's desk and he told her about Harry's intentions. Mildred said, "I liked him. He was fun to have around."

"Here's the problem—we don't have a room for him."

"Well, why don't you put him into one of the cottages?"

"That wouldn't work. Albert already has a lot of reservations."

"Miss Louise suggested you two share a room, so then, Mr. Leonard can have her room."

Mildred thought about it for a moment. I don't mind sharing... But... What if, instead of Louise moving in with me, Arthur moves in?"

Stanley's eyes widened. "Oh?"

"You know we've been sleeping together most nights, which leaves his room empty."

Stanley shook his head in recognition of the fact that they were sleeping together. "You sure you want to do that? That's kind of a commitment. Isn't it?"

"Stanley, I don't know if you noticed, but Arthur and I are very fond of each other."

Stanley didn't know what to say. "I'll need to ask him if he wants to do that."

"Well let's," Mildred suggested. "Let's go find him."

When they found Kulak, he was excited and more than willing to give up his room to move in with Mildred. Stanley notified Harry and told Miss Louise and the others at dinner that night. They were all thrilled to have Harry join the house.

For a short time afterward, Mildred, Stanley, and Kulak discussed Mildred moving into Kulak's room but then decided that Mildred's was a little bigger and Kulak had less to move. Over the next few days, they moved his things to Mildred's room; everyone adjusted to the changes and eagerly awaited Harry's arrival.

Just about one week later, Harry Leonard arrived on the island. Stanley and Miss Louise went to the airport to pick him up. He helped Stanley place his many pieces of luggage into the van.

Harry wore his white Panama hat and a white suit. He had new glasses that were thicker than the ones he had last time they saw him.

When they got to the farm, Mildred and the other residents welcomed him with *Alohas*. Harry was happy to see them all again. There were hugs and kisses all around.

*

That evening, everyone went to Jason's little league game to cheer him on. His team, the Serpents, was playing the Red Birds from the other side of the island. By the fifth inning, the Serpents were losing six to two, and the Red Birds had the bases loaded with one out in the inning.

Brado Palani was the Serpent's coach. He was Hawaiian in his late-twenties and had played minor league baseball for the Dodger's farm team. He still had the build of a player, despite his many injuries, including a slight limp from a hip fracture from a slide into a base.

The coach called Jason to come in from his position in center field to relief pitch. The Red Birds' best hitter was at the plate. He was probably the biggest kid on both teams.

Jason walked to the mound and took the ball from the coach. Neil was happy to see his son on the mound and yelled to him, "You can do it, Jason!"

"Put it right by him Jason!" Mr. Benson shouted.

Jason picked up the rosin bag to dry his sweaty hands. Then, he took some warm-up pitches. Albert leaned over to Neil and said, "It looks like he's got his stuff working." They both smiled.

Then, Jason threw three inside pitches to the right-handed batter, all balls, not one strike. The guy at the plate looked intimidating standing in the batter's box.

Jason's fans in the stands cheered him on and he put a fastball right by the big batter. He followed that strike with a low, inside curve that the kid took a mighty swing at and missed. Jason smiled in the direction of the stands. His fans were on their feet cheering and clapping. With his next pitch, he struck the batter out.

The next guy up wasn't as intimidating. He fouled the first pitch off but Jason's next two pitches were balls. The residents yelled at the umpire for calling balls. Jason pitched and the ball was hit hard on the ground to the shortstop who tossed it to the second baseman for the force out. That ended the inning. Jason proudly walked off the field to resounding applause from his friends.

The Serpents failed to score any runs in their at-bat and hadn't scored since the second inning when they got the two runs they had.

Jason's next inning on the mound was impressive. He got the Red Birds out one, two, and three.

In their last time at bat, the Serpents had men on first and second from a base hit and walk. The next batter struck out. The following batter ended the game when he hit into a double play.

Jason and the residents were disappointed but they all congratulated Jason on his pitching performance as well as the hit he got that helped score the two runs the Serpents got in the game.

Everyone went out to the Tahiti Nui for dinner and drinks. Even though they lost the game, Jason basked in the limelight. After all the praise he received from his parents and their elderly friends, he stood and said, shyly, "Thank you for coming tonight. I'm sorry we lost."

They all shrugged it off. "The coach said I'm the starting pitcher in the next game. The guys said, 'You pretty good pitcher for a *haole!*'"

Jason laughed and everyone joined in.

At dinner, the residents noticed how Harry had trouble seeing his silverware, and then, he had trouble seeing his plate when he went to pick up food. Miss Louise asked him, "Are you okay?"

Harry felt embarrassed and said, "My eyes are getting worse. I have macular degeneration. That's why I have these new glasses."

Stanley looked concerned.

The next morning something happened that upset everyone. Harry started down the stairs to breakfast, missed a step about halfway down tumbled headfirst, and landed with a thud at the bottom. His glasses sat on the floor unbroken a few feet from where he landed. Just about everyone in the house heard the crash. They came from all directions to see what happened and to help.

Stanley was the first to reach Harry who lay on the floor somewhat in pain. "Are you alright, Mr. Leonard?" Stanley asked.

"I think so. A little sore…"

Albert and the rest of the residents rushed to the scene. Stanley felt Harry's head, then gently felt around his neck and on down the body. Stanley wasn't convinced that Harry wasn't seriously injured. He and Albert helped Harry up carefully. Miss Louise picked up Harry's glasses and handed them to him. Aside from some bruises and a welt on his forehead, he seemed all right. They walked him into the living room and sat him on the couch. Mrs. Watanabe brought him a glass of water. "Drink this," she said as she handed him the glass.

Harry took it with shaky hands as he lifted it to his lips. Mildred came in with an icepack and said, "Here put this on that bump before it gets worse."

"I think we should go to the hospital," Stanley suggested."

Harry looking concerned said, "I'm alright. I must have missed a step."

"We should have you checked. Make sure there are no broken bones," Stanley told him.

"Stanley, I don't want to go to the hospital," he said in a panic-stricken voice. "I don't like hospitals."

Everyone discussed whether Harry should go or not. Harry was adamant about not going. "I'll be alright," he kept saying.

Over breakfast, Stanley raised the issue, "Maybe, you shouldn't be on the second floor?"

Karen asked, "Well, what can we do?"

They all looked around the table. Albert said, "We should move Harry downstairs."

"No... That won't be necessary. I just need to be more careful," Harry replied.

"Glo and I can move upstairs and Harry can have our room," Tony suggested.

Harry protested, "Oh, that won't be necessary."

Miss Louise said, "That's a good idea. You shouldn't be on those stairs. You haven't finished unpacking so it will be easy to move you."

"Yeah man, we can get you moved in no time," Tony said.

"We're just happy to have a place to stay," Glo added, "It doesn't matter whether it is up or down."

"You're all so kind. I didn't want to cause all this trouble."

"Thanks, you guys," Stanley, said to Tony and Glo. He was still concerned that Harry should be checked at the hospital but felt he had to respect Harry's wishes.

Following breakfast, everyone pitched in to move Harry downstairs and Tony and Glo upstairs. Without too much trouble, they finished the move before lunch. Miss Louise helped Harry with the rest of his unpacking and got him settled.

CHAPTER 33

Unbeknownst to their fellow residents, the Bensons had been going to the library every day to study for their real estate licenses. The day they received them they drove up to the house in an old U.S. Army jeep. Mr. Benson wore a short-sleeve khaki shirt and shorts. Mrs. Benson wore a similar shirt and trousers. They both had pith helmets on their heads.

It surprised Mildred and Kulak who sat on the porch as the jeep stopped. They stepped off the porch and walked over to the Bensons, still sitting in the vehicle.

"Where'd you get this?" Mr. Kulak asked while patting the army green drab hood. "This is some baby," he cooed. "It's an old Willy's MB from World War II."

"The gentleman we bought it from said this one was in Korea," Mr. Benson explained.

"Well it's a beauty," Mr. Kulak said admiringly, still rubbing the hood.

Mildred looked curiously at the Benson's garb and the jeep. Mildred asked, "What're you going to do with it?"

"We got our real estate licenses, today. We are back in the business," Mr. Benson said proudly.

"Oh, I hope you're not selling condos for that guy," Mildred said.

"No! As a matter of fact, we're not," Mrs. Benson answered.

"We're associated with his office. It's remote properties that we're interested in selling," Mr. Benson explained as he started to get out of the jeep. "You know more than eighty percent of this island is undeveloped land?"

Mrs. Benson stepped out, too.

"What do you know about these remote properties?" Mildred asked incredulously.

As they stepped onto the porch, "We've been out all day, riding around in the mountains and backcountry, looking at some of the listings," Mr. Benson said. "That's where the real peace and beauty of this island lies. We bought the jeep from an old *poi* farmer outside of town. He said he just replaced the engine. It runs like a charm."

"I heard how it purrs," Mr. Kulak said. "Well, that's great. We should tell the others and have a drink to celebrate."

Still skeptical, Mildred asked, "You sure you won't be selling condos?"

"We promise—Mildred dear. We won't do that," Mrs. Benson pleaded.

CHAPTER 34

Two days before the U.S. Bicentennial, one of the news items of the day upset Tony. He was in a funk because North and South Vietnam officially reunified. Over breakfast that morning, Tony complained to the residents, "We just wasted our time over there. I lost so many buddies. For what? We lost the war and they won. What about all those Vietnamese soldiers I killed? Most of them were just kids. I feel bad about them too."

The residents sympathized with him but couldn't offer any solace, except for Mildred who said, "The important thing is you came back."

"Yeah, and that's what I feel so guilty about. I came home. So many didn't. Or, they came back missing limbs, or with mental scars that last a lifetime. Why did I live through it and they didn't?"

"Only God can answer that," Mildred offered.

Tony looked at her with tear-filled eyes. "Thanks, Mrs. Meyers. I just have to get used to living with the pain." He hung his head as tears soaked into his beard. Glo, sitting next to him, put her arm around his shoulders and hugged him closer to her.

Stanley wanted to say *it wasn't your time to go* but remembered saying that to Mildred about her daughter's demise and regretted it so he kept his mouth shut. A solemn mood fell over the table.

Tony's reaction, that day remained in the hearts and minds of the Hanalei House residents and put a slight damper on the July Fourth, 1976 Bicentennial Celebration. Nevertheless, they planned a big party at the farm.

All over Kauai and the other Hawaiian Islands, most people anxiously anticipated the two-hundredth anniversary of the United States. However, some Hawaiian people still despised the U.S. annexation of the Hawaiian Islands. Those folks weren't as enthusiastic about the bicentennial. They remained bitter about the loss of their independence and the treatment of Queen Liliuokalani, the reigning monarch at the time, whom they imprisoned in her palace.

All over the islands, towns had parades, fireworks, concerts, and fun activities. Red, white, and blue decorations and flags were everywhere. The state issued new red, white, and blue license plates in honor of the bicentennial. In some towns, they painted the fire hydrants in patriotic colors as well.

Albert was happy that he had all the cottages rented for the big holiday.

The weather was picture perfect with temperatures in the eighties, bright blue skies, and comfortable trade winds. Hanalei Bay looked pristine with small waves, and the bright sun reflecting off the water.

After breakfast, that morning, the residents and some of the cottage guests headed out to the bay to watch the various competitive swimming and surfing events. Mr. Kulak participated in a paddleboard competition.

His friends and some of the cottage guests set their chairs on the beach along with a large crowd of spectators. Kulak wore a white tank top over red, white, and blue tight-fitting Speedo briefs. He leaned over to get a good luck kiss from Mildred before heading into the water. She said, "You be careful out there! You're not as young as you think."

"I'll be fine," Kulak said as he picked up his board and paddle.

There were two other men in Kulak's age group, both Hawaiians. One was as tall as Kulak but much more muscular with strong looking thighs and arms. He looked like a shoo-in for the win. The other man was very thin and bald like Kulak. Both Hawaiians had deep tans, much darker than Kulak's.

They entered the water and paddled out to where the waves broke. A flare shot into the air to start the race. Kulak got off to a good start but the other two more experienced men skillfully rode the waves and easily passed him. All three rowed efficiently and after a while, were abreast of one another.

Mildred watched them through binoculars. People on the beach cheered them on. As they got closer to the finish and the shoreline, the bigger man came in first, the other second, and Kulak, close behind in third.

Everyone on the beach roared with enthusiasm and applause as these old men got off their boards and carried them onto the beach. Kulak was a little disappointed that he didn't do better but he finished and didn't experience the embarrassment of falling off his board.

Mildred rushed over to Kulak who stood with the other two. She hugged him and said, "You did well."

"I didn't win," he said with a cocky smile.

The other two men heard what he said. The tall man said, "How long you doing this?"

"Oh, just a few months," Kulak answered.

The other man said, "Well you did good! We'll be watching out for you." He reached out and shook Kulak's hand.

The tall man did too. He said, "We see you here next year, buddy."

Kulak said, "Happy Fourth of July!"

The tall man looked at Kulak with disdain and said, "Not happy for us Hawaiians..." He pinched his nose shut and said, "Take our land... U.S. is just a country founded on sedition and slavery."

The other man said, "Oh don't listen to him. He's just a grouchy old man." The tall one clenched his fist and waved it at his friend.

Mildred and Kulak crept away a little disconcerted. "What's his problem?" Mildred asked.

Kulak said, "The U.S. overthrew the Hawaiian monarchy when Grover Cleveland was President. Sanford Dole of the Dole Pineapple Plantation masterminded the coup and then became the first President of the Islands."

"See? And now we have Calvin Daniels trying to take advantage of the people of Kauai," Mildred complained.

Kulak and Mildred joined the others who were eating. Mrs. Watanabe made pork *laulau* to eat at the beach. They spent the rest of the afternoon watching the other competitive events, including a volleyball tournament. Quite a few firecrackers went off throughout the day. Somebody on the beach had a small cannon. When it went off with a large explosion, it shook the beach and the sound echoed into the mountains.

Walking back to the farm that afternoon, the Hanalei House residents stopped at the construction site, which was quiet for the day. They looked in. "It doesn't look like they've done very much," Mildred said.

Everyone agreed that there hadn't been much progress made and that was another thing to celebrate.

Back at the farm that evening, Fourth of July decorations hung from trees, small American flags were everywhere. A local three-piece band set up and played Hawaiian tunes and rock and roll.

People arrived with all kinds of food, filling the table on the lanai. Mrs. Watanabe and Mildred prepared appetizers, baked ham, *teriyaki* chicken skewers, and desserts. Annie and Glo made beautiful *leis* with orchids from the farm. They bestowed them on the party guests with "*Alohas!*"

Some of Tony and Glo's hippie friends came to the party.

Miss Louise and Karen organized games. Folks participated in the one-legged sack race. They had a hula-hoop twirling contest. Mr. Watanabe borrowed a small pig from one of the local farmers. They greased up the pig and the kids competed to catch it and to hang onto it for as long as they could. That was a fun event for the kids that everyone enjoyed watching.

By the time it got dark, there were probably about one-hundred people in attendance. Colored lights lit the night along with *tiki* torches. People danced to rock and roll and Hawaiian tunes. Several young, beautiful girls in grass skirts performed a *hula* for the guests.

Fireworks exploded all over the area. Albert purchased a large number of fireworks. He and Tony set off an impressive display with Roman candles and rockets that shot high into the air.

Then the community fireworks were set off over the bay and seen all around the area. When the fireworks show ended, the partygoers began departing. Most people had the next day, Monday, off for the holiday, making it a three-day weekend. A small group of people stayed behind to help clean up.

Mildred and the other Hanalei House residents were still jubilant when they headed into the house for the night.

CHAPTER 35

A few days later, there was a rally at the building site. The protestors chanted their displeasure. "WHAT DO WE WANT? NO MORE CONDOS!" Mildred had an uneasy feeling when she saw the police arrive with Calvin Daniels. The police and Daniels surveyed the scene before moving into the crowd.

Daniels spotted Mildred. He turned to the police and said, "There she is," pointing in Mildred's direction. "Arrest her! She's the one who started all this."

Mildred saw them coming. Kulak noticed the police, too. Before they could reach Mildred, he stepped in front of her and thrust his sign like a bayonet at the cops and Daniels.

"Sir, I would advise you to put that sign down and step away before we have to arrest you," one of the officers warned.

Mildred felt the urge to run, then to fight. In the end, she decided to go peacefully. Mildred shouted from behind Kulak, "This is a peaceful demonstration."

Kulak stood his ground but only for a short time. He attempted to block the police with his body but they easily disarmed him of his sign and pushed him aside to get to Mildred. The crowd reacted by closing in on the police and Daniels.

The officers seemed unfazed as one of them roughly grabbed Mildred's arm, startling her. Her free hand shot out and touched the cop's chest. He slapped her hand away and Mildred tried to shrug herself free. Lucy Kapana, standing next to Mildred, got scared and jumped too. The other policeman forced handcuffs on Mildred and said, "You are under arrest for inciting a riot and disorderly conduct. And you just added resisting arrest." Then, he read Mildred her rights.

Daniels looked uncomfortable standing among his adversaries. There was a lot of pushing and shoving as the cops made their way through the crowd with Mildred. The protestors shouted after them, "WHAT DO WE WANT? NO MORE CONDOS! WHAT DO WE WANT? NO MORE CONDOS!"

Police reinforcements arrived to break up the demonstration. One of them announced through a bullhorn, "Please leave the area at once! This is an illegal demonstration. If you don't want to be arrested—leave now!"

The crowd ignored him and continued chanting. Albert noticed them dragging Mildred away. He rushed over to them, and asked the police officer escorting Mildred, "Where are you taking Mrs. Meyers?"

Indignantly, the cop turned to Albert and said, "What's it to you?"

Albert stood his ground and said, "I'm her attorney. Where are you taking her?"

"She's being arrested for inciting a riot, disorderly conduct, resisting arrest, and possible parole violations, and extradition to New York."

They pushed Mildred into the back of a police car. Albert couldn't stop them. Kulak and the residents of the house surrounded the car. "Don't worry, I'll follow you down and will get you out Mrs. Meyers," Albert shouted after the car.

Kulak became irate and shouted at the police, "These are Gestapo tactics! This isn't Nazi Germany! It's Kauai—in the United States of America. It's our right to protest."

The remaining police tried to disperse the crowd with arrest threats. The protestors enraged by Mildred's arrest wouldn't budge.

The police car slowly moved forward with Mildred staring out the back window and protestors banging on the car as it attempted to make its way through the crowd.

CHAPTER 36

The police booked Mildred and placed her in a solitary confinement cell. It had a bed, a toilet, and a sink. The only light came from the small glass window in the steel door that separated Mildred from the other inmates.

They let Albert in to see her before she was to go before the judge. He looked around the cell and said, "I can't believe they have you in here."

Mildred looked at him with a hopeless expression.

"I'm going to get them to drop all the charges. Treating a seventy-one-year-old woman like this…" He told her he would see her in court and left.

A little later, a guard led Mildred into the courtroom in ankle shackles and handcuffs. There was a communal gasp as Stanley, and the residents of the Hanalei House saw her. Mrs. Benson said, "She looks tired and stressed." Her friends agreed and looked concerned.

Albert stood immediately and objected, "Why is my client being treated so cruelly? I don't understand this. Is solitary confinement, handcuffs, and shackles necessary? She's a seventy-one-year-old woman. For God's sake. Come on! What do you think she's going to do?"

He received a boost of support from Mildred's friends when they applauded. Albert turned in their direction. Judge Paumakua, the same judge who presided over Stanley's case, banged his gavel and stared harshly at Mildred's friends.

Mildred felt confident about Albert's representation.

Albert continued, "Your honor, I request that you drop all the charges against my client. She was participating in a peaceful demonstration against a contentious condominium development."

The judge looked down at some papers on his desk. When he looked up, he answered, "From what I can see here, she is a convicted felon and a parole violator."

"Look at her your honor—she's a sweet old woman," Albert said.

The judge peered over the top of his glasses at Mildred. "I'm denying your request for a dismissal."

Albert felt a little deflated. "If you insist on continuing this abomination, please set bail so Mrs. Meyers can go home tonight."

"I'm afraid that won't be possible. Until we hear back from the parole authorities in New York, Mrs. Meyers will remain incarcerated."

"What?"

"She is a parole violator. They may want to proceed with extradition to New York."

"I wish you would please consider Mrs. Meyers' age. She is not well. She recently lost her daughter to cancer and has suffered extreme hardship as a result of her daughter's passing."

"We'll have a doctor examine her to see if she is fit to stand trial and extradition to New York."

Throughout this entire exchange, Mildred sat stone-faced, knowing from past experiences to keep her mouth shut and let her lawyer do the talking but biting her tongue didn't come easy to Mildred.

When Albert couldn't sway the judge, he asked, "Your honor, she's being held in solitary confinement. Isn't that a little extreme? Can we please move her into the regular population?" The judge seemed to soften as he turned to the bailiff and said, "Please see what we can do to get Mrs. Meyers into better accommodations."

The bailiff agreed to take care of finding Mildred a new cell.

"And can we please get the cuffs and shackles removed?" Albert asked.

"They will be as soon as she's in her cell," the judge claimed.

Albert, unhappy with that, requested, "Will you please let me know when you have the information, you need to release Mrs. Meyers on bail?"

"Yes! Please see that the bailiff has your contact information."

Mildred leaned towards Albert and whispered in his ear, "I need my medications."

Albert shook his head and said to the judge, "Mrs. Meyers is on several medications, which she will need."

"If you bring them to the jail, they'll see that they are administered," the judge responded.

"Thank you, your honor."

As Mildred was led from the courtroom, she attempted to wave to her friends by raising her handcuffed hands in their direction. They waved back with sad faces. Mr. Kulak stood with his arms folded across his chest and sadly watched them take Mildred away.

The mood around the dinner table that evening was somber. Mrs. Watanabe made baked *Mahi Mahi*. There were a lot of leftovers. Everyone claimed they had no appetite. As Mrs. Watanabe cleared away the dishes, she said, "It's not the same without Mildred."

They all agreed.

"I wish we could bring her some of this food," Mrs. Watanabe continued.

"Do you think you will be able to get her out tomorrow, Albert?" Mr. Kulak asked.

"I'm sure going to try. I plan to get down there early. They should have heard something from New York by the morning."

"If you can't, Tony and I are working on a plan to bust her out," Mr. Kulak said.

"What?" Stanley gasped.

"The justice system stinks. Arresting a seventy-one-year-old woman is disgraceful, man," Tony said. He shook his head. "It just ain't right. Locking up Mrs. Meyers. It just ain't right."

Albert said, "Mr. Kulak, please don't try anything foolish," while looking at Tony as well. "You'll only make it more difficult for Mrs. Meyers. We don't need anyone else going to jail."

Kulak listened but the look of contempt on his face hardened. A lull fell over the room.

"We walked past the construction site this afternoon. They're working! Unimpeded," Mr. Benson claimed.

"I don't understand how they could lock up someone Mrs. Meyers' age," Karen said.

"She's a pretty tough lady," Stanley told them "but I don't know after all she's been through if she can take this."

"The judge said they'd have a doctor look her over. I'll make sure they do that," Albert said. He looked at Mr. Kulak and asked, "Can you get all her medications together? I'll bring them with me."

Still disgruntled, Mr. Kulak said, "I will."

"And I'll put some food together to bring to her," Mrs. Watanabe added.

Stanley said, "I didn't eat anything while I was there. The other guys complained about the food. Said it was terrible."

Mr. Watanabe looked at Albert and said, "You think they'll let her have it?"

Albert had a perplexed look on his face. "I'll try to get the food to her. And I want to get her out on bail."

"That's good," Mrs. Watanabe said.

Mrs. Watanabe got up and picked up dishes and leftovers.

Unbeknownst to Albert, Mildred remained in solitary confinement overnight. They gave her a tray of food that didn't look appetizing. She poked at a piece of rubbery chicken, took a bite, then ended up only eating the chocolate cake and drinking the coffee.

She had been in jail several times in New York but this was the first time without cellmates. It made her feel alone, uncomfortable, and disconcerting. She wanted to go home.

Sleep that night was difficult. Dreams of different scenarios slipped in and out of her consciousness. When she fell into a deep sleep, it transported her back to her childhood on the Lower East Side. To the three-room tenement apartment where she and her family lived. A quick succession of images appeared and disappeared: the three flights of stairs; the toilet down the hall; the claustrophobic apartment with windows on each side of the kitchen that looked, not outside, but into the adjoining rooms where the family worked and slept.

There was the tight little kitchen in the middle of the apartment with its coal stove, sink, and bathtub. Her father Bernie Rabinovitz sat at the dining table with an impatient look on his face. He glanced at his wife, Rosie, sitting at the table, his younger son Hermie, Mildred, and her younger sisters, Marcy and Ellie. They were waiting for Sy, Mildred's older brother who delivered for a neighborhood butcher shop. They all looked up when they heard footsteps and the apartment door flew open and Sy rushed in. "You're late!" his father scolded.

"I got it," he said as he pulled a *Beitzah* (roasted egg) out of his jacket pocket and placed it on the table. He sensed his father's impatience over his tardiness. Under his other arm, he had a package wrapped in brown butcher paper. Still out of breath from running up three flights of stairs, he said, "Mr. Rogarshevsky gave me a small piece of cooked brisket, so we have it for our Seder."

"He's a good man, Mr. Rogarshevsky," her mother said.

"Tell him, we appreciate his kindness and will repay him as soon as God allows," Mr. Rabinovitz said.

Sy took his place at the table. His father looked impatiently at the boy. The youngster squirmed uncomfortably under his father's stern gaze. Finally, he said, "What?"

"Did you forget something son?"

Sy thought for a moment and then seemed to remember something. He sprung to his feet, went to his jacket, and pulled a lamb shank bone that was partially hanging out of his jacket pocket. Everyone at the table smiled. The boy placed the bone on an empty dish in the middle of the table and sat down.

Mildred's father nodded to his wife to light the Seder candle. Their father sat at the head of the table wearing his *Tallit* (prayer shawl) around his shoulders, his *Torah* opened in front of him to the Passover Seder ceremony. Mr. Rabinovitz put his hands together and said, "*Baruch Atah Ado-nai, Elo-heinu Melech Ha-olam, Asher Kid'shanu B'mitzvotav V'tzivanu L'hadlik Ner Shel Yom To*v. (Blessed are You, Lord our God, King of the Universe, who has sanctified us with His commandments and commanded us that we kindle the *Yom Tov* (holiday lights.))"

This would be the last Seder with their father. In the days that followed, he came down with the flu. The 1919 influenza epidemic killed millions worldwide. Mildred's father succumbed to it. Without his income, the family became destitute and had to move out of their apartment. They moved in with relatives in the neighborhood. Mildred was just thirteen-years-old. She and her brothers quit school to work and take care of her mother and her younger sisters.

The dream shook Mildred awake. She felt disoriented, soaked in sweat, tears running from her eyes as she looked around her cell, trying to figure out where she was.

CHAPTER 37

Albert got to the jailhouse early the next morning. He was surprised to find a protest going on in front of the building. As he got closer, he realized it was for Mildred's benefit. Twenty or thirty people marched in sympathy, chanting: "FREE MRS. MEYERS! FREE MRS. MEYERS! FREE MRS. MEYERS!"

Before entering the building, Albert smiled and flashed the peace sign at the protestors. The security guard at the front entrance looked skeptically at the medications and the small basket of food Albert brought with him.

"You could leave the medications here. We'll have the medical staff administer them. But you can't bring in the food."

Albert looked around to see if anyone was watching. When he noticed no one in the area, he slipped a twenty-dollar bill to the guard. The man looked down at it, then at Albert. For a moment, Albert wondered if he had made a mistake. Then the man quickly glanced around. Feeling safe, he snatched the money. Albert felt relieved. The guard examined the contents of the basket and said with a smile, "I'll have somebody take it into her."

As Albert headed towards the courtroom, a voice called out from behind him, "Mr. Cutler! Mr. Cutler!" Albert stopped and turned to see the bailiff from the court the day before. He was a short man with gray hair and a friendly face. "Mr. Cutler, I tried to reach you to save you a trip. They said you left already."

Right away Albert looked concerned. "Is Mrs. Meyers okay?" he asked impatiently.

"Well, I'm afraid Mrs. Meyers had to spend the night in solitary."

"What? The judge told me…"

"I know. But they said there was no room." The man moved closer to Albert and spoke in a confidential tone, "Yesterday, I saw that Calvin Daniels talking to the sheriff. I'm not sure, but I think he handed the sheriff some money to make Mrs. Meyers' life miserable."

"Son-of-a-bitch," Albert muttered. He felt a pang of guilt, having just bribed the guard.

"We can get her into a regular cell today."

"You said you tried to reach me, about what?"

"Ah, it's New York. We haven't heard from them. I'm sure it's the time difference. That's probably what it is."

Albert looked annoyed but he thanked the man. As the bailiff walked away, Albert called after him, "Hey, is there any way I can see the judge today?"

"I'll ask. Maybe later this afternoon. But I can't promise anything."

"Yeah, okay. Thanks!"

"How can I reach you if he can find the time?"

"I'm going to see my client. I'll stop at your office later."

When Albert tried to see Mildred, he found out she was at the Wilcox Memorial Hospital for an examination by a doctor. Albert looked frustrated. He left the building and went to a nearby restaurant for coffee. Mildred was on his mind. He had taken to her in a short time as much as Stanley had. He had never asked his brother how he felt about Mildred, but to Albert, she reminded him of their late mother.

Albert met briefly with the judge that afternoon. The doctor advised the judge to release Mildred. He also warned about sending her back to New York under any circumstances. The judge said the extradition was out of his hands and up to New York's discretion but released Mildred on bail.

CHAPTER 38

At dinner that evening, everyone was jubilant to have Mildred back. Albert said, "The judge refused to dismiss the charges against her and we still don't know if they will extradite her. But I'm grateful he let her out on bail. I believe he took pity because of Mrs. Meyer's age and based on the doctor's assessment." Albert took it as a small victory. He felt confident that when he presented the facts of the case, they would vindicate Mildred.

Mrs. Watanabe prepared meatballs, spaghetti, and salad for dinner. Tony and Glo sat at the table with the residents.

Mildred said, "I had a lot of time to think when I was in there."

Tony asked, "They had you in solitary confinement?"

"They claimed it was the only available place they could put me."

"You're my hero, Mrs. Meyers," Glo said.

"Thank you, but I don't feel like one."

"Some of us were arrested a few years ago. That jail is terrible," Tony said.

"I know," Mildred agreed. "It's not as bad as the Women's House of Detention in New York. Sue thank you for the food. Everyone complained about the food they served. I had the guard give some of what you sent to my neighbors. They told me to tell you it was delicious."

"But it was for you," Mrs. Watanabe claimed.

"I know but I couldn't eat it all by myself. Who wants to eat when you're confined like that?"

"When we were there the place smelled," Glo said. "It's hard to eat when the place smells of old urine, and I don't know what else."

"I know. If I had a mop, I would have mopped that filthy floor and cleaned the rest of the cell," Mildred told them.

Her fellow residents smiled, knowing her obsession with cleanliness.

Mildred continued, "I wish we could stop this development. The island needs tourists to grow economically but there will come a time when the infrastructure can't support its residents plus all the tourists."

"Peaceful protests aren't illegal," Albert said. "There's no reason for them to arrest you. They have no evidence that you organized anything or that you incited a riot."

"I know," Mildred answered.

"I was told Daniels gave money to the sheriff to make your life miserable."

"What?" Mr. Kulak asked incredulously.

There were a few grumbles around the table. Albert continued, "When I was in North Carolina, I saw a lot of these developments fail because of lawsuits and construction overruns. They usually end in bankruptcy."

"This Daniels' company may have a lot of capital," Mr. Benson said.

"They've had a lot of bad press and it hasn't stopped them," Karen added. "If they can't rent or sell their condos because of their reputation, wouldn't that hurt them in the pocketbook?"

"It hasn't stopped them yet," Mrs. Benson said.

Albert explained, "But on the other hand, when these projects fail, they leave a mess behind. It's just another unfinished project that becomes an eyesore."

"Yeah, man, and they felt us hippies were an eyesore," Tony insisted.

"At this point, it's going to take a miracle to stop them," Mildred said.

"I think Mildred's right. But the community is still against the project. They haven't been deterred," Albert added.

Then, Mr. Kulak said, "You know in ancient times, land disputes of this kind were settled by the chiefs."

The others stared at him and a silence fell over the table.

Later that night, Mildred and Kulak climbed the stairs to their room. Mildred looked affectionately at Kulak and asked, "Did you miss me?"

He took her hands in his as they faced each other. "Yes."

"I'm going to take a nice hot bath and then I'll join you in bed. Will you wait for me?"

Kulak smiled at her and kissed her cheek. "Of course, I will." A few minutes later, Mildred went to the bathroom carrying her bath towel and things while Mr. Kulak made himself comfortable in bed.

CHAPTER 39

For several days, protests stopped at the construction site and work continued unabated. They either replaced or repaired the damaged equipment. They used it to push dirt around, forming streets, sidewalks, and foundations.

Everyone sat around the dining room table eating breakfast. Mr. Kulak walked in with the newspaper. He had a curious look on his face as he read the cover story. Mildred asked, "Arthur, what is it?"

They all looked up at Kulak, and he said, "Our Joe Thomas broke another story about Daniels and the lawsuits against his company. It seems a number of them have been filed in New York and Miami for the use of asbestos in buildings and housing that was built by his father in the 1950s. Construction workers who worked on them as well as people that live in them have been diagnosed with Mesothelioma."

"What's that?" Mrs. Benson asked.

"It's a cancer caused by asbestos fibers getting lodged in the lining of the lungs," Mr. Kulak said.

"Is it curable?" Stanley asked.

Mr. Kulak sat down, looked up from the newspaper, and said, "There's no cure. It says it is one of the most aggressive cancers. Daniels used asbestos in their building materials for roofing and insulation. The lawsuits are in the millions."

"Do they say anything about the project down the road?" Albert asked.

"Just that it's the same Daniels Development Corporation," Mr. Kulak answered.

"Maybe we can pressure them to stop construction until they can assure the community that they're not doing the same thing here," Mildred suggested.

Later that day, Mildred, Kulak, and Annie were selling produce at the farmers' market. "*Aloha,* Mildred!" Lucy Kapana stood at the stand.

Mildred noticed her and said, "*Aloha!*"

"They're not working today. Did you see?" Lucy asked.

"I saw that when we passed. What do you think is going on?"

"I don't know. Maybe, something to do with that asbestos," Lucy said.

CHAPTER 40

Behind Jason's pitching, the Serpents had a seven and five record. It was enough to get them into the island playoffs. Their first playoff game was against the Dolphins who had an eight and four record.

Everyone from the Hanalei House sat in the stands cheering for the Serpents. Jason was on the mound pitching.

The score was five to three for the Dolphins in the top of the fifth inning. Jason seemed to be struggling on the mound with only one out and runners on first and third. He got behind on the batter with three balls and no strikes. The next two pitches the batter fouled off. Unfortunately, the next pitch resulted in a walk.

Coach Palani and the catcher walked out to the mound to settle Jason down. Whatever the coach told him must have helped because Jason struck out the next batter.

His fans cheered. The next kid up already had two hits in the game. Jason wanted to get him out this time.

The Dolphins goaded Jason, yelling, "The pitcher can't pitch!"

Jason tried to tune them out. His father shouted from the stands, "Don't let them get to you, Jason!"

He threw an outside pitch to the batter for a ball. The next pitch the batter fouled off. Neil shouted from the stands, "You can do it, Jas!"

Jason stayed calm and put a low fastball right down the middle that the batter hit on the ground. The shortstop caught it, tossed to the second basemen for one out, and the second baseman threw out the batter running to first.

When the Serpents got up, their first batter struck out. The next one grounded out. They had two outs, and the kid at the plate had a two and two count against him when he hit a home run over the right-field fence.

Before the inning ended, the Serpents had runners on first and second but failed to score another run when their batter hit a fly to right that was an easy out.

The coach wanted to take Jason out of the game but Jason convinced him that he was all right. He took the mound confidently and struck out the first batter. The next batter hit a long fly to center that the centerfielder caught at the wall.

Then, he got in trouble walking the next batter and the following one got a hit to shallow left field. The Serpents were able to hold the runner at third.

Jason was able to pitch himself out of the inning with another strikeout.

In their last time at bat, the Serpents got a lot of encouragement from their fans who were on their feet cheering. Their first batter walked. The next one up struck out. Things were looking up when the kid on first stole second with a headfirst slide. The batter with a two and one count against him hit a double to right field and the runner on second scored, making it five to four.

Jason was in the batter's box when the Serpent at the plate got a walk. Jason stepped up to the plate with a thunderous roar from the Serpent fans.

It looked like he was going to walk. With three balls and no strikes, the pitcher threw one right down the middle, Jason couldn't let it go by and belted it deep into left field, he had a double and two runners scored to put them in the lead six to five.

The place went wild. The residents cheered.

They didn't score any more runs and were the victors, going on to the next round.

The Serpents jubilantly jumped up and down in a group. The stands emptied and Neil and the residents went onto the field to congratulate Jason and his teammates. Neil and the residents shook Jason and his teammates' hands.

CHAPTER 41

Shortly after breakfast, Mildred put on a big straw hat and went out to the garden to help Mr. Watanabe, Annie, and Glo pick lettuce to sell at the farmers' market. They cut the lettuce at the stem and tossed it into a wheelbarrow.

Mildred was bent over and concentrating on the lettuce. She didn't hear the man's voice, "Mildred!" He said it again, "Mildred!"

Annie looked up and noticed Vic Meyers standing there. She tapped Mildred's shoulder, Mildred looked up and Annie said, "Someone wants you."

Mildred straightened up slowly and saw Vic. She dreaded another conversation with him. "*Aloha*, Mildred!"

She stood and he walked over to her. Mildred half-smiled. "Hello, Victor."

"I'm glad you're out of jail. How are you feeling?"

"Well, it took a lot out of me," Mildred said. "I'm not feeling that great. It's good to get out here and play in the dirt."

"Yeah, it is. I have a little garden that I tend in my backyard. I enjoy it."

"What do you want?" Mildred asked.

Vic looked at the others who were watching them and listening intently. "Can we talk somewhere?"

Mildred didn't want to talk to him but she did want to tell him about the divorce. She said, "Sure." She led him over to the table on the lanai. Mildred sat down and he went around to the other side of the table to sit. An awkward moment ensued as they both looked at one another.

Vic finally asked, "Yeah, did you think about what we talked about?'

Mildred didn't answer.

"About coming to live with me," he said hopefully.

Mildred took a long time to respond as she struggled with how to tell him about the divorce. She said, "Yes, I did think about it. I'm not going to come live with you. I will never forgive you for leaving us."

She wasn't sure if he expected her to say that or not. He just sat there staring at her. Mildred continued, "I'm filing for a divorce!"

"Oh, Mildred, can't we give it another try? We were both young. I was scared and foolish."

"No! You were an inconsiderate gambler who pissed away our money. You didn't even tell me anything about what was going on. You just left. No note. No nothing. You left me with nothing to hope for."

"I didn't want to scare you, yeah. You were pregnant and due any day."

"That's no excuse. It's bull and you know it."

"What if I won't give you a divorce?" he asked arrogantly.

"It doesn't matter whether you want it or not. I want one and I'm filing."

He looked frustrated. "I can't convince you otherwise?"

Mildred shook her head adamantly.

They sat there looking away from each other, not saying anything.

Mildred broke the silence and said, "I have to get back to work. We're taking our produce to the market this afternoon."

Vic stood slowly. "I wish you'd reconsider, yeah."

Mildred got up too. Vic looked at her for a response but she walked away from the table back to the garden. He stood there for a few moments watching her walk away. A feeling of hopelessness came over him.

As he left Vic passed Albert who was coming to talk to Mildred. He smiled at Vic as they passed. Albert walked over to where Mildred was picking lettuce. "Mrs. Meyers!"

Mildred looked up. "Oh, hi. Did you see him?" Mildred asked. "Vic. That was him."

"Oh, I wondered who he was. That's what I was coming to talk to you about."

"Vic?"

"Yes. We have to wait another month to file."

"Why?"

"You have to reside in the state at least six months before you can file for a divorce."

Mildred started counting in her mind. "Oh, I waited this long, another month isn't so bad."

"I'll have all the paperwork ready to go," Albert said. "What did he want?"

"The same old thing. He wants me to take him back."

"He doesn't look too healthy."

"I hadn't noticed," Mildred said and didn't really care to think about Victor anymore.

CHAPTER 42

Over the following weeks, more information about Daniels and his asbestos problems came out. Whatever was going on with his company put a halt to construction down the road.

Mildred was happy about that. She thought to herself that God must have intervened. The trial was still hanging over her head. She hadn't been to a religious service since she left L.A. Mildred felt she needed God's help now. She feared extradition and didn't want to return to New York and possibly jail.

As far as she knew, there were no synagogues on the island. She thought there might be other Jews living there. Then, she remembered Glo's last name was Goldberg, a nice Jewish name.

It was somewhat overcast that day as Mildred went out to the garden where she found Glo and Annie picking flowers for *leis*. "Hi ladies," Mildred said.

Annie and Glo looked up, smiled at Mildred and said, "*Aloha!*"

Mildred kept trying to remember to greet people with, *Aloha!* She thought it was a pleasant way to say hello and goodbye. For the life of her, she didn't know why she couldn't remember to say that. Mildred made a mental note to say it more often, so she said, "*Aloha,*" in return. "Glo, I wanna ask you something."

"What?"

"You're Jewish, aren't you?"

"I was. I'm an atheist now. Why do you ask?"

"I haven't been to services since I left L.A. There was a synagogue on our corner so it was easy. There must be other Jewish people on the island."

"There are. I know some of them."

"Where do they worship?

"There's a retired rabbi who lives around here," Glo said. "I'm pretty sure he still conducts services."

"How can we find when and where they are?"

"I know somebody that will know. They do it somewhere around here on Saturdays."

"Oh, yeah? Can you find out for me? I'd like to go."

"Annie and I are going into town in a little while. I'll find out for you."

"Thanks! Can I help you?" Mildred asked.

"No, I think we're almost done," Annie said.

Glo was correct about the Jewish services. That Saturday, Mr. Kulak escorted Mildred to service at the Waioli Hui'ia Church meetinghouse. There were a handful of people, men, and women in attendance. Rabbi Moskowitz had a white beard. He was in his eighties, a big man with a round mid-section. Even at his age, he still had a strong, husky voice. His eyes were dark and sunken and he had a big black mole on his nose.

After the service, he greeted Mildred and Kulak. "I read about you, Mrs. Meyers. You've gained quite a reputation around here in the short time you've been here."

"That's my problem—I would like to live a quiet, peaceful life, but I can't keep my mouth shut when I see people like Calvin Daniels destroying communities without any regard for the people that live there."

"Well, that's quite an accusation. You'll get no argument from me. I'm on your side. These islands are overrun with people trying to make a quick buck. If I can be of any help, please let me know."

"I will, and thank you for the service. We will be back."

The rabbi looked at Kulak and asked, "So are you two married?"

Mildred smiled self-consciously and said, "No."

The rabbi nodded. Kulak said, "We're in love and may want to get married someday."

"That's nice to hear."

Mildred turned to Kulak and smiled. That's the first time she ever heard him say that. Mildred wondered if he meant it or he was just saying it for the rabbi's benefit. It also reminded her about her divorce from Victor.

Mildred and Kulak said goodbye and walked back to the farm. Mildred felt a lot better. She had prayed for her daughter at the service.

CHAPTER 43

A few days later at the farmers' market, Lucy Kapana approached the produce stand and said, "*Aloha, Mildred!*"

Mildred looked up and said, "*Aloha!*"

"You hear the news about Calvin Daniels?" Lucy asked

Mildred shook her head, no. Lucy had also grabbed the attention of Kulak and Annie. They all waited patiently for her to continue. "He settled some lawsuits out of court for millions."

Mildred and her friends looked surprised. "So, how's it going to affect this project?" Mildred asked.

"You see them working?" Lucy asked sarcastically.

"No," Mildred answered.

Lucy suggested, "I think it's over."

"I sure hope so," Mr. Kulak said.

"What about you Mildred? They still trying to put you in jail?" Lucy asked.

"Well, my trial was postponed a month because the judge had surgery."

"Maybe that softens him up a little for you."

"I sure hope so. Even if they find me not guilty, they may still try to extradite me to New York."

Lucy looked worried as she picked through the produce on the table. "I hope that don't happen. We need you here. They're building all over this place. I wish more people were like you. Most of them complain but they don't wanna do nothing. They just want to sit in front of their TV and drink beer."

"A lot of people are like that," Mildred said as she stuffed Lucy's items in a bag.

"Hey, I heard about your apple strudel."

"From who?"

"Let's see… You know I don't remember. It was probably over the coconut wireless."

"Oh, and it's not apple. I use apricot preserves. It tastes like apple, but there's none.

"You should sell them here."

"I hadn't thought of that."

"That's a good idea, Mildred," Mr. Kulak added.

"You should, Mrs. Meyers." Annie claimed, "Nobody around here sells anything like that."

"Yeah." Lucy advised, "Make a little money for yourself."

Mildred finished packing Lucy's produce and collected the money. Lucy said, "I'll let you know if I hear more about Daniels."

"Thanks."

Lucy smiled at them and walked away.

"Well that was interesting," Mildred said. "You think they're really shutting down the project?"

Kulak and Annie looked hopefully at Mildred.

CHAPTER 44

On an overcast Saturday afternoon in late summer, the Serpents played in the island championship little league game. The game was in Lihue against the Devils, a very good team from the south shore. All the residents of the Hanalei House sat in the stands to cheer on Jason and his team.

Coach Palani told his team before the game, "You guys are better than them. The fact is you are good enough to be here today and good enough to be the island champs. I want you to go out there and play your best. And remember, whether you win or lose, have fun."

The coach's words still resonated in Jason's head as he took the mound in the bottom of the fourth inning. There was no score for either team. Jason held the Devils to one hit. The Serpents had two hits to their credit.

Jason's first two pitches were balls, followed by two strikes. More than anything, Jason didn't want to walk the batter. Unfortunately, he did. With a man on first and no outs, Jason felt the pressure.

With the next batter, he got behind on the count again. He threw a fastball that the batter hit on the ground. It looked like an easy double play but the shortstop bobbled the ball and was only able to get the batter out at first. The runner from first was safe on second.

From the stands, Neil shouted, "Settle down Jas!"

"He'll be okay, man," Tony said to Neil.

"I don't know. He's getting a little wild," Neil responded. "He may be getting tired."

But Jason settled down and struck the next batter out. He got out of the inning when the following kid hit a fly ball that the right fielder caught.

The Devils took the field at the top of the fifth. They had a new pitcher on the mound. The first Serpent hit a line drive down the left-field line and ended up on second. Between pitches, he stole a base and was on third—intimidating the Devils pitcher with a long lead down to home.

Unfortunately, by the end of the inning, the Serpents couldn't bring in their man. The coach told his team before they took the field again, "We can still win this! So, don't make any mistakes out there."

At the bottom of the fifth inning, the Serpents ran out on the field. The first batter was the Devils' best hitter. He was a big *haole* kid with muscular arms. Jason had a one and two count on him when the kid hit a long fly ball over the left fielder's head. When the fielder retrieved the ball, he threw it to third but the runner had a standup triple.

The hit seemed to rattle Jason because he walked the next batter. In between pitches, Jason tried to pick off the runner on third, who was taunting him with a big lead to home, but the runner on first took the opportunity to steal second base.

The coach and catcher went to the mound to talk to their pitcher. Coach Palani wanted to take Jason out of the game but didn't have anyone better. "Don't worry about the guys on base. Just concentrate on the batter."

Jason nodded and struck out the next two batters. The next one up had a three and two count when he hit a slow roller to the shortstop who bobbled the ball. When he finally picked it up the batter was safely on first, the guy on second went to third, and the man on third scored making it one nothing Devils.

The inning ended with a fly ball to shallow center, which the centerfielder had to hustle to grab.

The Serpents had to scramble to catch up in the sixth and final inning. Jason led off with a base hit to left field. The next kid got a walk.

The following batter bunted. They threw him out at first for an easy out, but it successfully moved runners to second and third.

The next batter had no balls and two strikes against him when he hit a long fly ball that dropped between the center and left fielders. Jason easily scored from third and the kid on second ran like hell to get in before the throw to the plate. It was close and he was safe. It put the Serpents in the lead two to one. That's how the score remained when the Devils took their last at-bat in the bottom of the sixth inning.

Their first batter grounded out. The next kid walked. Jason struck out the following batter. He wasn't as lucky with the next guy up who got a base hit to right field. It put men on first and second with two out.

Tony turned to Neil and said, "He'll be okay, man."

Jason felt uncomfortable and walked another batter. The coach, catcher and the infielders met on the mound. Jason was certain the coach was going to pull him out of the game. Instead, he said, "Jason all you need to do is get this guy out. Anything hit on the ground is a force out at any base. I want you to keep your heads up and give Jason the support he needs behind him."

Everyone patted Jason on the back. "You can do it!" the catcher said as the coach left the field and everyone went back to their positions.

Jason felt good but once again fell behind on the batter with three balls and no strikes. He kept reminding himself, *I got to get him out!* He took his time getting ready. He figured the batter was feeling as much pressure as he was. That filled him with confidence. Jason picked up the rosin bag and powdered his sweaty hand until it felt dry around the ball. When the catcher flashed the sign for a fastball, Jason nodded. He focused all his attention on the catcher's mitt and fired in a searing pitch for a strike.

The Hanalei crowd cheered.

Jason felt a little calmer. Once again, he took his time. He threw another fastball for a strike.

The Hanalei fans went wild. They could smell victory. Jason wanted to strike him out. The catcher flashed him the sign for a low outside curveball but the ball didn't go where Jason wanted. It crossed the middle of the plate and the batter slammed it to left field. The fielder had to run and made a spectacular running catch over his head.

The crowd cheered. At first, the Serpents stood in their positions. It seemed they didn't realize they won until the Hanalei fans roared. It snapped Jason and his team back to reality. They jumped up and down on the field, hugging each other. They were ecstatic.

Neil, Annie, and the rest of the Hanalei House people rushed onto the field to congratulate the winners.

Mr. Benson said, "You boys did great."

Mildred added, "Jason, you have a lot to be proud of."

Jason's heart was still beating out of control during the trophy celebration that followed.

When everyone got back to the farm that night, Albert walked out to Neil and Annie's cottage to see Jason. He carried a basketball. Albert knocked and Neil opened the door. "I have something for Jason," Albert said.

Neil invited him in. Jason's adrenalin was still pumping. His winning trophy sat on top of the television. "I got something for you," Albert said, and held out the ball.

Jason looked at it enthusiastically. "For me?"

"Take a look at the signature," Albert said. He handed over the basketball.

Jason quickly rotated the ball in his hands, stopped it, and then stared at the signature. He quickly looked up and said, "Hank Aaron? Wow!"

"It's yours."

"You're kidding."

"Nope."

"Why is it on a basketball?"

"He was at one of my college basketball games. He came into the locker room after the game and signed autographs for us. I had this ball in my hands and I held it out for him to sign."

"Wow!"

"You were great out there today. You deserve it."

Jason put the ball down and hugged Albert. "Thanks."

CHAPTER 45

Now that baseball was over, Karen and Annie convinced Jason to join Miss Louise's acting class. At first, Jason did so reluctantly. But Miss Louise had a knack for drawing out the best in her students. Jason was very shy, but with each new success in class, his confidence grew and he started doing scenes from plays, and even some scenes from TV series scripts that Miss Louise had acquired over the years.

Some of the other island boys around the same age as Jason thought acting too sissy for them until Jason convinced his friend Mark, an athletic-looking surfer with shoulder-length hair, to come audit a class. Mark immediately got hooked on the adrenalin rush that acting provided and it seemed to come naturally to him. He said to Miss Louise, "You mean I should be myself?"

With Mark in the class, some of his other surfing buddies joined too. Miss Louise was happy with the group she cobbled together. The boys seemed to love her.

She taught them sensory exercises to get them in touch with their environment, their bodies, minds, feelings, and emotions. She taught them how to use sensory work in their scenes.

As for Karen, her students were all girls ranging from four to twelve-years-old. She enjoyed working with them. Karen taught them the proper way for dancers to stretch as well as limbering exercises to warm up using the barre. Her lessons were a mix of classical ballet and some modern dance.

One afternoon, Miss Louise and Karen sat in their office. Miss Louise said, "I think we should put on a little holiday show with some dance and some theatre."

"That would be nice. It would have to be around Thanksgiving. I'm going to Vienna shortly after that."

"That would be alright. I would probably do a short Christmas play. I have something in mind," Miss Louise said.

"And there are some nice dance scenes from the *Nutcracker* that would be lovely."

"That's good. We'll pick a date, notify the children and their parents of our plans, and set a rehearsal schedule," Miss Louise said.

"Yes, and we have plenty of time to get the kids ready."

CHAPTER 46

The day before Mildred's trial, she worked in the garden with Mr. Watanabe and Annie. Each of them had a different task. Mildred picked orchids for *lei* making. Mr. Watanabe sat on the ground under his umbrella on the other side of the garden planting onion starters. Annie picked flowers for bouquets for the hotels: carnations, birds of paradise, anthurium, pikake, plumeria, and hibiscus.

Mildred heard Albert's car come up the drive, stop and park. She heard the doors open followed by a familiar voice, "*Madone!* This place is beautiful."

Then she heard a woman's voice that had a slight Italian accent. "Oh, I like it here already."

"Let's get you settled in your cottage and we'll go find her," Albert told them.

Annie said, "Sounds like Albert is back."

"And somebody's with him," Mildred said. She was a little too far away to make out who the man and woman were, but they sounded like New York people. Mildred gathered her orchids in a basket and walked over to the cottage where Albert took the new guests.

From inside the cottage, the man said, "Aaa, this is very nice."

Mildred stepped onto the porch and peered inside. To her surprise, she saw her old friend from New York,

Angelo Sambucci, and his wife Helen. She opened the door and said, "Oh my God! I thought it was you."

"Son-of-a-gun! Look at you," Angelo said. "Look at that tan. You was always so pale-faced in New York."

Angelo Sambucci was Mildred's boss from the West Side Produce Market. He wore a brightly colored Hawaiian shirt. It looked like a tent over his large frame. He was balding and in his mid-sixties. Angelo and Mildred hugged.

"What're you doing here?"

Albert answered for Angelo, "He's here to testify at your trial as a character witness."

"Yeah, he told us you were in trouble again. He wanted me to write a letter. Aaa! Me write a letter? Helen and I needed a vacation. I told 'im I'd come for a visit and testify. That's alright, right?"

"Yeah, I didn't expect to see you."

"Hey, this is my wife Helen."

Mildred turned to Helen, and said, "We talked on the phone so many times, yet we never met," The two women hugged. "So nice to finally meet you."

"Nice to meet you too, Mildred," she said.

Mildred couldn't believe how pretty Helen was. Her face had a smooth olive complexion with only a few wrinkles around her eyes. Her gray hair was shoulder-length and looked recently styled. She was slim, just a touch taller than five feet, a wisp of a woman next to her husband. Her bright blue eyes glanced around the room.

"I'm trying to retire—believe it or not," Angelo said.

"You, retiring? I can't believe it."

Helen said, "I tol 'im to stop a working before he dies."

"I'm gonna try to enjoy myself a little," Angelo said.

"Work, work, work—not so good for you when you get too old," Helen said.

"Tell me about it," Mildred agreed. "So, who's minding the store?"

"The kids… My son Michael and my nephew Andy. My brother Frank's oldest."

"I remember when he was a baby," Mildred said.

"So—what—you like it here?" Angelo asked.

"Yes. I'm getting used to it. I'd like it better if Calvin Daniels wasn't here building his condominiums."

"I told you about that guy," Angelo said, shaking his head negatively.

"Yeah, I know you did." Mildred smiled warmly at the couple. "It's so nice to see you. Thank you for coming to my defense. I might be coming back to New York, too."

Angelo looked concerned. "Hey, I hope not. I can see already—you're better off here."

Albert said, "We're hoping it doesn't happen. Hey, I'm going to take off. You people have a lot to catch up on. Dinner's usually around seven." He smiled. "Sometimes we have cocktails on the porch earlier. I'll come and get you if we do."

"Thanks for pickin' us up, Albert," Angelo said.

Albert walked out the door. Mildred asked, "Did you know about Nancy?"

"Mildred, we were so sad," Helen said with a frown.

"It was all over the New York papers," Angelo added. "I didn't know how to get in touch with you." He walked over and put his arms around her. Mildred seemed to collapse into his strong embrace.

She said, "I got so much to tell you. Let's go sit down." They walked over to the couch and living room chairs and sat.

Mildred felt so at home to be around New York friends again.

CHAPTER 47

The residents of the Hanalei House, Lucy Kapana, and many of Mildred's supporters sat in the courtroom gallery. Albert was prepared to plead his case for Mildred's innocence. Judge Paumakua sat on the bench.

The same prosecutor from Stanley's trial opened by presenting the evidence against Mildred. They dropped the parole violation since that had to do with her New York case, leaving extradition still on the table. The remaining charges against Mildred were inciting a riot, disorderly conduct, and resisting arrest. The prosecution called the policemen to the stand and they testified to the circumstances of Mildred's arrest.

Albert cross-examined them to demonstrate that the charges against Mildred were baseless and untrue.

Albert said, "Your honor I have witnesses who were present and can corroborate Mrs. Meyer's actions on the day in question."

Albert's first witness was Lucy Kapana. She testified, "Mildred didn't do what the cops say. I was standing next to her. The police came out of nowhere. He grabbed her arm."

Albert asked, "Who grabbed her arm?"

Lucy pointed to the policeman in the gallery. "Him! He scared her. Scared both of us. I felt her jump. I jumped too. No jokes!"

The prosecutor cross-examined Lucy but she stuck to her story that Mildred wasn't resisting arrest, only reacting to the rough treatment.

Albert called his other eyewitnesses to the stand one-by-one. They each supported his position that Mildred's conduct could not be characterized as inciting a riot nor did she engage in any disorderly conduct or resisting arrest. She only participated in a peaceful demonstration. Upon cross-examination by the prosecution, the witnesses all stuck firmly to their story.

Albert called Angelo Sambucci to the stand. "Mr. Sambucci how do you know Mrs. Meyers?"

"She worked for me for, what, thirty-five-years," he smiled at his friend sitting at the defense table.

Mildred nodded back to him. Albert continued, "What's your opinion of Mrs. Meyers?"

"Oh... She's the best."

"What do you mean by that?"

"Well for instance—her job was to take care of my books. You know! Accounting and all that... But she did everything. I could depend on her to organize the office, mop floors... You name it she did it."

"So, you're saying she was a good worker."

"Oh, yeah."

"How about as a person?"

"Geez, she's always helping somebody out!"

Albert said, "No further questions, your honor."

The prosecutor on cross-examination asked, "Mr. Sambucci are you aware of Mrs. Meyers' activism?"

"Yeah, she's always fighting something. She has very high principles."

"I see. Would you say she's a troublemaker?"

Sambucci smiled, and then answered, "I wouldn't say that."

"What would you call her?"

"A good person who sees injustice and stands up against it."

"Thank you, Mr. Sambucci." To the judge, he said, "No further questions, your honor."

Albert in his closing remarks proceeded to disprove the charges. "My client was not the organizer of this demonstration as the prosecution has claimed. She was just a participant. Other individuals had already organized the demonstration as has been stated by my witnesses.

"As for the charges of disorderly conduct and inciting a riot, you heard what my witnesses said. They did not see any disorderly conduct on Mrs. Meyers' part. She was one of many people peacefully demonstrating against a very unpopular condominium development. And since no other demonstrators were arrested, Mrs. Meyers was unfairly singled out for her participation. Therefore, she must be vindicated and found not guilty."

The judge took a recess and twenty-minutes later returned with his verdict. "Mrs. Meyers, I'm aware of your past record in New York and I don't want you creating any more trouble here. Do you understand that?"

"I do."

"In my opinion, the prosecution has not proved its case beyond a reasonable doubt and I find you not guilty. But—"

A cheer rose from the back of the courtroom where Mildred's friends reacted to the verdict. The judge banged his gavel to silence them. When they quieted down, he continued, "I don't believe New York City will extradite you. I have spoken to the New York judge about your case. I explained that you have suffered extreme hardship when you lost your daughter and you left Los Angeles. Since you didn't fulfill your probation requirements in L.A., your probation has been transferred here. You need to be under the supervision of the probation authorities. The bailiff will provide your attorney with the necessary information. If you do not contact the probation department in the next two weeks, a warrant will be issued for your arrest. Do you understand that?"

Mildred said, "I do."

"If you don't report to the probation department, you could be sent back to New York. Do you understand that?"

"Yes, your honor."

"Very well. You are free to go." With that, the judge banged his gavel, and the bailiff called the next case. Mildred hugged Albert, and then joined her friends in the gallery. Mildred and her group left the courtroom smiling.

Early that evening, back at the house, Mrs. Watanabe prepared food for a party. Mildred, Mrs. Benson, Karen, and Annie helped. Mrs. Watanabe said, "It's going to be a beautiful full moon tonight."

"That sounds lovely," Karen said.

Mrs. Benson rolled her eyes and said, "Very romantic, too, my dear."

Karen blushed. She thought Mrs. Benson intended it for her and Stanley but the Bensons might have had their own ideas for a romantic moonlit evening.

Stanley entered the kitchen and asked, "Mrs. Watanabe have you seen that folding table?"

She pointed and said, "Look in that closet over there."

Stanley opened the closet door on the other side of the room. He sighed when he saw how much was in there. As he removed objects, Mr. Kulak entered carrying a beach umbrella. He noticed Stanley and said, "Stanley, I found this umbrella in the upstairs hall closet."

Stanley stepped out of the closet. He looked at the umbrella. "Take it outside and see if it's still good."

"Okay. What are you looking for?"

"There's a folding table in here. I just have to get to it. It's somewhere in the back. If the umbrella still works, put it in the van."

Mr. Kulak headed out the back door. Karen and the women wrapped food and put it in several picnic baskets on the counter. Mildred and Mrs. Watanabe finished sliding pieces of marinated chicken onto wooden skewers and placed them in a plastic container.

As it turned out, it was a beautiful night on the beach. Medium-sized waves crashed to the shore. A warm trade wind mixed with the slightly salty air. Mildred and her friends weren't the only ones enjoying the beach that evening. Other groups of people gathered nearby and all along the sandy shore. Aromas of grilling fishes, meats, and veggies permeated the air as well.

Mr. Kulak brought his paddleboard. He was out on the water but as night began to fall, he paddled to shore. Mildred met him at the shoreline. As he came to a stop in front of her, he asked, "You want to try?"

Mildred laughed. "Me! You gotta be kidding."

"It's not that hard to learn."

"Well, I'd have to learn to swim first."

"You don't know how to swim?"

"Never learned."

"I could teach you."

"Never mind. Come on food is ready."

As they walked to where the others sat, Mr. Watanabe grilled *teriyaki* chicken skewers on a small hibachi grill while Mr. Benson played his ukulele. Everyone was in a festive mood. Some sat in chairs, some sat around the folding table eating, and some of them sat on blankets on the sand. "Arthur, sit down and have something to eat," Mr. Watanabe said.

"I will."

"You were looking pretty good out there," Mr. Watanabe continued.

"Yes, I think I've mastered this sport in a relatively short time. These are nice waves. I don't think I can handle those ten-footers. They're still a little scary for me."

"I might have to give it a try sometime," Mr. Watanabe said.

Mr. Kulak picked up his towel and dried himself then slipped on a shirt. Tony and Glo arrived and everyone greeted them. "I made a key lime pie," Glo told them as she put the pie on the table.

"Oooh, that looks delicious," Mrs. Watanabe complimented.

"I used the limes Annie gave me."

Annie, overhearing, walked over to look. "I can't wait to try it," she said, smiling.

Albert picked up his *mai-tai* and said, "Here, here!"

Everyone looked up.

"I'd like to make a toast to Mrs. Meyers."

"Oh, please," Mildred said.

Albert continued, "I wasn't finished, Mrs. Meyers."

Mildred made an innocent face and then said, "Sorry."

"I also want to toast the Sambuccis for coming all this way to help Mrs. Meyers."

Everyone turned to the Sambuccis and cheered.

Angelo said, "Hey, it was nothin'. We got a great vacation out of it. And we got to meet and spend time with all of ya."

Albert raised his glass and said, "We might not be celebrating tonight. We were lucky today that we came out on the winning side. To Mildred and the Sambuccis!"

They all clinked glasses and drank. Mr. Benson strummed *"She's a jolly good fellow"* on his ukulele and the others joined him in singing the old tune. People nearby on the beach heard them singing and joined in.

As serving dishes circulated, Glo warned, "Hey everyone! Leave room for my pie."

There was general agreement that they would. There were other desserts too. Mrs. Watanabe had made a tropical fruit and jello mold and a coconut pie.

After they had filled themselves on all the food and desserts, they praised and thanked Mrs. Watanabe for what she had done. Glo received kudos for her pie. In their intoxicated, bloated state, everyone sat around waiting for the moon to come up. They listened to Mr. Benson strum tunes on his ukulele. Tony accompanied him on the guitar.

The full moon rose and it didn't disappoint. It was large and bright as it hung over the bay and lit the beach. It almost looked like daylight it was so bright out.

A limbo stick was set up and they all had a fun time dancing under it. Somewhere down the beach, another group of people set off flying Chinese lanterns that glowed and floated up over the bay.

Mildred said, "I'm pretty tired. I need to get some sleep. It was an exhausting day."

"Well let's get going," Mr. Kulak suggested.

Everyone agreed it was time to go. They were surprised when the Bensons said they wanted to spend more time on the beach. Stanley, of course, was concerned and said, "Karen and I will stay with you."

Albert left his car for them and drove everyone home in the van.

Stanley and Karen sat in the sand on a blanket holding hands as they watched the Bensons stroll down the beach hand-in-hand. The love the Bensons showed for each other inspired Stanley and Karen. Stanley took Karen in his arms, lowered her to the blanket, and locked their lips in a passionate kiss. They made love on the beach.

When the Bensons hadn't returned. Stanley and Karen decided they better go look for them. They crept down the beach through the trees. They spotted the Bensons, lying in the surf at the water's edge, locked in an embrace, and kissing passionately.

Embarrassed, Stanley and Karen snuck away. When they were out of earshot, Stanley said in an incredulous voice, "It looked like the love scene from *Here to Eternity*."

Karen giggled.

Later, when the Bensons re-joined Stanley and Karen, their hair was wet and Mrs. Benson's makeup was gone. "Sorry we took so long," Mr. Benson apologized. "We took a swim!"

"The water was so lovely tonight," Mrs. Benson said.

On the drive home, they passed the construction site. Stanley slowed the car when they saw someone walking around with a flashlight. Stanley said, "It must be the night watchman."

CHAPTER 48

The Sambuccis went home after two weeks. Mildred enjoyed their visit and felt their absence. She was grateful to Angelo for his testimony on her behalf and she had gotten to know Helen a lot better. They shared recipes and Helen, Mildred, and Mrs. Watanabe prepared some of Helen's delicious Italian meals during her visit. She showed them how to make manicotti, pizza dough, Fettuccini Alfredo—the residents loved it.

At the condominium project, days passed with no activity. There was no longer a nightwatchman. Rumors that the project shut down spread quickly over the coconut wireless, but it was not clear that it was permanently abandoned. The residents of the Hanalei House waited to hear something conclusive.

Mildred and Mrs. Watanabe were in the kitchen making strudels to sell at the farmers' market. Rounds of dough sat on the table where a large jar of apricot preserves was open. They scooped gobs of preserves and spread them over the dough, then raisins and nuts. They heard a car coming up the drive and stop.

A few minutes later, they heard a man's voice at the back door. "Is anyone here?"

"Yes, we're here," Mildred answered.

Joe Thomas opened the door and walked in. "*Aloha,* Mrs. Meyers… and Mrs. Watanabe."

They stopped what they were doing to look at him. "Oh, hi Joe," Mildred said. "What are you doing here?"

"Well, I was in the area. I thought I'd stop and deliver some good news."

"What is it?" Mildred asked.

He walked over to the table and stared at the rounds of dough. "What's all this?"

"Strudels. We're making them to sell at the farmers' market," Mildred said.

"Oh, they must be delicious."

"So, what's the big news?" Mrs. Watanabe asked.

Mildred anticipated it had something to do with Daniels.

"Well, it seems our Mr. Daniels has filed for bankruptcy because of all the asbestos lawsuits against him. He's had to pay out a lot of money to the victims."

"What about this project?" Mildred asked.

"That's the good news. He's shutting it down."

Mildred's eyes almost popped out of their sockets with excitement. She asked, "For good?"

"It sure sounds like it," Joe answered.

"I don't know what to say," Mildred blurted.

"I'd say that's pretty terrific," Mrs. Watanabe offered.

With a big smile on her face, Mildred said, "Wait till we tell the others. They'll be happy about that."

"Yes, a lot of people around here will be excited to hear about it. It will be in tomorrow's paper."

"I hope it's true," Mildred speculated.

"Well, unless he sells the land to another developer. But I don't think that will happen. People still claim it's sacred land. I'm sure no other developer wants to touch it after what Daniels went through."

"Maybe he'll let the hippies move back," Mildred said.

"I don't think that's going to happen," Joe said.

Mrs. Watanabe started rolling up the strudels and Mildred placed them on a baking pan.

Joe continued, "There's some talk about turning it into a park."

"That sounds like a good idea," Mildred said.

"That's if Daniels will sell it."

Mildred thought there must be another way.

"You think I can buy one of your strudels?"

"We'll give you one," Mildred said. "You've done so much to help. That's the least we can do."

"Oh, thanks. I'm just doing my job."

"Well you've been an ally," Mildred said. "I always tried to get the press involved in my protests. There's nothing like good publicity."

Mrs. Watanabe looked at Joe and said, "These are going to bake about an hour. Can you wait that long?"

"I have some other people to see. Is it alright if I come back in an hour?"

"Certainly," Mrs. Watanabe said.

That night at dinner, everyone was jubilant about the news. It lifted Mildred's spirits. Mrs. Watanabe made chicken tetrazzini in a creamy mushroom sauce over egg noodles along with garlic bread and salad. For dessert, they saved two strudels.

By dessert time, there were moans and groans all around the table. Karen said, "Mrs. Meyers and Mrs.

Watanabe the food you've been making is going right to my waistline."

Mrs. Benson jumped on that. "You sure it's not something else my dear?" she said while staring at Stanley.

He blushed and so did Karen. "Well, I hope not. I still have a performance to do in December. I need to stay in shape."

"Oh, you should see what she does at that barre. My aching back," Miss Louise said and touched her hand to her brow, "if I ever did that…"

"Are you going along, Stanley?" Mildred questioned.

"I want him to," Karen said. "We didn't get to have our honeymoon."

"Well, there, there… You both must go, then," Mr. Kulak said.

"Hey, we have a lot of bookings for that month, right through to New Year," Albert said. "I told him I can handle it."

"It shouldn't even be a consideration, Stanley." Mr. Benson said.

Stanley who had been sitting quietly listening spoke, "We've never had that many guests since you started." Turning towards his brother, "It's going to be a lot of work."

"Stop being such a martyr, Stanley," Mildred chided.

Harry, who had been eyeing the strudel in the middle of the table, finally said, "Can someone please pass a piece of that delicious looking strudel?"

They all laughed and started passing the dessert.

Albert looked at his brother then turned toward Tony and Glo, and said, "Tony and Glo can help."

Stanley started shaking his head. Tony and Glo looked uncomfortable.

"What? What's the matter?" Albert asked.

With doleful eyes, Tony turned to Albert and said, "I told Stanley today… that we're leaving, man."

There was a communal buzz around the table, followed by sad faces.

Tony said, "We're moving to Chicago."

"My mom is sick," Glo explained. "She had a stroke and needs someone to be with her twenty-four, seven."

Everyone expressed their sympathy.

"Could you stay around till the end of the year?" Albert asked.

"That's a long time," Glo responded.

"Listen everyone!" Mr. Kulak got their attention. "We are grateful to these young people for the spirit they've brought to our lives. And Tony is truly an American hero."

Tony looked surprised and a little bit of embarrassment crept in. "Oh, yeah, I love all of you like family," he said.

"Me too," Glo said with tears forming in her eyes.

"Maybe, we'll return someday. I love this island, man. I don't know how I will do in a big city like Chicago."

Various responses and reactions went around the table. Most were feeling the same thing—that they were a family.

Mr. Kulak said, "Well I think we should throw a big party to celebrate the end of the condo project and give these two lovely children a fond send-off."

"That's an excellent idea, Arthur," Miss Louise said.

Mildred chimed in, "There are lots of people around here who will want to join the celebration.

As Joe Thomas had promised, the paper the next day contained a story about Daniel's asbestos lawsuits and the demise of the Hanalei condominium project.

At the breakfast table, Mildred read from the paper and said, "It says, he shut down projects in New York, Florida, Honolulu, and here."

"Well he must be hurting to take such drastic action," Mr. Kulak added.

"I'm going to try to get him to donate the land for a park," Mildred stated.

Albert said, "I'm pretty sure he's still on the island. He has that office in Lihue."

"I'll call him and see if I can get a meeting," Mildred said.

"You think he's going to do that?" Stanley asked.

"Who knows? But I'm sure going to try," Mildred answered.

CHAPTER 49

The following Saturday, a big celebration took place at the farm. Cars lined the driveway and spilled down the road. Mildred and her fellow residents were thrilled about the enthusiastic turnout. People from the community were in a celebratory mood. They brought food and drinks, a small Hawaiian band provided music, and a pig roasted in the ground. Mrs. Watanabe baked a big chocolate layer cake.

A few guests were staying in the cottages. They seemed thrilled to meet locals and join the celebration. The party started in the late afternoon of a lovely fall day with high clouds hanging over the island. People continued to arrive all afternoon and into the evening.

Mr. Benson played his ukulele with the band. Mildred, her fellow residents, and locals danced. Lucy Kapana walked over to Mildred and said with a big smile, "*Aloha!*"

"*Aloha!*" Mildred responded.

"See Mildred, I told you it was over." She hugged Mildred.

"I know. But I have to admit, I'm surprised."

Lucy looked up at the sky; the sun was shining and darting in and out of the high clouds. She said, "I think *Pele* lined up the stars in our favor."

"I don't know who it was, but I'm sure glad they lined up. Did you get some food?"

"Not yet, but I see them opening the *imu*. I bettah get in line for some."

"Thanks for coming," Mildred told her.

"You're the one we should be thanking," Lucy suggested. "You went to jail for this."

"I'm just glad it's all over."

Mr. Kulak joined Mildred and Lucy and said, "Mildred, let's get some of that delicious pork."

There was a heated volleyball match in progress. Tony, Glo, Annie, Neil, Jason, and Albert played on one side. Karen, Stanley and several locals, two guys and two girls, played on the other. The game terminated when the pig was unwrapped and everyone got in line for it.

Besides the pig, there was a bounty of food. The table under the lanai had all kinds of salads, fruit dishes, *poi*, barbeque chicken, fish, and desserts, including Mrs. Watanabe's cake.

While everyone stuffed themselves, the afternoon wore into evening. Mildred stood on a bench and requested the attention of the crowd. Then she said, "This is such an exciting day. I want to thank all of you who made this celebration possible. The odds were against us and we prevailed. The anthropologist, Margaret Mead once said, 'Never doubt that a small group of thoughtful, committed, citizens can change the world. Indeed, it is the only thing that ever has.' That's us. We're that small group of dedicated people that accomplished a great victory. We've been able to change the tide of development on the island. Let's not fool ourselves. Let's not be complacent. Calvin Daniels may be out of the picture but this island remains ripe for development. We must remain vigilant because there will be other developers coming to line their pockets. We will be ready for them. Thank you all for putting up a good fight."

The crowd cheered enthusiastically. Mr. Kulak joined Mildred. He held a *mai-tai* in his hand, turned to the crowd and said, "If you will indulge me for a few moments. We are also here today, to say goodbye to our good friends, Tony Santos and Glo Goldberg. They are leaving us for a family emergency. We enjoyed having them here on the farm. They contributed so much to this place. They will be missed. He raised his glass in the air. To Tony and Glo! We hope you return someday soon."

Everyone in the crowd raised glasses in unison.

Several hours later, the party wore down with only a few remaining hangers-on. A more intimate group moved out to the back of the property to Annie and Neil's place. A bonfire burned and everyone sat around the fire. The clouds from earlier were gone and the night sky was filled with shiny stars.

Miss Louise, Harry, Stanley, Karen, Annie, Neil, Tony, Glo, Albert, Mr. Kulak, and Mildred sat around the fire on blankets, chairs, and logs. There seemed to be an endless marijuana joint being passed around. Everyone indulged except Mildred. She kept passing the joint until finally, she said, "I'm going to try this stuff. You all look so happy. How can it be bad for you?"

"That's it, Mrs. Meyers!" Tony said enthusiastically.

The others encouraged her. Mildred put the joint to her lips and took her first drag. She inhaled a little too much and started to cough, then blew out a cloud of smoke.

"Not so much," Mr. Kulak said.

"Yes, take it easy Mrs. Meyers," Stanley said, a little nervously.

"I don't feel anything," Mildred replied. "Should I try some more?"

The others laughed. Once again, Mildred put the joint to her lips and inhaled.

"Now, hold it in," Neil said.

Mildred followed his direction, then exhaled.

Karen asked, "How was that Mrs. Meyers?"

"Well, I feel the same."

Annie wanted to know, "You've never done this before?"

Mildred shook her head but started to feel the effects of the drug.

Stanley turned to Tony and Glo and said, "You know Glo, if you want, maybe, you can bring your mom back here to live."

"I don't know if she's even able to travel," Glo said. "But thanks for the offer."

"Yeah man, we'd love to come back," Tony said. "We're leaving you the sewing machine and my truck if that's alright?"

"Oh, sure," Stanley answered.

"Well you always have a place here," Albert said.

"What are you going to do in Chicago, Tony?" Mr. Kulak asked.

"I'll try to get some work. I hate big cities. I've never been to Chicago."

Karen said, "I've performed there many times. I think it's a nice city."

"I've never been there either," Mildred said. "I hear it's colder than New York in the winter. I can't take cold winters anymore. That last winter I was there... I couldn't take the cold. You should try to get an inside job. You got plenty of warm clothes?"

"Well, no I've been living here since I got out of the marines."

Mildred continued, "Get yourself a warm hat and a coat. You'll need gloves, too. If you were going to New York, I could tell you some good places downtown to get things at good prices. Oh, and a good wool scarf. You got one of those?"

"No, I don't. I'll have to get one.

Everyone noticed the change in Mildred's behavior, especially since she couldn't stop talking. Mildred asked, "Is there any of that delicious chocolate cake around?"

CHAPTER 50

Albert drove Mildred to Lihue to meet with her probation officer. It was a rainy day and at times, it came down so hard the car's wipers were ineffective. Because of the weather, they arrived fifteen minutes late.

Albert wore a black raincoat and a rain fedora. Mildred had on a clear plastic raincoat and a clear plastic kerchief over her head and tied under her chin.

The office was across from the Lihue Courthouse. As they entered the office, Mr. Yamamoto, the probation officer, a short man in his forties, with black hair whose sides were turning gray, greeted them. He had dark sunken eyes and a mustache. His face was kindly looking and he wore a pleasant smile. "I'm sorry you had to come down here in this terrible weather."

He shook Albert's hand, then Mildred's. "It's very nice to meet you, Mrs. Meyers. I've been looking through your file. You have quite an interesting story."

Mildred wasn't sure how to take that. "Have a seat," the man directed.

Albert and Mildred removed their wet clothes and hung them on the clothes tree, then sat in the two chairs in front of Mr. Yamamoto's desk.

"I must congratulate you, Mrs. Meyers, on closing down that condo development. Developers are running rampant all over these islands. I'm glad you were able to stop one of them."

His reaction surprised Mildred. "Thank you. But it wasn't just me. It was a community effort."

"Well, I have some good news for you."

He removed an envelope from the file folder sitting on top of his desk. Albert and Mildred wondered what he was getting at. "Judge Paumakua sent this over yesterday." He handed it to Mildred. "It's from New York. They're not going to extradite you." He smiled and continued, "I didn't think they would do that."

Mildred gasped with delight. Albert peered over to see it.

"That's good news," Mildred said.

"I thought you would be happy to see it," Mr. Yamamota told her. "Now about your probation… It will last one year. During that time, you will report here on or about the first of every month. If you can't get here, a phone call will suffice. You don't have to come in this kind of weather. No associating with criminal types, and no travel outside the State of Hawaii without my permission. You must obey all laws, including minor ones. Do you drink alcohol in excess?"

"No."

"I'm sure you don't use illegal drugs."

Mildred felt a little uneasy because of the marijuana she recently smoked.

"I don't think I will have to drug and alcohol test you. Do you have any questions?"

Mildred thought for a moment and said, "No, I don't"

Albert added, "I'm sure Mrs. Meyers won't have any problem complying with the conditions you've specified.

"Very well, I think we are through here. If you move or change phone numbers, make sure you let me know."

Mildred and Albert stood up and they each shook Mr. Yamamota's hand. Albert said, "Thank you!"

Mildred thanked him too. They put their wet clothes back on.

Mr. Yamamoto warned, "Be careful driving home. Watch out for flash floods."

Mildred and Albert left the office feeling a whole lot better.

CHAPTER 51

Mildred was determined to get a meeting with Calvin Daniels about donating the condominium land for a park. She had reservations about offering to name the park in his honor but was prepared to do so if necessary. It was something she would keep in her back pocket and only use it in a last-ditch effort.

For the past few days, she had called his office several times and left messages to get back to her. She had just put down the telephone on Stanley's desk. Mildred wanted to complain to somebody, but she sat by herself until Albert walked in and noticed her. "What's the matter? You look frustrated."

"I keep trying to get in touch with Daniels."

"No luck?"

"He's either ignoring my calls or he doesn't want to talk to me."

"Well, maybe this will cheer you up." He handed her a folded paper.

Mildred looked at it curiously, then opened it and read. She looked up. "It's my divorce."

"Yes, it is."

"That means it's final?"

"You're no longer married to Victor Meyers."

"Hallelujah! I guess he got one of these too?"

"I'm sure he did."

"Thanks for your help."

"I was happy to do it."

Albert sat in a chair in front of the desk.

"I want to pay you," Mildred said.

"It won't be necessary."

"But you did a lot of work to make it happen."

"It wasn't that much. Believe me.... Maybe, I can help you get that meeting with Daniels."

"You think you can?"

"Dial the number then give me the phone."

Mildred did as he suggested. She handed him the phone. Albert took it and someone answered. He said, "Hello my name is Albert Cutler. I'm an attorney on the north shore. I'd like to set up a meeting with Mr. Daniels to discuss purchasing the land he has in Hanalei."

There was a pause at the other end and the woman said, "Hold on a minute. I'll talk to Mr. Daniels."

Albert winked at Mildred.

When the woman came back on the phone, she told him that Calvin Daniels would meet with him. Albert thanked her and hung up the phone.

"He'll meet with us tomorrow morning at eleven."

"Yeah, but he thinks he's just meeting with you. What's he going to say when he sees me? He hates me."

Albert said, "But he thinks I'm going to purchase the land. The almighty dollar will motivate him. You can make your proposal for a park."

"I hope you're right."

The next morning, Mildred and Albert drove to Daniels' office. When they entered the modest office, they noticed stacked shipping boxes along the walls. A bored-looking secretary in her forties, chewing gum, sat behind a desk outside of Daniels' office. Albert said, "I'm Albert Cutler. We're here to see Mr. Daniels."

The woman looked curiously at Mildred. Mildred thought that maybe she recognized her from the TV news. The secretary pressed the intercom.

"Mr. Daniels, I have Mr. Cutler and his party here."

Daniels hesitated at first, then said, "Send them in!"

"Right away." She released the intercom button and said, "You can go in now."

As soon as Mildred and Albert entered Daniels' office, they noticed more shipping boxes. Daniels took one look at Mildred, stood up, and asked, "What is this some kind of trick? What's she doing here?"

Albert tried to diffuse the situation by extending his hand. He said, "How do you do Mr. Daniels? I'm Albert Cutler."

Daniels said, "Yes, I remember meeting you a few months back. You own that property next to mine. Don't you?"

"Yes."

"Nice to see you again, Mr. Daniels," Mildred said. She decided not to shake his hand, figuring he wouldn't want to shake anyway.

"Mr. Daniels, may we sit?" Albert asked.

Daniels looked hesitant and then indicated for them to sit. He sat back down.

"We're here to make you an offer," Albert said.

"What kind of an offer?"

Mildred jumped in and said, "We're here to ask you to donate that land you have in Hanalei for a park."

"A what?"

"A community park," Mildred said.

Daniels sat up straight in his chair. He laughed. "You want me to donate it for a park? Do you know how much that land is worth? I've already sunk large sums of money here. What do I have to show for it? Nothing! And you want me to just give it away."

"Look the way I see it," Albert said. "You have already lost a considerable amount of money on the project. You'll be paying tax on undeveloped land. Why don't you cut your losses, donate the land, and take a big tax deduction?"

Mildred smiled across the desk. She hadn't even thought about the benefit of a tax deduction.

"It's absolutely out of the question."

"What are you going to do with it?" Mildred asked.

"That's none of your business."

Mildred said, "We're just asking you to please consider it."

Daniels looked angry and said, "I may still develop it in a few years."

"If you ask me, I don't think you want to continue to try to develop the land," Albert said. "The community is still against it. It may very well be sacred land. You will be fighting the same uphill battle."

"Look, we're just asking you to consider it," Mildred told him.

Daniels sat silently staring a Mildred, then said, "I'm not promising anything, but I'll give it some consideration."

"That's fair enough," Albert said.

"Yes, it's a good start," Mildred agreed.

"Now if you'll excuse me, I'm very busy."

"Oh, sure. Thanks for taking the time to see us," Albert said.

Mildred and Albert stood. Mildred smiled and nodded at Daniels. "Thanks," she said.

"Here's my business card." Albert handed it to Daniels. "Just call me whenever."

Daniels took the card. They left his office with a touch of optimism. When they got in the car, Albert said, "Well that went pretty well."

"Yes, much better than I expected. What do you think he's going to do?"

"He's a businessman. He already has financial problems. He doesn't have too many options left for the property. I think we have a pretty good chance."

"I hope so. That would be a big victory for our side."

CHAPTER 52

That night over dinner, Albert and Mildred told everyone about their meeting with Calvin Daniels. The residents were surprised.

"Bravo!" Mr. Kulak said.

Stanley turned towards Mildred and said, "So how are you feeling about it, Mrs. Meyers?"

"I hope he does it."

"That's wonderful news, Mildred," Mr. Benson said. "And you've gotten your divorce."

"Yes, another pleasant surprise. Something else I have to be thankful to Albert for." Mildred related to them how Albert got the meeting with Daniels.

"We have some news of our own," Mr. Benson said. Turning to his wife, "Don't we dear?"

Mrs. Benson nodded.

"My goodness, what is it?" Miss Louise asked.

Mr. Benson continued, "After a couple of months back in the business, we've decided, it is not for us, anymore."

"What do you mean? You were so excited about getting back into it," Mildred said.

"I know... I know," Mrs. Benson exclaimed.

"We just don't have the passion for it that we thought we would," Mr. Benson said. "There's so much paperwork involved now. We've been there. Done that. You know what I mean?"

Miss Louise perked up. "That's what happened to me. Once I got a taste again for what I loved to do—I found I didn't have as much passion for it as I used to have. I was tired, too."

"I guess we don't know when we've had enough," Harry said. "As a writer when I got older, I couldn't remember things. How to spell certain words... I would forget my characters' names. I became very unproductive."

"That's the problem. We don't always know when to stop working," Mr. Kulak added.

"Same with me," Karen offered. "Here I was all set to retire from dancing and now, I'm doing another performance halfway across the globe."

Mrs. Benson said, "But you're still a lot younger than us."

"How is your show coming along?" Mildred asked.

Miss Louise answered with an enormous smile, "The children are just wonderful."

"Yes. We can't wait for you all to see it," Karen told them.

Mr. Benson said, "We haven't given up completely on working. We've decided to start a new business."

"What kind of business?" Stanley asked curiously.

"Well, we learned so much about the island over the last few months. We've been to so many interesting, beautiful and out of the way places that we are going to start a tour business," Mr. Benson said.

"Won't that be a lot of work?" Mr. Kulak asked.

"Not as much as doing real estate," Mrs. Benson said, "and not as much paperwork. And more fun."

The conversation continued around the table about when was the right time to retire.

CHAPTER 53

Several days later, Albert walked out to the lanai where Mildred and Annie where sitting, making *leis* for a wedding. The women were placing orchids on a long needle then pushing them onto a string. There was a completed pile on the table. Albert approached and said, "Wow, you have a lot done."

Mildred looked up at him. She said, "Oh good, we were just talking about you."

"Uh, oh."

"We're thinking this might be a fun activity for your guests. We can teach them how to make them," Mildred suggested.

"I like the idea. I'll see if I can drum up some interest."

"They could keep some for themselves and the rest we could sell," Annie said.

"I came to tell you that I got a call from Daniels. He's trying to get the county to appraise the land at a higher rate so he can take a bigger tax deduction."

Mildred shook her head. "That guy's something else."

"He's a businessman. He's trying to find a way out of this without losing his shirt."

"The main thing is getting the land for the park," Mildred said.

"Yes. And it sounds like he's thinking about it."

Later that afternoon, Mildred, Kulak and Mr. Watanabe were at their stand at the farmers' market. It was another warm, beautiful day. It made Mildred thankful that she wasn't back in New York. That day, there was a lot of activity because it was getting closer to Thanksgiving. Potatoes, squash, and string beans were the big sellers.

Mildred was finishing up with a customer when Mr. Kulak poked her. Mildred turned to him. He nodded toward the people standing in front of the table. Mildred noticed Vic Meyers among them. Vic walked up to Mildred. He gave a perfunctory nod to Kulak.

Victor smiled at Mildred. "I guess we're divorced now."

"Yes, we are," Mildred answered.

As he helped other people, Kulak kept an eye on Vic.

For the first time, Mildred felt sorry for him. He looked like an old, lonely, little man. Later she would question herself as to why she said, "Do you have plans for Thanksgiving?"

"No, I usually just stay home and have a turkey TV dinner."

"Would you like to come to our house for dinner?"

Kulak couldn't believe his ears. His head swung from Mildred to Vic. He wanted to say something but was too flabbergasted and couldn't find the words.

"You don't want me to come," Vic said.

"Listen, I wouldn't invite you if I didn't mean it."

"Thank you, yeah. Thanks. What can I bring?"

"Oh, I don't know. We'll have enough food."

"Are you making any of your strudels?"

Mildred smiled. "Yes."

"Well, I'll bring something."

"That's good."

Kulak said in a sneer, "Not a TV dinner."

"What?" Vic asked.

"I was just joking," Kulak said.

"Come around four," Mildred suggested. She helped Vic with his purchase. He paid and left.

Kulak asked, "What'd you do that for?"

"I don't know... He looked so lonely. Nobody should spend Thanksgiving alone, even an ex-husband."

Kulak questioned her bad judgment but hugged her anyway. "You have a good heart, Mildred."

CHAPTER 54

As usual, Thanksgiving Day arrived before anyone was ready for it. That day turned out to be another beautiful one on the island with sunny skies, light trade winds and temperatures close to eighty. Because of the time difference, Mildred got up early to watch the New York City Thanksgiving Day parade on TV. The New York weather teetered around freezing. Mildred was glad to be on Kauai.

Mildred and Mrs. Watanabe planned and prepared the entire Thanksgiving dinner with plenty of help from the residents. They started several days in advance. Annie, Neil, and Mr. Watanabe harvested from the farm most of the dinner vegetables. They provided squash, corn, potatoes, yams, spinach, string beans, and turnips.

Mildred made her strudel, which was already becoming a popular dessert among locals. She and Mrs. Watanabe could hardly keep up with the demand. At all the farmers' markets, the strudel sold out every time.

Mrs. Benson made pumpkin, apple, and pecan pies for the dinner. Miss Louise oversaw the table settings. The men had their duties, too. Stanley and Albert cleaned the grounds and the porch. Mr. Kulak and Mr. Benson were in charge of the wine and drinks. Harry because of his bad eyesight volunteered to help Miss Louise. He polished the silverware, folded the white linen napkins, helped set the table, and decorate the dining room. They created a beautiful centerpiece with flowers, ferns and baby's breath from the farm and placed little pumpkins and gourds on the table and around the room. Harry inscribed place setting cards and put them on the table where Miss Louise directed him.

Guests started arriving around four o'clock. Mr. Kulak had a bar set up in the living room where he prepared to serve drinks. An overflow table in the living room butted up against the end of the dining room table.

Vic Meyers arrived with a large flower bouquet and a bottle of wine. "*Aloha* and Happy Thanksgiving!" Kulak politely returned the greeting but still felt put off by Vic's presence. Vic hugged Mildred awkwardly. She felt a little uncomfortable about the hug. Mr. Kulak watched with disdain. Mildred introduced Vic to some of her fellow residents, the ones who hadn't met him yet.

Stanley said, "Nice of you to join us, Mr. Meyers."

"Yeah, thanks. I would have just been home with a TV dinner if Mildred hadn't invited me."

"Well I'm glad you could make it," Karen said.

"Would you like something to drink?" Kulak asked, a little impatiently.

"I don't drink," Vic said.

"How about some apple cider?" Kulak asked, looking rather annoyed.

Mildred took notice. She didn't like how Kulak treated Vic but she just shrugged it off.

Lucy Kapana arrived and brought a big bowl of *poi* and a pineapple upside-down cake that she made.

Before it was time to sit down to dinner, everyone sipped cocktails, wine, beer, apple cider, and soft drinks while they munched on appetizers. There was a lot of chatter as all were in a celebratory mood.

By five o'clock, Miss Louise clapped her hands to get everyone's attention. "If you all would take a seat, look for your place card. That's where you will be sitting."

There was a little confusion at first until they all found their assigned places and then a few people exchanged seats. The cottage guests sat at the overflow table. There was an elderly couple in their sixties from Ohio; a family from Los Angeles with two children, a boy and a girl around eleven or twelve; an elderly professor and his wife from Cal State Berkeley, who Albert knew; and two middle-aged women from Philadelphia.

Karen, Stanley, and Albert helped with the food. Stanley carried in a large turkey, Albert a ham, and Karen a big serving dish with dressing. People commented on how delicious it smelled and looked. Then the side dishes with potatoes, yams, and other vegetables came out.

Lucy Kapana, sitting next to Vic Meyers, asked, "Oh, you cook the turkey in the *imu*?"

"We talked about it," Mr. Watanabe answered. "But then we decided to cook it in the oven."

"It looks good," Lucy commented.

When everything was on the table, Stanley went back into the kitchen and said, "Okay, you ladies, out of the kitchen now." He escorted them to the dining room. Mildred carried a basket of biscuits and placed them on the table. Mrs. Watanabe had a string bean casserole that she put on the table before sitting next to her husband.

Mildred sat between Mr. Kulak and her ex-husband, Vic. She didn't like how she felt and wondered why she invited him. She just knew that she didn't like anyone to be alone on Thanksgiving, even Victor. When she touched Mr. Kulak's arm, he abruptly moved it away.

Mildred looked curiously at him but he wouldn't make eye contact. As she looked over at Vic, he and Lucy were absorbed in conversation. Mildred wondered what Lucy and Vic could find to talk about.

Mr. Kulak asked, "Does everyone have something to drink? There's wine, red and white if anyone wants some."

Albert opened bottles of wine. The bottles along with a carafe of homemade apple cider passed around the table and people filled their glasses. Albert said, "Thank you all for being here today. This is our first Thanksgiving on Kauai. So, it's a special day."

Joe Thomas and his girlfriend, Mary, a pretty woman in her early thirties with long black hair and blue eyes sat across from Mildred.

Joe said, "Have you heard? Calvin Daniels is trying to get the county to reassess his property at a higher value. He's looking for a bigger tax deduction for his donation."

"Yes, we heard that. So, what's going on?" Mildred asked.

"From what I hear, the county's not going along with it," Joe answered. "They think he paid too much for the land, to begin with."

Lucy Kapana looked at Joe and said, "I wish he just leave us alone."

"He'll try anything," Mildred said. "Let's not talk about him anymore. We all have a lot to be thankful for today. Would someone like to say grace?"

Stanley said, "I will!"

Everyone got quiet, and Stanley became solemn and said, "Today, we are grateful for the food on our table, our good friends and neighbors, and for all the other blessings we have received throughout the year. Amen!"

They all joined in with "Amen!"

Mildred winked at Stanley and said, "Very nice Stanley. Thank you!"

"Now let's eat," Stanley directed.

Mildred asked, "Clark, would you like to carve the turkey and Albert can you slice the ham?"

Mr. Watanabe picked up a carving fork and knife and started to cut away. Albert did the same with the ham.

Vic turned to Mildred and said, "Thanks for inviting me, Mildred, yeah."

"You're welcome."

"I haven't had a home-cooked Thanksgiving dinner since I moved here," Vic said.

Kulak made a disapproving face.

Mildred felt good that she had invited Vic. "Well I hope you enjoy it," Mildred said.

Dishes went around the table. Everyone piled their plates. As people started to eat, the table grew quieter. There was the occasional, "Hmm," "Delicious," "This turkey is so tender."

Mr. Benson stopped eating, picked up his wine glass, and said, "I'd like to make a toast to Mildred and Sue who prepared this lovely meal and to everyone else who helped and brought a dish."

They all clinked glasses and toasted.

It didn't take long before everyone sat back, filled with food. Mildred did too and said, "Would any of you like to share what you are thankful for today?"

There were a few grumbles around the table. Mildred looked at Jason, sitting between his father and Annie. "I know you have something to be thankful about, Jason. You want to share it with all of us?"

Jason felt put on the spot but, surprisingly, he began, "Ah, um, I'm grateful that I was able to pitch on my baseball team and we won the championship."

They applauded. Jason blushed and then said, "And I'm also…" He hesitated, then asked, "Can I say another thing?"

There were a few chuckles.

"Of course," Mildred told him.

"Well, I'm learning how to act. Thanks to Miss Louise."

Miss Louise smiled proudly at him. He continued, "And come see our play and dance performance Saturday night at our theatre!"

Mr. Kulak laughed and said, "You're training him right, Louise."

They clapped, Jason smiled and looked relieved.

Miss Louise said, "Well let me say what I'm thankful about. It's being here with all of you and living in this beautiful place. Thank you, Stanley and Albert, for getting us here."

Mr. Benson looked around the table and asked, "May I?"

"Of course," Mildred said.

"I second Louise's sentiments. I am especially grateful to my wife Pauline who puts up with me. I'm glad we have relatively good health. That's it."

Mrs. Benson chimed in, "He doesn't know what a job it is to put up with him."

Laughter broke out.

"I would like to say how lovely it is to be here with all of you. I'm so grateful for your love and friendship," Mrs. Benson said.

"What about you Karen?" Mildred asked.

"For me, the best thing that ever happened is marrying this wonderful man sitting next to me."

Stanley blushed.

"I'm also very happy to share this place with all of you."

Karen poked Stanley, trying to encourage him to speak. He got the hint and said, "Wow! So many terrific things have happened this year. But I have to say the best thing to happen to me was," he turned to look at his wife, "marrying this beautiful lady. I feel so lucky."

There were various comments. Mr. Kulak said, "Bravo! You're a beautiful couple."

Albert smiled and said, "I'm so glad to be here with all of you. I'm thankful for the success of my new business," looking at his cottage guests, "and for having such wonderful guests."

Joe Thomas looked around the room and said, "May I say something?"

Mildred encouraged him. "Yes, of course."

"I want to say how thankful I am for meeting all of you. Mrs. Meyers taught me a lot about what it means to fight for something you strongly believe in. And I want to thank Mary for being the love of my life."

Mary jumped in and said, "And I'm thankful for Joe and his love." She smiled and kissed Joe's cheek.

Annie looked around the table and said, "I have something… I'm grateful for my wonderful husband, Neil," she turned to Neil and touched the back of his hand. "I'm also glad to have a say in Jason's life. It's so great to live here on this farm with all of you."

"I guess it's my turn," Neil said. "I'm so proud of the young man Jason is growing into. I'm grateful to Annie for all her love and for helping Jason and me to get through life every day. Oh yeah, and we had such wonderful success with the farm this year. I'm very proud of that. Thank you to all who helped."

Mr. Watanabe looked around the table and then said, "I'll say something. I'm thankful this Thanksgiving for being here on Kauai. Thankful for my wife," he smiled at Mrs. Watanabe, "and my wonderful children. I wish they could be here with us too. I'm so happy to spend every day with all of you."

Harry looked up and said, "As for me, I'm just happy to be anywhere at this age."

Everyone laughed.

Mrs. Watanabe said, "I'm very happy to have a new friend, Mildred. I'm happy to be back in the homeland that I remembered as a little girl. Like my husband, I'm happy to have him. I miss the kids, too. But I'm sure they will be visiting soon."

Lucy Kapana said, "I'm thankful that condo project goes away."

Some at the table applauded.

"I'm glad I'm healthy too." She pounded her chest with her two little fists ala Tarzan.

Laughter erupted again.

"What about you, Arthur?" Miss Louise asked.

"Well, you all know me. I'm happy to be naked whenever I can. This place lends itself well to that pleasure." Turning to Mildred, he said, "I'm enjoying the relationship I share with Mildred. It's been a long time since I've had a relationship. Oh, and I've mastered a new sport, paddleboarding and haven't killed myself doing it, yet."

Victor and Kulak exchanged unpleasant gazes. Vic seemed to want to say something. "I'm a newcomer here, yeah." He turned to Mildred and said, "The biggest and best thing to happen to me this year was to reconnect with Mildred who I haven't seen in over thirty years."

Mildred tried not to look surprised.

He continued, "I don't know all of you very well, but I hope I can get to know you better. I've had health problems in the past, but," he knocked on the table and continued, "fortunately, I've been a-okay this year. Yeah, so I'm thankful for all of that."

Kulak listened, then smirked.

Mildred said, "For me, this year has been another big transition. Most of you know, I lost my only daughter last year. I miss her so much."

Victor seemed to share Mildred's emotions.

Mildred continued, "I used to say it should have been me but Stanley warned me about saying that. I feel truly at home here with all of you. I have to thank Stanley and my fellow residents for all their love and support." She turned to look at Victor and continued, "I had a big surprise this year, too. I thought the man sitting next to me was dead. I'm glad I finally found out he isn't."

Kulak seemed annoyed that Mildred said that. Victor dabbed at his eyes with his napkin and bowed his head.

Mildred didn't notice Vic's reaction. She looked over at the cottage guests and asked, "Would any of you like to say something?"

"I would, please," one of the Philadelphia women said. She was heavy-set with short gray hair. "I think you all have something wonderful going on. I want to know how we sign up to live here."

Laughter erupted around the table.

The woman next to her, also gray-haired had a round face with a sweet smile. She said, "I second that. I want to live here with you. You have such a warm and pleasant home."

The husband of the elderly couple from Ohio had a thin face with sharp features. "I survived a heart attack this year. I'm thankful to still be around and feeling great. I'm grateful to my wife for taking good care of me."

His wife, an attractive woman with salt and pepper shoulder-length hair said, "I'm glad he's still with me." She stretched out her arm and put it around his shoulders.

The family man from Los Angeles was handsome with the build of a football player. "This is our first trip to Kauai. We're so glad we did it. We love being here with all of you. Thank you for this wonderful dinner." He looked at his wife and asked, "You want to say something?"

She was thin, pretty with red hair, and looked very athletic. "I would add to what Doug said. This has been a fabulous trip for our children. This is one of the best vacations I can remember." She nudged the boy. He was about ten-years-old and had a swatch of red hair. The young man was shy and didn't want to say anything.

Their daughter, however, was willing to express herself. She was cute with freckles. "I'm not leaving."

Everyone laughed.

The girl continued, "I want to stay here with all of you. You look like you're having so much fun. I'm thankful for being on my soccer team."

There were a few chuckles.

The Berkeley professor said, "It's been a pleasure to share this lovely place with all of you. Albert was one of my best students. You always remember the good ones. This is my last year of teaching. Maybe, we'll move here too." He smiled.

Stanley looked a little worried because they already had a house full of seniors.

The professor's wife a petite woman with black-framed glasses and white hair said, "We're both thankful for this vacation. I'd like to move in with you, too. And, Albert, our cottage is so cozy. Thank you for having us."

Little conversations started up among the guests. Mildred said, "And now, I think we should have dessert and coffee."

They cleared dishes and leftovers of which there weren't many. Several people helped carry in the desserts and coffee. There were oohs and aahs at the sight of the delicious looking desserts.

Later that night, Mildred climbed the stairs slowly. The cooking and all the excitement of the day took a toll on her. She looked forward to getting into bed with Mr. Kulak and having a good night's sleep.

As she reached the second floor and turned towards her room, she met Kulak carrying some of his belongings. He looked uncomfortable. They stopped and Mildred asked, "Arthur, what are you doing?"

He looked hesitant and then said, "I'm moving back into my old room, now that Tony and Glo are gone."

"Why in the world do you want to do something like that?"

Kulak didn't want to have this conversation. Finally, he said, "I think it's best for both of us."

Mildred shook her head, not comprehending any of it. "What brought this on?"

"Mildred, I think we went into this relationship a little too quickly."

Mildred's head started spinning. Her exhaustion weighed heavily. She couldn't believe this was happening. "I don't know what brought this on. I'm happy. You seemed happy." Something else suddenly occurred to her. "Does Victor being here today have something to do with it?"

Kulak's face flushed.

Mildred said, "It is Victor. You're jealous."

"I am not."

"I'm too tired to discuss this tonight."

"Yes, it was his presence that got me thinking about it. I don't like how I felt. I'm probably not ready to carry on a relationship. Maybe, it's for the best that we end it now."

Mildred didn't know what else to say. Finally, she said, "Can we talk about this tomorrow?" She just wanted to throw herself on her bed.

Kulak said, "Sure," and stepped around her. "Goodnight! I'll get the rest of my stuff in the morning."

Mildred stood motionless for a moment. She watched him walk away before going into her room. Mildred flopped down on the bed, felt like she wanted to cry but tears wouldn't come. As tired as she was, sleep wouldn't come easily either. She was so pleased with how the day had gone, but Kulak's reaction was crushing.

The next morning, Kulak knocked on Mildred's door. "Who is it?"

"It's me," Mr. Kulak answered.

"Come in."

Kulak opened the door and walked in. It surprised him to see Mildred still in bed. "Good morning!"

"Good morning."

"I woke you?"

"Yeah, I was still sleeping." Mildred looked at the clock on her night table. It read eight-thirty. She was usually up way before that. It surprised her.

"Mildred, I'm sorry about last night. I don't know what came over me. Can you forgive me?"

"Maybe I was wrong to invite Victor."

"No, it was my own foolishness." Kulak hung his head.

"Come over here." She patted the bed next to her. Kulak squeezed in. "I had a restless night."

Mr. Kulak said, "I didn't sleep a wink, either. All I did was toss and turn."

"Listen I forgive you. I won't invite him anymore."

"No, no… I was wrong. I'm sure he's a lonely old guy. He seemed to enjoy himself. And he and Lucy seemed to strike up a relationship. I'll try to be nicer to him next time."

Mildred turned her face to him and they kissed.

"You think I can move back in?"

"You sure you want to?

"Yes, of course."

"Well get your stuff and come back."

He smiled at her and kissed her again. "Thanks."

Mildred smiled mischievously. "You still eating that noni fruit?"

CHAPTER 55

It was a full house the night of the children's play and dance performance. Parents and friends filled the folding chairs set up in rows. The room had a festive holiday look. The kids had decorated the walls with pictures of Santa Claus, reindeers, snowflakes, and winter scenes that looked nothing like Kauai. Colored lights hung from the ceiling. A decorated Christmas tree sat in the front corner of the room. A makeshift black curtain that Stanley and Albert rigged hung between the stage and the audience.

All the Hanalei House residents were present, plus Annie and Neil. Mildred and Kulak sat next to each other. Lucy Kapana and Vic Meyers sat on Mildred's other side. Mildred was happy that Vic and Lucy had struck up a relationship at Thanksgiving dinner.

Karen and Miss Louise took the stage. Karen wore a black pantsuit and her hair in a ponytail. Miss Louise dressed in a loosely fitting black dress, wore black flat shoes, and her hair tied tightly in a bun.

Karen stepped onto the stage, looked out at the audience and said, "What a nice turnout. The children have worked very hard to make this evening possible. We're very proud of them. Their ages are as young as four and as old as twelve. I'm sure you will be as proud of them as we are." She turned to Miss Louise.

Miss Louise said, "Yes, this is a wonderful turnout. Thank you all for coming. Our little play will be on first, followed by an intermission and then the dance performance. I believe you will have an enjoyable evening.

It was Karen's turn again and she said, "Now if you will just sit back and enjoy the show."

Everyone in the audience applauded. The house lights went off, the stage lights went down, the curtain opened, the stage lights came up again, revealing a manger with makeshift farm animals.

The actors entered. A tired-looking Joseph dressed in robes, played by Jason, held a rope and pulled a makeshift donkey on wheels. Mary, with her head covered in white muslin and wearing blue garments, walked alongside.

Another boy about twelve entered from the other side of the stage. He wore floor-length, brown robes. Joseph, happy to see the man, said, "We are weary travelers who need a place to stay."

The boy looked them up and down and said, "I'm sorry but my inn is full. I have no room for you."

Joseph and Mary looked disappointed. The man pointing at the manger said, "I can only offer you this humble abode."

Joseph looked to Mary for help. She nodded to her husband that it was all right. Joseph went into his robes and removed a handful of coins from a small purse. He extended his open hand to the man and said, "Please take what is required."

"Keep your money for food."

"Thank you, kind sir," Joseph said.

The lights went dark. When they came up again, baby Jesus lay in a makeshift crib in the manger, wrapped in swaddling clothes, surrounded by Mary, Joseph, and the makeshift animals. The lights went down on the manger and white stars sparkled all over the stage. The lights came up slowly on another part of the stage, revealing shepherds watching over their sheep.

The stage lights got brighter transforming the stage into daylight. A young girl in an angel costume appeared before the shepherds. The shepherds looked frightened. The angel said, "Don't be afraid. I bring good news. Your savior has been born. You can find the baby lying in a manger in Bethlehem."

The angel exited. One of the shepherds said, "Let us go see what has happened." The lights went dark again. When they came up, the shepherds stood at the manger admiring Baby Jesus. In unison, the shepherds said, "Praise God for sending his Son to be our Savior."

Before they left, one of the shepherds told Mary and Joseph, "We must tell everyone of this blessed event."

The lights went down and a bright white star hung from the ceiling over the manger. Three Wise Men appeared on stage and studied the star. One of the Wise Men said, "We must follow this star."

The stage got dark again and when the lights came back. The Wise Men stood in the manger, admiring Baby Jesus. The gifts of gold and spices that they brought were on the ground next to the child.

The Wise Men left and the lights lowered. As Mary and Joseph slept, a young girl dressed as an angel appeared on stage and woke Joseph. The angel said, "Get up! Take Jesus and Mary to Egypt where you will be safe."

Joseph asked, "Why must we leave Bethlehem?"

"Herod can be the only King of this land. Your child is in danger. Herod looks to kill him."

"Thank you, we will leave." Joseph shook Mary awake and said, "We must leave immediately, or our child will be murdered."

Mary gathered up the baby and she and Joseph exited stage right.

The lights went down. The audience applauded enthusiastically. When the lights came back on, the actors came out on stage. The angel and the Wise Men took their bows; the shepherds came out and took theirs, followed by Mary and Joseph. The entire cast stood at the stage's edge, held hands and bowed in unison.

The house lights came up and the actors exited stage right.

Miss Louise stepped on stage applauding. "That was wonderful. We'll take a fifteen-minute intermission before the dance performance."

During the intermission, people stood around both inside and outside the theatre. Annie and Neil stood with Mr. Kulak, the Bensons, Harry, and Mildred. Mr. Kulak said to Neil, "Looks like you have a baseball-playing actor."

Mr. Benson added, "Another Chuck Connors."

Neil laughed and then said, "He was more nervous about this than pitching in the championship."

"Jason did wonderfully," Mrs. Benson said.

"I think he's a natural," Mildred added. "Is he dancing in this next performance?"

"He wouldn't say much about it," Annie chimed in. "Just that it will be a surprise."

The intermission went by quickly. The theatre lights flashed signaling the performance was about to resume. People rushed to their seats.

The stage was bare, the house lights lowered, and the stage lights came on revealing three adorable little girls dressed in white tutus over white tights who sat on the floor with their legs straight out.

The Sugar Plum Fairy music from *The Nutcracker* began to play. As the music got louder, the girls began slowly waving their arms from side-to-side in time with the music. They all turned in the same direction, not completely in unison; then laid on their stomachs flat on the floor with their knees bent and their feet in the air.

They stood up, danced with their feet forward and back, back and forward, then pirouetted several times across the stage. From a pirouette, they jumped in the air and pirouetted again. They raised their right legs out from their side and, then, raised their left legs.

The audience giggled because they were a little shaky and hardly in unison—but oh so cute.

As the tempo picked up, so did their movements. They danced across the stage, then back. They held hands and danced in a circle, then fell to the floor, bent forward from the waist, then up again.

In their final movements, they danced around the stage holding hands. They came to the front of the stage as the music ended. They froze in-place.

They took their bows. The audience erupted with applause and shouts of "Bravo!"

The next act was a girl around ten, with long legs, and a pretty smile. She wore a sailor suit and tap dance shoes. The music was jazzy and quick-paced. She was very talented as she tapped her way around the stage. The audience seemed to love it and gave her resounding applause. She bowed and quickly left the stage.

Hawaiian music started to play and two Hawaiian girls about ten-years-old dressed in grass skirts wearing *leis* around their necks sidled onto the stage. They waved their arms in unison and swayed their hips to the music.

The audience loved them, too, and expressed it with enthusiastic applause.

When it was time for the final dance performance, Brenda Lee's, *Rockin' Around the Christmas Tree* played. Three couples came out on stage and began dancing a Lindy Hop. The big surprise was Karen dancing with Jason. The other partners were a twelve-year-old girl with long black hair and a skinny boy about the same age. The third couple consisted of Jason's friend Mark and a short petite girl with her blonde hair in pigtails.

The girls wore hoop dresses, white blouses with red silk scarves around their necks, bobby sox, and saddle shoes. The boys wore black pants, white shirts, and high-top black sneakers on their feet.

The audience applauded halfway through their dance number. When the music ended, the six of them went to the edge of the stage and bowed.

The response was overwhelming. Karen and Miss Louise felt proud. Jason and the other kids were all smiles. Parents praising them and wanting to enroll their children besieged Karen and Miss Louise.

CHAPTER 56

Several days later, Stanley and Karen finished packing for their honeymoon. At breakfast, the usual suspects sat around the table. It was an overcast day outside. Stanley looked worried. He was concerned the airline would cancel their flight. He also worried that Albert would not have enough help with his holiday guests who would be arriving soon.

"How many performances will you be doing, my dear?" Mrs. Benson asked.

Karen seemed to count in her head. "I believe it's seven shows with two matinees."

"And what will you be doing in Vienna while your lovely wife is working, Stanley?" Mr. Kulak asked.

"I'll probably be at most of the performances," Stanley said.

Karen smiled, "That's if he doesn't get bored."

"It's such a long trip," Mildred claimed.

Mr. Benson asked, "What's your travel itinerary?"

Karen turned to Stanley. "He's got all the arrangements."

"It's Lihue to San Francisco. San Francisco to New York."

"We're going to spend two days in New York. We'll do some shopping for winter clothes. Help my mother get ready for the trip."

"Oh, your mother is coming along?" Mrs. Watanabe asked.

Karen smiled and explained, "She always wanted to see Vienna. And since this is my first performance in *The Nutcracker*, she wanted to see it. And it will be my last dance performance."

"Never say it's your last, my dear," Miss Louise warned. "I thought I would never work again, then I had such good fortune."

"You're right," Karen agreed.

She turned towards Stanley, put her hand on top of his and said, "We want to have a family. I think with a baby and the school I'll have enough to keep me busy."

Everyone encouraged them.

"What's on the agenda after your show," Mr. Kulak asked.

"Well, mom will leave the day after Christmas," Karen said. "We'll spend one more day doing some final sightseeing around the city."

"Where do you go from there?" Harry asked.

"We fly to Venice," Stanley answered.

"Oh, that's such a lovely place," Mrs. Benson said. "You're going to love it. And the food is to die for."

Stanley continued, "We're going all over Italy. You know all the big cities and a lot of the countryside."

Karen said, "We're also going to rent a car and drive through Switzerland to France."

"Yes, a few days in Paris, then we fly over to London," Stanley added.

"There's a lot to see in London," Harry offered. "And don't miss the theatre. They have these wonderful old theatres."

"I know," Karen said.

Albert entered the dining room. He said, "I got everything in the car. We should get going soon."

Stanley and Karen stood up.

"When will you be back?" Mildred asked.

"We leave London, on January twenty-second. We should be back here on the twenty-fourth," Stanley told them.

Mildred stood up and hugged Karen, then Stanley. "You have a wonderful trip," Mildred wished them.

Kulak and everyone else gave them hugs.

Mildred said, "I've never been to Europe."

"We'll have to go some time," Kulak offered.

"I've never been out of the United States," Mildred claimed.

They all looked at her curiously.

Finally, Albert grabbed his brother's arm and said, "Okay, we've got to get going now."

As they drove away in Albert's car, the residents stood outside waving and watching them leave.

Shortly after Karen and Stanley left for the airport, the phone in Stanley's office rang. Mildred happened to be walking by and picked up the receiver. "*Aloha!*"

"*Aloha!* Is this Mrs. Meyers?"

Mildred recognized Joe Thomas's voice and said, "Hello Joe!"

"Mrs. Meyers, I just got off the phone with Calvin Daniel's secretary. He's agreed to donate the land."

"Yeah?" Mildred asked doubtfully. "The county reappraised the property?"

"No. They refused. They claim he overpaid for it, anyway."

"So, he's still going to give it to the community?"

"Apparently, he wants to get out of here. He's closing up his office and going back to New York."

"Well, Joe that's very good news."

"I thought you'd be happy about it."

"There's some kind of dedication of the land tomorrow or the day after. I'll let you know as soon as I find out when."

Mildred smiled. She felt a sense of victory. It was the first time in a long while that she felt that way. They said goodbye. Mildred hung up and rushed off to share the good news with the others.

CHAPTER 57

Just as Joe had mentioned, several days later they scheduled a ceremony for the dedication of the new park. The residents of the Hanalei House along with many community members gathered at the defunct condominium site. Joe Thomas was there to report for the newspaper and a TV news crew was present with cameras.

Lucy Kapana and Vic Meyers squeezed through the crowd when they spotted Mildred and the others. "Mildred!" Lucy shouted.

Mildred turned around and Lucy said, "Mildred isn't it exciting?

"I know I can't believe it's going to happen," Mildred said with a big smile.

"You should feel proud, Mildred. Yeah," Vic said.

Mildred offered, "It was a community effort. I was just one of the cogs in the wheel."

"Yeah, but you went to jail," Lucy reminded Mildred.

The county officials and Calvin Daniels arrived. Two workmen carried a large sign wrapped in a shipping blanket. There was a lot of chatter among the crowd.

A low wooden platform was set up, a microphone on a stand, and speakers set at the front of the platform.

The mayor, county officials, and Daniels gathered on the platform.

The mayor stepped forward and tapped the microphone. "Can I have your attention? Please!"

The crowd settled down and focused on the mayor. He continued, "Today is a special day in Hanalei. We are all here to celebrate the dedication of our new park."

Lucy Kapana whispered to Mildred, "It's still sacred land. At least, it won't have people living on top."

Mildred smiled at the shorter woman and put her arm around Lucy's shoulders.

The two workmen put posts into two holes made in the ground.

The mayor continued, "I know this has been a contentious project for the community. I'm glad it has come to a satisfactory conclusion."

Mildred wondered if he meant that.

"One we can all live with. I would like to thank Mr. Calvin Daniels for his generous donation of the land."

Boos and hisses rose from the crowd. Daniels frowned when he heard them.

Mildred said to Mr. Kulak, "They shouldn't do that."

"You can't blame them. They don't like the guy."

Mildred made a disapproving face.

"Mr. Daniels would you like to say something?" the mayor asked.

Daniels walked up to the microphone. There were more boos and hissing. Daniels didn't appreciate their reaction. Some people clapped. "Thank you. I would like to say thanks to the mayor and the county officials for their swift and decisive action. I had other plans for this site as you well know. Unfortunately, for me, things didn't fall into place as they should have. I'm more than happy to donate this land back to the people of Hanalei."

"You know that's bullshit," Mr. Kulak whispered to Mildred. "Since when does he care about the people?"

Mildred shook her head in agreement.

Daniels continued, "This land will be placed in perpetuity for the people of Hanalei to use as a community park."

This time the crowd cheered.

"Thank you." He handed the microphone back to the mayor."

The workmen nailed the still covered sign to the posts. Everyone waited anxiously for them to unveil the sign. The mayor turned to Daniels and said, "Mr. Daniels would you like to do the honors?"

"Oh, sure."

Daniels stepped off the platform. The workmen got out of the way. Daniels pulled the blanket off revealing the sign. It read, THE PEOPLE'S PARK, under that it said, OF HANALEI, and below that, in larger lettering, it said, ON LAND DONATED BY THE DANIELS DEVELOPMENT CORPORATION, and the next line read, CALVIN DANIELS, CHAIRMAN & CEO.

The crowd applauded. The mayor took to the mic again and said, "And that concludes our dedication. Food and beverages are available behind you. Compliments of the county."

As they turned around to look, there were serving tables with food on them. At another table, soft drinks were available.

"We appreciate your being here today. *Mahalo!*" the mayor said.

Mildred's friends turned towards the food and beverages. Mildred said to Kulak, "I'm going to say something to Mr. Daniels."

Kulak looked apprehensive. Mildred said, "Don't worry I'm not going to say anything bad."

"Okay, but I don't want you to get arrested again."

"I'm not," Mildred said, impatiently.

Kulak went to join the others. Mildred strode towards the platform. Daniels looked nervous when he saw her. Right away, Mildred smiled at him, extended her hand and asked, "Mr. Daniels can I have a word with you?"

Daniels shook Mildred's hand and said, "Hello, Mrs. Meyers."

"Thank you for donating the land. I know it must have been a difficult decision. I want you to know that I personally plan to oversee the use of the park and to make sure people use and enjoy it."

"Well, that's very considerate."

"I know we've had our differences over the past few years. I hold no animosity towards you and hope our paths don't cross again."

"Me too," Daniels agreed.

As Mildred turned away, he called after her, "Mrs. Meyers!"

Mildred turned around. Daniels leveled his gaze at her, "Would you like a job? I can use someone with your determination and skills."

Mildred thought it funny that her arch-nemesis would offer her a job. She smiled before answering, "Thank you for the offer but I think I'm a little too much over the hill."